Sins & Temptation

BOOK 3 OF ENZO'S TRILOGY

LEXXI JAMES

SINS & Temptation
Book 3 in Enzo's Trilogy
SINS of the Syndicate
Copyright © 2024 Lexxi James

www.LexxiJames.com
All rights reserved. Lexxi James, LLC.
Independently Published

With Grateful Appreciation to My Remarkable Editing Team
KE
Jaime Ryter, The Ryter's Proof Editing Services
With Special Thanks to the Lexxi James VIP Beta Readers

Cover by Book Sprite, LLC
Image by Wander Aguiar
Wander Aguiar Photography LLC
Models Stephen & Dina @ ZINK MODEL

No part of this publication may be reproduced, distributed, or transmitted in any form or by any means, including photocopying, recording, or other electronic or mechanical methods, without the prior written permission of Lexxi James LLC. Under certain circumstances, a brief quote in reviews and for non-commercial use may be permitted as specified in copyright law. Permission may be granted through a written request to the publisher at LexxiJamesBooks@gmail.com.

This is a work of fiction. Names, characters, places, and incidents are the product of the author's imagination. Specific named locations, public names, and other specified elements are used for impact, but this novel's story and characters are 100 percent fictitious. Certain long-standing institutions, agencies, and public offices are mentioned, but the characters involved are wholly imaginary. Resemblance to individuals, living or dead, or to events which have occurred is purely coincidental. And if your life happens to bear a strong resemblance to my imaginings, then well done and cheers to you! You're a freaking rock star!

Please Note...

This is the final book of a trilogy. Please begin at Book 1 of Enzo's Trilogy "SINS: The Deal."

If you are a fan of my work, please be warned:
This trilogy is dark. It is darker than the first three books in the *SINS of the Syndicate* series and is my darkest romance to date.

On the morally gray scale, Enzo D'Angelo veers to black. His adversaries have no morals. Bodily harm and graphic violence will be described.

Like haunted houses and carnival rides, only you know your limits. Your mental health matters.

Welcome back to Enzo's world.

Sins & Temptation

Chapter One
ENZO

"Teach him the ropes, Mullvain," my uncle ordered, heading out as the mountain of an intimidating man finished tightening the glove around my wrist.

"Aye, sir," Mullvain replied, his voice a gravelly rumble. Then, he slipped on his own gloves, eyes locking onto mine.

The first blow landed on my cheek with a crack, pain radiating but not overwhelming. It should have been blinding, considering it came from a three-hundred-pound giant. But here I stood, a scrawny fifteen-year-old punk, defiant. I shook it off.

"Hit me back, lad," he taunted, his Scottish brogue both endearing and infuriatingly incomprehensible.

Italian was where I felt at home—the fluid, rapid-fire pace of it, the expressive arm gestures, the unapologetic volume. English felt foreign on my tongue, a clumsy substitute, though I was adapting.

His words were calming enough, but the amusement in his eyes set my blood boiling. I wanted to hit him. Wipe that smug *grin off his face so hard, he'd see stars. But every instinct screamed that it was a trap.*

"C'mon, boy. Yer uncle says you need training if you're going out on your own." Smack. This time, my left cheek was on fire. "Running away? What's the matter? Not enough maids to wipe yer ass?"

I swung twice at his head and missed. "I'm not running away," I huffed, struggling with the weight of the red boxing gloves. Bastards were heavier than they looked. "One day, I'll be the King of Chicago. My father thinks I need to learn the business. I need to learn to fight."

"King of Chicago, eh? Wi' the way ye hit, ye look mair like king o' the pussies."

That did it. This time, when I swung again, my fist connected with a satisfying thud. Direct hit. The giant doubled over, and for a moment, fear seized me—had I actually hurt him? But then, his booming belly laugh echoed through the room, shattering my concerns.

"I guess when you're a wee guy, the best ye can do is hit ma gut."

For that, I hit him again. An uppercut that stopped his laughter cold. Easy to do when he's bent over. His smile vanished as he cradled his cheek. "Look at that. Not even sixteen, and I'll be kicking your ass in no time."

The amusement in his eyes darkened. "Fifteen years old." His gaze traveled over my face, the same way my father's had done countless times. "And already too big for yer britches." His arm shot out, tapping my belly with so much speed and force, the pain didn't actually register until my ass was on the floor.

I struggled to breathe as his laughter grew, my embarrassment and annoyance blurring until I found myself laughing too. His left-handed glove ruffled my hair. "Well, if I didn't owe your uncle a mountain of debt, I wouldn't do it. You're too young to be fighting your way to the top."

With that, I jumped to my feet, chest puffed out. "I'm ready."

He chuckled, ruffling my hair. "Aye, that ye are, young Jedi. That ye are. And if it gets me out of debt with yer uncle, consider it done."

My eyes lit up. "So you'll train me to be the best fighter in the world?"

He clapped a hand on my shoulder, his grip firm. "Kid, I'm about to make you the deadliest devil that ever walked the earth."

I bounced on my toes, eager. "Can we start with that move? What you did that put me on the ground. Show me, please."

With a grin, he stepped back and assumed a fighting stance. "Alright, wee lad, pay attention. This is where it begins."

THE WHEELS TOUCHING DOWN DRAG ME FROM MY thoughts—memories I'd long ago buried. *Mullvain*. It had been an eternity since I'd heard the name, though his voice has continued to haunt and annoy me in equal measure from beyond the grave.

Looking at Kennedy now, her pink lips swollen from our kiss, her body still trembling with desire beneath my robe, and her eyes burning with enough anger to set the world on fire—I wonder if any sane man would feel something at this point.

Guilt.

Remorse.

Regret.

"How about love? Aye, there's one ye haven't tried on for size," the Scotsman taunts from the darkest corner of my mind.

"Possession is more my speed," I growl to the empty air.

"I am not your possession," Kennedy snaps back, tightening my robe around her luscious curves as she crosses her legs.

As if any part of her could ever be off-limits. As if I can't still taste her on my tongue.

"I own you, *Bella*."

"For a week," sweet Kennedy corrects. "During which time I get to see my sister. Every day," she demands, her fire and petulance damn near combustible.

She glares at me, the tension thick and electric. With any other woman, she'd be on her knees by now, wrapping that smart mouth around my dick.

I consider commanding her to do just that, then check my watch. Shit. I need hours with Kennedy, not minutes. Ruining her for life takes time. I can't fuck her senseless with a stopwatch.

And trust me, I will be fucking her senseless. Every. Goddamned. Time.

Plus, I see a man outside the plane I prefer not to keep waiting. "Get dressed."

"Why Bother?" she asks, fussing with her belt. "If you're just going to tear them off me, then half-naked would save time and give me more precious moments with my sister."

I let her and her luscious curves fuss with the seatbelt for only a minute before I undo it for her. I tip her chin up to meet my gaze. "Don't tempt me, *Bella*. Unless you want me to take my time fucking you while a dozen security guards listen as you scream my name, I suggest you get dressed."

She rushes off, and I don't bother watching her. One glance, and I'd be lost in her all over again, impulse and instinct ready to explode.

And right now, there are bigger battles to fight. Like the text I'm currently staring at.

GIO
Guess who lands later today?

Giovanni is more than a *Capo*. He's my eyes and ears in Italy. No one knows what's going on more than he does.

ME
I don't pay to guess.
Just tell me.

GIO
The biggest cocksucker you know.

Even without hearing Giovanni speak, his thick Italian accent usually lifts my spirits when he refers to my uncle as a cocksucker.

Right now, it's just pissing me off.

Chapter Two
KENNEDY

"*Bentornato!*" an older man with salt-and-pepper hair and a sweater vest greets us enthusiastically as we step off the plane.

For a moment, I'm blinded by the sun—a casualty of chasing it around the globe, I guess. I fumble for my sunglasses, taking in the stunning landscape with awe.

Thankfully, the flight attendant handed me a pair earlier—nice and dark with "please, no paparazzi" vibes. She mentioned it would be mid-morning here, but she didn't mention just how gorgeous it is.

Considering it was around the same time she calmed me down with my third glass of champagne, maybe she did and I'm too drunk to remember. And since she helped me into this gorgeous pale blue dress that hugs my curves perfectly and has a gazillion buttons down the back, I'm pretty sure she's become my new best friend.

What was her name again?

I sway a little, still feeling the champagne, and gaze out at the Italian coastline in the distance. The azure waters and rugged cliffs, bathed in golden sunlight, are absolutely breathtaking.

Another wobbly step off the stairs, and I crash into Mt. Enzo, his rock-hard body steadying me. He tries to tuck me under his arm like I'm some kind of newspaper. I push him off. "I don't need your help."

His breath is hot against my neck, sending shivers down my spine. "Behave, *Bella*. And tonight, I'll give you exactly what you need."

And when he kisses me, that sensual blend of hot lips and rough stubble, I suddenly can't breathe. The world fades away until it's just him and me and—

"And you must be Kennedy," the sweet man says with a warm smile.

I extend my hand for a shake, but he gently cups my cheeks and kisses each one. He then turns to Enzo, repeating the gesture, which Enzo reciprocates. "Kennedy, this is Giovanni," Enzo introduces.

"Gio," he corrects, patting my hand as he takes it again. "You must call me Gio." His accent is thick and warm, wrapping around me like a cozy pashmina in fall. "Anything you need, you call Gio, *eh?*"

Enzo checks his phone, a hard line forming at his brow. Jaw clenched, he looks up. "Which one is mine?"

I glance around, confused. *Which one what?*

Ahead of us are two sleek black cars, each with its own driver. They're lined up like they're about to kick off a parade, with a dozen armed guards standing by for a gun salute.

Gio kisses my hand and, with a paternal touch on my back,

leads me forward in an old-world manner. "You come with me, *bellissima*."

Enzo instantly yanks me from the man's hold in an uncharacteristically playful tug of war that makes me grin. "Get your own girl, Giovanni. This one is mine."

For a week, I silently remind myself.

Gio laughs a hearty laugh, his eyes sparkling. He playfully nestles my hand into his arm and leads me away from Enzo. "We'll see, *ragazzino*," he says with a wink.

"*Ragazzino?*" I ask.

Enzo cuts in. "It means Italian stud."

"More like little boy," Gio teases.

Enzo mutters something under his breath with enough fervor that it has to be an Italian swear word. But when his golden eyes lock onto mine, there's a playful glint. It's clear he and Gio are close. "Don't push me," Enzo threatens, a hint of a smile tugging at his lips.

Gio waves him off, completely unfazed, and leads me to the first car. "We take this one," he whispers, loud enough for Enzo to hear. "Drive him insane with jealousy."

The growl that rumbles from Enzo's chest could register on the Richter scale. He slips on his sunglasses with a sharp glare. "I don't get jealous." Sure, keep telling yourself that.

As the driver opens the car door, I spot my sweet pup Truffles already in the back seat. Then it hits me. "Where's Savannah?"

Enzo straightens his tie, a smirk playing on his lips. "Her services were no longer required." He leans in, his lips brushing my cheek. "Dinner is at seven. Don't keep me waiting."

I slide into the back seat, my mind spinning. Does Enzo know what Savannah told me? Did he do something to her?

"Where is she?" I ask nervously.

"Being slowly tortured for the next ten hours."

What?

The door shuts as a knot of worry tightens in my chest.

Is that mob humor?

Or is he serious?

Rather than Enzo getting behind the wheel, Giovanni slides in. I watch as Enzo gets into his own vehicle and speeds off without a backward glance.

I shake off the small pang of hurt at that and focus on the road as we head in the opposite direction.

"Where are we going?" I ask, forcing a small smile.

Gio smiles warmly, his eyes filled with comforting reassurance. "You'll see, *bellissima*."

Chapter Three
ENZO

"Drive," I command the moment I slide into the car, barely restraining myself from ripping that blue dress to shreds and ravishing her right then and there.

"*Sì, signore*," the driver responds promptly, and we speed away. As we leave the tarmac, he asks, "Where to, sir?"

"Home." The word feels almost foreign on my tongue. I've made it my life's mission not to grow too comfortable anywhere, but this is different.

After Uncle Andre dug his claws into me as a teen, Villa Luca became my sanctuary. The one place I could let my guard down, shed my skin, and just breathe. But not this time.

This time, the walls are too thin, and the shadows too deep. Uncle will be landing within the hour, and I need to be ready.

I glance out the window, trying to shake off the tension as we glide through the gates to the villa. Or rather, a cluster of villas nestled in the secluded Italian countryside.

The rolling hills are peppered with olive groves and vineyards, ancient stone buildings, and sprawling gardens. Beautiful. Private. It's the perfect place for *Bella* and me, or it would be if I wasn't on my way to a fucking welcoming party.

I narrow my eyes as the car winds through a long, cobblestone driveway, and rolls to a stop.

My brother Dante stands front and center, beaming like the cat that ate three canaries. The fucker knows I'm here with a woman, and he just won't let it go.

Sin is to one side—because apparently, this occasion calls for an attorney—and Dory on the other.

How my meddlesome, insufferable secretary managed to finagle her way into an all-expenses-paid vacation to Italy is anyone's guess. Though by the thickness of the folder in her hands, she's about to give me work.

And, with any luck, my next piece of business to attend to. And when I say attend to, I mean kill.

The car pulls to a stop, and my driver rushes to open my door. I step out, calm and collected, adjusting my cuff as I wonder if Dante would prefer granite or marble for his headstone.

Before I can take a breath, Dante strides over, a smirk plastered on his face. "What's the matter, bro? Not expecting us?" he teases, clapping me on the shoulder with far too much enthusiasm. "Did you know the D'Angelo super-jet can overtake a small transatlantic plane?" He grins, enjoying his little jab.

I grit my teeth, brushing off his hand. "Really? I guess I should've asked more questions when I was buying it with your black card," I retort. "What are you all doing here?" My gaze flicks to Sin and Dory, who are both watching with far too much amusement.

"We figured whatever you're running from would catch up eventually, and you'd need reinforcements." He rubs his hands together eagerly. "So, where's Savannah Whitaker, Dog Trainer to the Stars?" Dante asks, trying to peer through the darkly tinted window.

I straighten my tie as he casually plops his ass on the hood of the car, too comfortably. The last thing I need is for them to learn about Kennedy staying with me. "I'm not running from the boogeyman. That's your department. As for Savannah, she got under my skin, so I'm doing what I do best."

"Fucking things up?" Dante asks.

"Underwhelming her with your intellect?" Sin offers.

"I'm torturing her," I snap.

Dory gasps, Dante crosses his arms, and Sin simply cocks his head. "How?" Sin scoffs. "You'd sooner eat canned spaghetti sauce than torture a woman. Perhaps you're boring her to death?"

Dante smirks, not missing a beat. "Or suffocating her with your cologne?"

Dory smartly says nothing, her one hand up in surrender as if she wants no part of this. Her other hand is still clutching the folder.

"If you must know, I sent her back to the States," I say, a smirk playing on my lips.

Dory blinks her big, clueless eyes, confusion etched across her face. "How is that torture?"

My grin widens. "I sent her back coach. Middle seat. With two layovers."

They all wince in unison. Dante shakes his head, chuckling. "You sadistic bastard."

"I also let her fly without any of her credit cards or toiletries, including her over-the-top makeup. And I kept this." I pull out Savannah's cell, flipping it in the air with a careless flick of my wrist. "A little punishment for her snitching to Caleb Knox." I unlock the phone and toss the phone to Sin. "I reprogrammed the passcode."

We all know the passcodes. Whoever sets it, it's the first four digits of our name. ENZO equals 5-6-9-6.

He unlocks it, the lines of his brow hardening. "Agent Knox," he says, exhaling sharply. "So the FBI is not only watching you, they're infiltrating your operation with a snitch. And a high-priced, high-profile one at that."

Dante's hand lands on my arm with a sharp smack. "You must be doing something right."

"Knox," Sin says, the name rolling off his tongue like it's laced with bitterness. "Now there's a guy I'd like to torture slowly. Just to find out what he knows about our family and the disappearance of your father."

"In due time," I assure him. "But I have bigger fish to fry."

"We," Dante says, slinging an arm around my shoulder. "There's nothing the D'Angelos like better than a fish fry."

"We're all in this together," Dory says, her tone sweet and delusional as usual. She links her arm in Sin's, and we look so much like the quartet from *The Wizard of Oz* it's embarrassing.

I wrench myself free from their clutches and jab a finger at their smug grins. "Look, I didn't fly my ass halfway around the world to be suffocated by familial warmth. I need my space."

And my privacy, because God only knows how loud Bella might get.

Sin sweeps his hand across the expansive landscape. "The

grounds of the villa are vast. Two main houses. Seven smaller ones, if you can call ten-thousand-feet small. The furthest one is over that hill," he points out. "Secluded, private entrance, lakefront views. It's also far enough away that we won't be disturbed by your victims' screams in the night."

I snatch the folder from Dory's hand and snap my fingers. Instantly, my driver opens the car door. "Then that's the one I'll take."

Chapter Four
KENNEDY

"Ahhh!"

I cling to my seatbelt for dear life, my knuckles turning white as Gio whips through the narrow streets of the Italian town at hair-raising speeds.

The engine roars as we pinch around tight corners, his occasional fist slamming against the steering wheel accompanied by what I can only imagine are colorful Italian profanities.

Of all the ways I imagined meeting my demise because of my association with Golden Eyes, this wasn't one of them.

If this were an amusement park, I'd be thrilled. As it is, my pulse is thudding so hard in my ears, I barely hear his question. "You like Gio as your tour guide, *eh?*"

I nod in haste, surprised Truffles isn't puking all over the back seat. "Uh-huh."

We enter a traffic circle where a swarm of scooters dart past us like angry bees, their drivers shouting and gesturing wildly. Cars honk impatiently as Gio cuts across what would be lanes of traffic if there were any lines, and I have to shut my eyes.

His maneuvers are executed with such precision that I can't decide if he's a remarkably skilled driver or certifiably insane.

"You hungry?" he asks sweetly, one hand on the wheel and the other relaxed over the arm of my seat, as if navigating through the chaos of the streets is just a leisurely drive through the park.

Considering it's taking everything I have in me not to upchuck last night's meal, I simply shake my head.

We emerge in a corner of the city with cobblestone streets and a beautiful townhouse. Gio doesn't slow, but somehow expertly squeezes into an impossibly tight space between two vehicles before coming to an abrupt stop. "Here we are."

Huh? Is this Enzo's place?

Before I can ask, Gio has already rounded the car, lets Truffles out on his leash, and opens my door. Swiftly, he presses the doorbell. "Now, this is for you," he says in his charming Italian accent, handing me the leash, a credit card, and a business card that simply says "G."

There's a crazy long string of numbers beneath it, which I'm guessing is his local phone number.

"If you need me," he says, "I'll be nearby and can take you anywhere you want to go." With that, he plants a kiss on both my cheeks and gently guides me towards the door.

I give the building another once-over, and I'm not sure why, but I imagined Enzo's place to be colder somehow. All sleek and modern, with clean lines and sophistication, radiating an unmistakable aura of one-percenter wealth.

Yet, with the light stone and the Romeo and Juliet balcony adorned with Bougainvillea, the place is absolutely adorable.

Cozy and Tuscan, like something plucked straight out of a fairy tale.

When the balcony door swings open, I half expect strands of shimmering spun gold hair to come flying at my face from Rapunzel. Instead, Riley appears, waving and screaming so loud I'm sure the neighbors will think a murder is happening. "Kenni?"

I wave up shyly, trying not to attract too much attention from the nearby houses as people are starting to look. It's obvious Riley could care less about that. "Oh, my God. What are you doing here?" She leans out of the window, then disappears back inside. "I'll be right down."

She reappears at the front door, looking so beautiful and happy, I get a little choked up. We hug so tight, a surge of relief washes over me, and tears well up in my eyes. It feels like we've been apart for a year.

Thank God for this internship. I've never been so grateful for anything in my life. Having Riley safe and sound, a million miles away from Jimmy's debt and the D'Angelo's, feels like a weight lifted off my shoulders.

"Truffles!" she squeals, scooping up the excited ball of tail-wagging fur. Before I can introduce her to Gio, he's already around the other side. "I'll pick you up at 6:30," he calls out before disappearing.

"Wait, you can only stay until 6:30?" Riley asks, frowning.

"But I'll be back every day," I assure her. My words do little to erase the crease in her brow or the cute *I always get my way* pout, which means she's no where near satisfied with that answer.

It's hard to explain why I can't just stay here the entire time.

And even harder to admit that I've offered my body up to a dangerous mobster just to spend precious hours for seven days with her.

But if Savannah Whitaker is right, and Enzo is merely using me before tossing me back to Andre, the cold, hard reality is that I might not be able to change it.

If I run, they go after Riley and have her take my place. And it will be over my dead body that anything ever happens to my sister. I push out a heavy sigh. My death is definitely a possibility.

But I have seven days to figure out a way for both of us to escape. Agent Knox somehow seems in the middle of all this. Maybe he really can't offer us both an escape.

But even if he can't, and if this is truly the last chance I have to see my sister, I want every moment to count. I want to make our time unforgettable. I want to shower her with love, to let her know just how much she means to me.

When we lost our father, we didn't have that chance. We didn't have the opportunity to show him how much he meant to us, to say the things we wanted to say. To tell him one last time, "We love you, *Da*. And we always will."

I won't lose that chance again. Not with Riley. Not when it matters most.

"AND THIS IS MY CLOSET!" RILEY PRACTICALLY HAS jazz hands as she concludes the tour of her lavish home, ushering me into a closet that's bigger than my entire Chicago apartment.

Granted, there are only a few clothes hanging on the hangers, and most of it is bare space, but it's still jaw-droppingly incredible.

As Riley continues to gush about living there, I can't help but notice a worn pair of jeans tucked away in the corner, a stark contrast to the luxury surrounding them. "And your internship pays for all this?"

"Yup." With a deep breath, she sighs. "It's almost too good to be true."

It really is. Riley's been living it up in Italy in a fairy tale, while I've been trapped in a nightmare, and all I can feel is a profound sense of gratitude. That and relief.

Her hands clasp together, pleading. "Please. Can't you stay here tonight?"

I want to. I really do. But Enzo giveth, and a pissed-off Enzo would certainly taketh away. "I wish I could," I admit. "But I'll be back tomorrow. Maybe earlier." I nibble my lip. "But I don't want you to get in trouble with your school."

"It's no trouble." She leads me back to the bedroom and flops on the bed.

I sit beside her, taking in the luxurious king-sized bed with its plush pillows and silk sheets, the headboard adorned with intricate carvings. It's a bed fit for royalty.

The walls are lined with original looking art and the rug might as well have the word expensive embroidered across the center. "They do?"

"Yup. My boss is amazing. He pretty much lets me come and go whenever I want. I can just call and request a few days off."

"What do you do for him exactly?" Okay, that totally came out wrong. "Is this his place?" I ask before I can help myself.

She shoots me a snarky glare. "Not that." She rolls her eyes. "It's completely innocent. Half the time, he's not even here. He travels non-stop. All I have to do is text him."

Right. The first chance I get, and I'm breaking into her phone, scouring every text between her and this lech. And if I find even one dick pic, the asshole is toast.

If Riley thinks I won't use whatever ounce of mafia power I might have at my disposal by sleeping with the enemy, oh, she can think again.

When I sneak a glance over her shoulder, the message isn't exactly scandalous. Just a polite request for a few days off because family is in town.

But then, my gaze lands on the digits. The Chicago area code jumps out at me, but it's the rest of the number that sends shockwaves through me like a hurricane ripping through a calm sea.

That number.

I know that number.

The damned thing is seared into my memory like a brand. It was a lifeline dangled in front of me like a carrot—a promise of escape when Uncle Andre and Rocco closed in.

It was my ticket out, scribbled hastily on the inside of a matchbook and shoved into my hands with a warning: if Uncle Andre or any of his goons touched me, that lifeline was gone.

I take in the Italian townhouse, its opulent furnishings, and the extravagant perks of an all-expenses-paid internship in Italy, and realization hits me like a mack-truck full of bricks.

Enzo.

"Squee," Riley squeals. "My boss said take all the time I need." She grabs me by both arms. "You're about to see Italy, Riley-style."

Riley-style means we're eating, and we're eating a lot. I flash the credit card with E. D'Angelo written across it. "And I'm about to treat you to anything you want."

Riley claps her hands and bounces on her toes like she's won the lottery. Not that she'll have me splurge on anything beyond lunch and a gelato.

Hell, we could probably waltz into the nearest Lamborghini dealership, and Enzo wouldn't even bat an eyelash.

Right?

Chapter Five
ENZO

No sane person would do this. But then again, sanity isn't my strong suit.

For an hour straight, I pore over the images, one after another, suppressing the nauseating churn in my stomach. Dory's search didn't uncover any more pictures of my sister, Trinity, which is the good news.

The bad news is that she stumbled upon ten more of Kennedy. All nude. All underage. And all of them death warrants for the man—or men—who did this.

When I hunt down the scum responsible for this, I won't rush. I'll relish every moment as I strip them of their sight and crush every single one of their 206 bones.

It's not Kennedy's image that captures my attention as much as the backdrop behind her. The scenes, familiar rooms from the dance studio Kennedy teaches at, are unmistakable.

And since Clive Weston, former owner of said dance studio, has been my guest in a soundproof torture chamber just outside of Chicago, I'll be wringing his body of more information as soon as I return.

I blow out a breath and send a text to Striker.

> **ME**
> Keep that bastard alive.

> **STRIKER**
> Which one?

Annoyed, I pinch the bridge of my nose.

> **ME**
> Andre's banker.

> **STRIKER**
> Yes, sir.
> I have a defibrillator on standby.

"Good," I mutter, a twisted smile dancing across my lips as I snatch a cigar from the humidor. There's a mountain of business Clive and I still need to hash out. Which is why my instructions are clear: do what you want to the eyes, teeth, and ears. But for the love of God, save the tongue for last.

I light the cigar, drawing in a deep drag, fighting the urge to incinerate the damning photos in my hand.

The Scotsman decides to haunt me some more. "*They're evidence,*" his whisper in my mind, drawing out the subtle, rolling *r* that's his trademark.

"I. Am. Not. A. Cop," I growl through clenched teeth, loud enough to reverberate across the empty room.

"You'll never take down Andre without those," his ghostly whisper taunts, firing me up on all cylinders.

I shoot from my seat, words spilling out in a fierce snarl. "What the fuck does that mean?" I snap, frustrated.

"So, we've finally cracked," Dante interjects, his sudden presence whipping me around to face him.

I can't gauge how long he's been lurking there, witnessing me unraveling like a defective burrito, but I swiftly shove the images back into the folder and draw a sharp puff from my cigar. "I lost it ages ago, Dante," I retort, my voice tight. I narrow my eyes. "Is there something you want?"

"I want to know what's in the folder. Dory wouldn't say a word."

"That's because she values her life."

He strides across the room, yanking open the heavy silk drapes. "It's freakin' gorgeous out on the Italian shores. Why the hell are all the curtains closed?"

I suppress the urge to snap at him, my head throbbing like a jackhammer and sunlight feeling like a barrage of thumbtacks pelting the backs of my eyes. "I need to concentrate," I grind out, the words strained and unconvincing.

"You need a swift kick in the ass if you think you're gonna take on Uncle Andre solo," he retorts, nodding towards the file on the desk. "Whatever that is, you can't keep it under wraps forever."

"I can try," I mutter dryly.

His hand brushes his chin thoughtfully. "Knowing you, that pain in the base of your neck is agony by now—like an ice pick being slowly driven in. Probably, because you're tiptoeing towards the edge of the worst decision of your life."

"And what decision is that?" I ask, attempting to push past the pain he's so astutely highlighted.

"You're either going after Andre or something equally as idiotic. We don't need a war," Dante reminds me.

"That's the thing about wars, Dante," I counter. "No one ever needs them. They have them because if they take another ounce of shit, their back will break." My phone pings. I glance at it and shake my head. "Speaking of shit."

Dante simply raises a brow, then exhales a heavy sigh. "I know you came here with a girl. I know said girl is at the heart of some major issue between you and Andre. And I know that without my help, you're gonna get yourself killed."

I'm sleep-deprived, near exhausted, fueled by nothing but adrenaline and rage. I lack the strength to combat the relentless nagging of a D'Angelo brother hell-bent on the truth—Dante being the grandmaster of sniffing out skeletons.

He takes a step closer. "It stays between us, I swear."

At this point, I'm in too much pain to keep sparring with my brother. He's right. I need his help. So, I make the reckless decision to show him my phone.

He stares at the text from an unknown number, confused. "Six?"

"It's the number of days I have left with said girl before I have to return her to Uncle Andre."

"Why?" Dante's brow furrows in confusion.

"Her worthless son of a bitch of a stepfather owes him, and vanished. So now she owes him," I explain, preemptively raising a hand to ward off what he's about to ask.

"So buy her debt."

"You think I haven't tried?"

"Why does she mean so much to you?" Dante probes.

"Because she does," I reply flatly.

After a minute of scrutinizing me, he nods in agreement. "Okay. Then she means so much to me too," he concedes, reaching for the folder of images. My fist slams down on the file and against the desk with such force, we both hear a crack of the fine wood. He takes a step back. "What?"

"She's nude in these," I confess, the words heavy and forced. It causes physical pain, saying what I'm about to say. "And too young to consent to them."

"Then you're too close to this to be objective," Dante asserts with enough common sense, I stand down.

I've been going cross-eyed, staring at the photos as if the pieces of a ten-thousand-piece puzzle will miraculously come together. I'm missing something. Something that's right in front of my fucking face.

"Trust your gut, lad. And trust your brother. All the clues are there."

For fuck's sake, not you too. It's bad enough that the Scotsman I murdered has haunted my thoughts since I was fifteen. Now he's siding with my brother?

Dante pauses, as if he can tell, I'm already swimming in the deep end of insanity, then takes another step, reaching out a hand in a gesture of reassurance. "Just . . . cover her private parts up with a ton of sticky notes and let me take a look."

Chapter Six
ENZO

"I'M TELLING YOU, THAT—" Dante points to the tenth image we've pored over repeatedly with a fine-tooth comb—"is wrong. There's something off about it."

I grab a colossal vintage magnifier we had delivered from town. It magnifies the images twelve times, enough to make Sherlock and Poirot size envy, and try to refocus my eyes. "Are you pointing to the window or her face or what?"

I stare at him, wondering how my brother keeps the wheels turning at a multi-million dollar nightclub without getting lost in the bathroom.

"Hear him out."

Argh. With the obnoxious Scottish brogue nagging persistently in one ear and Dante's unwavering insistence in the other, I choose to ride the current and go with it.

Maybe, just maybe, if I squint hard enough, I'll finally see it. If I don't go blind first.

"What's going on?" a sweet voice interrupts from the door.

"Bella," is all I manage to say. Her sun-kissed skin glows,

and I breathe in the scent of jasmine and vanilla, nearly forgetting that these are *her* half-naked photos Dante and I have scattered across my desk.

Thankfully, Dante doesn't miss a beat and swiftly gathers them all into the folder, tucking it securely under his arm. He extends his hand to hers without skipping a beat. "It's good to see you again."

"Hi." Kennedy doesn't hesitate for a moment, kissing him on both cheeks like she was born Italian. It boils my blood enough that I have to clench my fists in my pockets. "It's nice to see you when, uh . . ."

"You're don't need rescuing," he replies smoothly.

"Yes," she nods, embarassed. "Thank you."

She's thanking him? Annoyed, I check my watch. "You're late."

Her mouth falls open. "Late? We had no clue where to go. Gio drove me to the main house."

"The main house is a two-minute drive from here."

"Where I met this charming man named Sin and your secretary, Dory."

Shit.

She pauses, fidgeting with her purse strap. "They had so much to spill about you." Her eyes dart to mine, then back down. "Took quite a while." My *Bella* beams with delight, oblivious to the rage simmering just beneath my skin like lava.

Sin *and* Dory.

If Sin knows, Smoke will know. And if Dory knows, my entire family will find out, which is just perfect.

And by perfect, I mean inconvenient as fuck. Especially if I actually have to hand her back to Uncle Andre.

Her smile widens so big, it squeezes my heart in the strangest way. Fuck, I better not be having a heart attack.

I clutch my chest as Kennedy goes on. "Plus, Dory practically fell in love with Truffles. She insisted on feeding him, bathing him, and taking him for an extra-long walk. Even begged to keep him overnight."

Finally. The crazy old woman is good for something.

"Oh my gosh," Kennedy continues, laughing lightly. "The stories they have about you when you were a kid..."

"Lies," I insist. "Everyone knows I was never a kid. Now, before I have to strangle the life from my brother for not releasing your hand, it's time he left."

"He could stay for dinner," *Bella* offers, all coy and begging to be punished.

"I'm not hungry," I lie. I'm fucking famished. I haven't eaten since before we left for Italy. It's a good thing Dory kept Truffles. I swear the damned dog is sounding more like a crudités by the minute.

"He never eats dinner," Dante whispers loudly to *Bella*. "Haven't you heard? Vampires only feast on the blood of their victims."

When I shoot him a death glare, Dante quickly takes the hint, kisses *Bella* on both cheeks just to spite me, and moves at a snail's pace to the door. "I'll have the chef deliver dinner. Pleasure to meet you, Kennedy. *Arrivederci*, bro."

WITHIN FIFTEEN MINUTES, DINNER IS SERVED promptly on the terrace of the cliffside house overlooking the sea, where flecks of amber and gold dance across the water in the early evening light.

The chef presents a rustic Italian feast: bruschetta topped with ripe tomatoes and fresh basil, tender lamb chops grilled to perfection, and handmade pasta served fresh in a wheel of Pecorino Romano.

Kennedy's eyes light up as the chef prepares *cacio e pepe*. "I've never seen anything like this," she says as she watches in awe.

I explain. "The hot pasta is tossed in a creamy sauce made with cheese and freshly ground black pepper, which allows the cheese to melt and coat the pasta in a way to create a rich and indulgent dish straight from the wheel of Pecorino Romano." The chef twirls a serving onto her plate, and I take a bit with my fork and feed it to her.

"You've become the sexiest man alive," she says, opening her mouth.

"As if there was any doubt, *Bella*."

Her bite of the pasta is accompanied by a moan so erotic, the bulge in my pants was instant. I took several deep breaths as I watched her eat, steadying my pulse against the rhythmic pounding in my chest and throbbing of my painfully stiff cock.

I've never been so turned on by a woman in my life, let alone one that was just *eating*. Her lips were pink and full. Eyes deliciously satisfied. And somehow, watching her swallow became the highlight of my night.

With a quick, "*Questo è tutto*," I excuse the chef.

He nods with a knowing glance. Maybe too knowing. "*Molto bene, signore*."

Very good sir.

Then bids us both a good evening with, "*Buona serata a voi,*" and makes himself scarce.

Kennedy manages to squeak out a "*Grazie mille,*" thanking the chef profusely before ravenously shoving another forkful into her gorgeous mouth. I stare in awe as her next moan is damn near orgasmic. "*Mmm.*"

At this point, I have to blow out a breath. *Fuck.* This woman will be the death of me.

With an unsettled furrow in her brow, she murmurs, "You're barely touching your food." She twirls a forkful of creamy, cheesy pasta and gently offers it to my lips. "Here."

I lean closer without thinking, allowing her to feed me. It's a gesture laden with unexpected intimacy, a vulnerability I rarely show. This closeness, this ease with her—it's unsettling, and there's a strange comfort in it.

It's not my style to let anyone get this close, damn sure not close enough to fucking feed me.

Yet here I am, unexpectedly docile and oddly at ease. It's comfortable. Too comfortable. Like the deceptive grip of a noose moments before it tightens and snaps my neck.

"*Home, lad. Yer home.*"

Shut up.

Chapter Seven
ENZO

As the food touches my lips, an involuntary moan escapes, deep and resonant. "*Mmm.*"

"Right?" Kennedy eagerly prepares another bite. "You look exhausted," she adds softly.

"You look beautiful," I say because it's true. From her tantalizing overbite to the heart shaped freckle on her neck, I've never seen a woman more beautiful in my life. But I mostly say it to avoid the conversation about why I look as beat down as I do.

She tipped toes further in the deep end of this conversation. "Are you going to tell me how you got the bruises on your face?"

This is the point at which I sit back and eat my own pasta. "Defending your honor, obviously."

"Obviously."

Her giggle flutters lightly, a fragile butterfly's wing against the stillness of my heart. I swiftly drown the stirring emotions with booze.

Pouring a glass for her and then for myself, I gulp down the

1982 Château Lafite with haste. As I refill my glass, she quips, "Thirsty?"

I glance at her, my gaze lingering on her breasts. "You have no idea."

For the next few hours, we eat, talk, and laugh, our conversations flowing alongside the steady pour of wine—glass after glass.

She points to my chest, her lips grazing that tempting lower lip. "Be honest with me," she requests.

"Always," I assure her, a vow I intend to keep with *Bella*. But the *truth* and *the whole truth*—two entirely different beasts.

"How did you know my sister was in Italy? Or where she lived?" Her eyes glint with a knowing that she's pieced together most of the puzzle. Instead of my usual evasion and a round of twenty questions, I choose to fill in the gaps of the picture for her.

For a price.

"Kiss me, and I'll tell you."

Her smile turns puzzled, a flicker of curiosity lighting up her eyes. "We've kissed before. Plenty of times. Why are you making a deal over a kiss?"

"Because right now, out of everything in the world I could have, it's the only thing I want."

I set down my glass and lean back, a smirk playing on my lips. She finishes off her third—no, fourth glass of wine, before trailing her finger along the table as she slowly makes her way to my chair.

Her body sways hypnotically as she moves, each step deliberate yet teasingly slow. The curve of her hips catches the soft light, accentuating every subtle shift as she closes the distance.

Her dress clings in all the right places, a blend of elegance and allure that commands attention without needing to ask for it.

I don't need to instruct her. Braver than she would be sober, she takes a seat on my lap, her eyes widening as the round curve of her ass nestles softly on my hard cock.

And when her lips meet mine, there's no hesitation. No restraint. No barriers left standing. A collision of heat and need—her lips, her breath, her tongue entwined with mine in a seductive dance.

For one fleeting moment, the world falls away. We are a heartbeat of connection—her shivering in my hold. Me, breathing in pure oxygen.

When she finally pulls away, the air crackles with electricity, and so much sexual tension you could cut it with a knife. Kennedy shifts on my lap, a move that's literal torture, and an awkward silence lingers between us.

I want her. And I'm pretty sure by the way she's squirming on my lap, she wants me to. Why we're not already fucking like bunnies is beyond me.

Her eyes meet the intensity of my gaze briefly before looking away. "Your turn," she whispers.

My turn? Right. How I knew about her sister.

I blink away the lust fog, clearing my throat. "I promised you I'd protect your sister, just as if she were my own. And, I did."

She shakes her head incredulously. "By sending her halfway around the world to Italy? And you fabricated an entire internship? With a salary and an extravagant place to stay?"

"Yes."

Her gentle fingers run through my hair, her eyes searching mine. "Why?"

"You wanted her safe. With my connections and my family ties to the region, nowhere in the world is safer than here. You and I made a deal, *Bella*. Remember?"

The faint blush tinting her cheeks tells me she definitely remembers me devouring her sweet pussy.

Sure, the bill to ensure her sister's safety in Italy skyrocketing towards six figures in just a few weeks, the price tag is staggering.

But in exchange for Kennedy willingly offering herself to me on a platter, legs spread and telling me to eat her out?

Fucking priceless.

"I always keep my word," I remind her, brushing a few strands of hair from her face.

Normally, my words would be cold, distant, and transactional—neither warm nor personal. But now they spill out oddly tender, infused with a depth of genuine care that even I don't recognize.

Fuck. Who am I?

My phone pings, giving the control freak in me the chance to step in.

It's a desperate attempt to detach myself from obsessing over Kennedy for even a minute more. A lifeline to reality I instantly seize.

I don't make excuses or provide an explanation. I just grab it.

> **STRIKER**
> Followed your uncle and Rocco all day. Photos attached.

Rocco. The bastard who attacked Kennedy. Just the mention of his name has my jaw clenching so hard, I'm liable to crack a tooth.

I imagine his torture session starting with him dangling from a meathook and me etching "Thou Shalt Not Rape" twenty times into the flesh of his back with a soldering iron.

Rest assured, vengeance will be mine. It's just won't be today.

In the first image, my asshole uncle hands the local *prete*—or priest—an envelope, likely stuffed with cash. The moron still believes he can buy his way into heaven. Last I checked, St. Peter doesn't do pay-to-play.

I flip through a few more images of him, barely registering Kennedy's question of whether she should leave.

Random shots capture Andre and Rocco maneuvering around town, conferring with his army of Capos and his trusted Consigliere.

Hmm. The bastard is up to something. But what?

Kennedy is already on her feet, moving toward the door. "Savannah and I had an interesting chat on the plane."

That grabs my attention, though I continue to focus on another cluster of images that pop up on my phone as I make my way to the sofa. "Did you?" I ask, distracted.

By this point, I'm so absorbed in the image on the screen that I only half hear what *Bella* says. "She told me you were handing me back to Andre the moment we return to the States." A beat later, her timid voice asks, "Is that true?"

But her words don't register above the rage pounding in my ears.

I'm staring at an image of Uncle Andre at a restaurant, flanked by Rocco and his useless entourage, and lo and behold, there's Jimmy fucking Luciano among them.

He's the reason Kennedy is in debt to begin with. "Debts will be honored," I mutter under my breath, white-hot anger simmering just below the surface.

I wipe my face and tamp down my overwhelming need to get in a car, drive into town, and hunt down that man like it's opening day in the *Hunger Games*.

Then, I try zooming in on the blurry image. Seriously, did Striker take this photo from space?

My pulse pounds out of my chest, a needle of doubt prodding at my gut. Douchebag Jimmy is the one who owes my uncle a hundred grand. His disappearance is the entire reason why Kennedy's in debt in the first place.

What's Uncle Andre up to?

Could he be up to something at all? I mean, Kennedy and I met by chance.

I scrutinize the image once more. Those brooding, shadowed eyes, the lean figure, that exaggerated mustache. If I'm right, and I'm damn near certain I am, then Kennedy's off the hook.

I start to speak, ready to spill the beans to Kennedy. Uncle Andre's been pulling the wool over her eyes—and mine—all this time. Which means I don't have to settle her debt after all.

But what if I'm wrong?

What if this is just my shattered, desperate mind grasping at the faintest glimmer of hope, the one elusive miracle that might release Kennedy from Uncle Andre's ironclad grasp.

But, then what?

If she has no debt, there's no reason for her to stay.

If she believes she's free, I know exactly what she'll do. She'll run.

And my *Bella* can't run.

I'm not done with her yet.

I slide my phone into my pocket, my thoughts spinning in every direction until they land on what I must do next. When I lift my gaze, the silence in the room is suffocating. Too quiet.

It's then that the control freak in me goes ballistic. Kennedy is gone.

In three quick strides, I cross the room and rush down the hall. The soft rustling from behind the bedroom door tells me she's inside. But when my hand grips the handle, it's locked.

My fist slams against the door. "Let. Me. In," I demand.

"No!" Her refusal is a bonfire of raw heat and defiance. My cock instantly responds.

"She deserves the truth," the Scottish voice urges.

"The truth?" I scoff bitterly to no one. "No. What *Bella* deserves is to be punished."

"You said you were giving her back to Andre," the voice warns.

I did?

I mentally replay the conversation and shake my head in disgust. Goddamnit, he's right. I roll my eyes. The son of a bitch is always right.

Exhaling deeply, I straighten my cuff and knock once more, my voice firm yet controlled. "Open the door, Kennedy."

"The only way you're getting through that door is if you break it down," comes her defiant response.

What?

All the instincts I've kept suppressed suddenly surge to the surface, full force.

Stepping back, I gather all my pent-up frustration into one forceful kick.

With a resounding crash, the door flies open, and I stride inside.

Chapter Eight
KENNEDY

I SWEAR, this man is a goddamn nightmare.

Sure, he's a beautiful nightmare, all power and control with golden eyes that pierce you like daggers and a body chiseled from stone, but a nightmare nonetheless.

And I'm the idiot who kisses him. Slid my ass right onto that colossal cock of his and imagines he's . . . what? A knight in shining armor? A guy plucked from the pages of a romance novel ready to rescue me?

Ha! Prince Charming my ass. More like Duke of the Dick's.

Frustrated, I start packing. It doesn't matter that I'm in a foreign country and have no idea where I'll go or what I'll do. I'm not staying here another second. Not when he's treating me like a book borrowed from Andre D'Angelo's sleazy porn library.

Ugh!

I snatch my duffel and hastily cram it with clothes. Mostly brand new clothes with very expensive price tags on them, but who knows where my own clothes are in this fashionista closet.

And since I'm fleeing with little more than a thimble of dignity, I need something to wear.

When I spot my vibrator, you bet I'm taking it. One, it's mine. And two, I need something to cool down all this pent-up heat melting off my panties. Because when an Italian God makes his moves, my traitorous body responds, damnit.

Snatching my old denim jacket from the hanger, a card flutters out of the pocket—Agent Caleb Knox's card. As much as I'm tempted to dial him up now, it's past midnight, and I doubt the man's sitting around, waiting for confidential informants to blow up his phone.

But wait. That's local time. What time is it in Chicago?

Out of nowhere, a booming voice echoes from the hall. "Let. Me. In."

I clutch the card in my hand, bolstered by the courage from that and the bottle of wine I downed, and retort boldly, loudly, "No!"

What does Enzo expect me to say? When I pressed him about returning me to Andre after this trip, all he bothered to say was, *"Debts will be honored."*

What a total fucking asshole.

I tuck the card in my bag and refocus on packing. I'll spend one final day with Riley and strategize my next steps afterward. But one thing is absolutely certain: I won't be sacrificed to his uncle for the greater D'Angelo good.

Just as my false sense of confidence is making me feel all zen in my decision, I hear three gorilla knocks and his stupid voice sounding through. "Open. The. Door."

I swear, this man makes me thermonuclear. I shout back, "The only way you're getting through that door is if you break it down." Which, considering it looks like it's from the 17th century and made of solid oak, I doubt he will.

Though, and I hate to admit this, that does sound hot.

The mere thought of Enzo Ares D'Angelo, the living, breathing God of War, smashing through that ancient door, pinning me up against the nearest wall, and ravaging my body mercilessly sound so insanely hot, in fact, I actually give my vibrator a second glance.

I shake my head. *What's wrong with me?*

In an instant, the door flies open with a violent slam. I jolt —there's Enzo, demolishing the massive door as if it's cardboard.

He strides in, his expression brutal and dark, his overpowering presence instantly filling the space.

I stagger back—dizzy and transfixed. The room tilts, spinning in a heady mix of fine wine and raw Alpha male dominance.

My heart hammers against my ribs as he glides through the room, each movement a deliberate, predatory prowl of a panther zeroing in on his prey.

It's at this point I realize I'm too intoxicated to fully grasp the situation. Enzo is dangerous. Ruthless. And right now, all that formidable wrath is laser-focused on me.

If I had a shred of common sense, I'd be scared. Terrified, even. In any sane scenario, I'd turn and run. But that's the problem. The closer he gets, the more my brain cells dissolve into dust.

With his next step, I'm pressed against the wall. A solid wall of muscles and tension, impossibly hot against mine.

And as a raging river of alcohol surges through my veins,

too swiftly to stop, I blurt out, "What do you think you're doing?"

"What am I doing?" Without warning, he grabs both my wrists. Hard. "I'm doing as you wished, *Bella*. You demanded I kick the door down to get in, and so I did." In one swift move, he yanks both arms over my head, pinning me in place. "Be careful what you wish for."

A sudden knot of panic tightens within me. My body recoils, twisting and writhing against his. Desperately wrenching to break free. "Enzo."

"*Shh*," he breathes, his sturdy arms lifting me higher until I'm on my toes, barely touching the ground.

Not much of a challenge for me, given my years of dance, yet I gasp. It's not pain or fear that grips me. Is it . . . a thrill? Am I twisted enough to actually enjoy this?

"You were a bad girl, *Bella*," he murmurs, his teeth nipping at the heart-shaped freckle on my neck just hard enough for tears to prick my eyes. "And you will be punished."

I suck in a sharp breath, releasing a single, trembling word. "Punished?"

"Consequences." This time, his lips nip my shoulder, and his thick thigh wedges between the two of mine. "Ride my leg, dirty girl."

I freeze. "What?"

"I'm not releasing you until I feel every last ounce of your dripping hot honey soaking through my slacks."

He wants me to dry hump his legs. Because, what? I haven't earned his dick?

"Fuck yourself," he murmurs, his heated breath a hypnotic caress against my skin.

It's degrading. And definitely breaches the barrier between naughty and down right filthy. What's worse is that I can feel the pool of wetness forming at my sex, but I'm not telling him that.

When his thigh presses up against my clit, my body moves involuntarily, thrusting slow. Desperate not to give in, I force through a series of rough, mechanical moves along a thigh. It's enough to quell the ache of desire throbbing between my legs, but it's not enough to come.

His golden eyes darken, smoldering with heat. "Still being bad, *Bella*?"

What is he, a mind reader? It's like he knows I'm deliberately saving off my gratification. And my angry fuck god is having none of it.

Ladies, meet Enzo D'Angelo—the living lie detector. He can spot a fake orgasm from ten paces, no mercy, no mistakes.

He swiftly lowers my hands, guiding them to rest on his broad shoulders as he rips open the front of my dress. Both his hands land on my bra, massaging my breasts so perfectly, I have to bite back a moan.

"Faster," he coaxes.

I try to fight my body's desperate need to obey. "No."

The sharp smack on the side of my ass is instant. The pain morphs to pleasure as he caresses the sting with the heat of his hand. "Has your pussy ached for me all day?"

And then some. "No," I pant. My defiance comes out more like a whimper than a roar.

His chuckle rumbles low, thick with amusement candy-coated in a threat. "The things I will do to that mouth for your lies."

One hand on my hip, he begins to control my movements. His free hand dives into his pocket—smooth, quick. My blood chills as he pulls out a switchblade, and flicks open the knife.

My gaze is locked, unblinking. My rhythm slows only for a beat before my body takes over. She has a mind of her own now. As if she knows everything he wants.

Or, knows everything *I* want.

With steady precision, the cool tip of the knife barely presses against my chin. The distant pinprick of sensation forces my eyes to his deep gold ones.

A steady stream of tears spill over, barely registering as simmering heat builds beneath my skin, spreading like wildfire.

Will he cut me?

Hurt me?

Kill me?

"That's it." He growls. His voice is so satisfied. So pleased. It kind of pisses me off. "Only good girls get my cock."

Girls? Plural? "Go to hell."

"Without your breathtaking body fucking mine, every day is hell."

The knife slips beneath one strap of the bra. Snip. Then the other. I watch, breath held, as he slices it off. My heavy breasts fall free. My nipples, embarrassingly hard and tight.

By this point, I'm flooded with enough arousal, I'm a damn water slide on the man's lap. Soft kisses land along my neck, shoulders, and chest as he teases my nipples with his tongue. "Beg me to let you come, *Bella*. Or, I stop."

I want to resist. I do. But I can't. It's like every fantasy I've ever had about a professor walking in on me fucking my pillow.

His wrath? Ten punishing smacks on the ass before making me beg to let my pussy come.

So close.

The sharp bite of pain on my nipple makes my eyes squeeze shut. My stride ratchets up, "Please . . ." escapes my lips before I can help myself.

His deep voice plucks the tightest chord. "Come," he says, the knife at my throat as a million stars explode behind my eyes.

The supernova orgasm hits me in waves. "Enzo!" I scream, over and over, my voice cracking like a desperate plea. A prayer.

Because even as his soft kisses feather my lips and cheeks, and his thumbs wipe every tear from my face, all I can think is, how can he do this to me?

Use me.

Seduce me.

Shatter me.

Fuck me.

Only to let me go.

Chapter Nine
ENZO

God, I could do this all night.

The satisfying crack of bone meeting fist is like magic for easing tension.

Mine. Not his.

I cock a brow and study the man strapped to a forklift. I'm pretty sure tension is the least of his worries. Considering I've moved from punching his face to a hard jab to his throat, he's probably praying for death about now.

After a minute of wheezing, he speaks. "I swear, I d-don't. Know. Anything . . ." he eventually sputters out. Actually, he's talking pretty good for a guy with six teeth on the floor.

And yet he's not telling me what I wanna know. "At the risk of sounding repetitive, I'm going to ask again. Where's Jimmy Luciano?"

The stubborn bastard shakes his head. For one of Uncle Andre's foot soldiers, he's surprisingly loyal.

I handpicked him because he's high enough up to have the

intel I need, but low enough that his absence won't raise any alarms. Like, ever.

He was also in the midst of beating a woman I presume was his wife, so I doubt she'll miss him either.

I crack my neck and give it another shot. This time, my foot connects with his knee, a sharp pop echoing loudly enough that it has to hurt like a motherfucker.

He howls in agony, followed by an obstinate "Fuck you!"

It's like watching the stages of grief unfold before my eyes: denial, anger, bargaining, depression, and acceptance. Right now, he's stuck in anger. I need him at bargaining.

Spoiler alert: no one ever gets past bargaining.

I check my watch and blow out an indecisive breath.

Push.

Don't push.

Six of one, half dozen of the other.

I examine his breathing and slumped physique. He's so out of shape that, frankly, just saying boo might give him a heart attack.

Besides, either way gets me there around the same time. Not that it matters.

It's not like *Bella* is waiting for me to come home and spoon her. Not that spooning would ever be on my agenda. I'm more of an *on your knees, suck my cock* kinda guy.

But every time I go to take her—really, truly fuck the girl senseless—my brain derails.

Make no mistake, I want her. There is no part of me that doesn't want to pry open the gates to *Bella's* heaven and slam in to the hilt. Repeatedly.

Fuck. What's stopping me?

"You seem a little"—Dante blows out a breath—"I don't know. Frustrated," he says suggestively.

Both bodyguards smirk.

Great. You want to announce it to the world?

The fact that I still haven't fucked Kennedy and my balls are three sizes too full and desperate for relief has nothing to do with it. "This guy has answers," I quip back.

"Uh-huh," Dante replies, unimpressed. "Is that why you've been pounding him like veal off and on for twenty hours straight?"

Yes. That, and I'm avoiding *Bella*. I need answers before I see her again. If that means an entire day of taking out my frustrations on this scumbag, so be it.

"Hey, it's okay," Dante says as he strolls over and placates me with a paternal pat on the shoulder. "Women have needs." He smacks my cheek playfully. "The right girl who's into needle dicks will come along one day."

"And when she does, I'll be sure to hand her your card." I snatch my phone from my pocket, flip to the image, and point it at Dante's face. "That's Andre. That's this guy." I gesture to the mass of blood and broken bones barely breathing. "And *that*," I point to the center of the image, "is Jimmy Luciano."

Dante squints at the images and scratches his chin. "I feel like that could be anyone."

I narrow my eyes and thrust the image toward the man clinging to life, forcing him to focus on it with his good eye—not the one that's all kinds of jacked like a swarm of bees went ape shit on it.

"Could this be anyone?" I sneer.

Exhausted, he strains to look, then lets out a sigh. "That's

J.," he manages between labored breaths. "He's . . .the . . . Shipper."

Shipper. Both Dante and I exchange a glance. We've always known Andre's achilles heel was seeded in distribution. We could never sniff it out.

I pull out my steel-cased Glock and weigh it in my hands. "Let's cut to the chase. You spill the details on the next shipment, and I'll end it fast and clean with a bullet between the eyes."

I'm not sure if he's nodding or his body is going into convulsions, but I take it as a yes.

"Good. Let's start with an easy one. What's he shipping?"

"*Pelle*," he utters with a gasp and what might actually be his last breath.

Fuck.

Pelle. As in skin. It confirms my uncle's despicable human trafficking operation is in full swing.

"When?"

Silence.

I smack him harder. "Where?" I shout.

No answer.

My mind goes into a tailspin, and I'm not even fully aware of pounding the man's lifeless body over and over again until Dante and the guards forcibly pry me off him.

"How many women? Dozens? Hundreds? Are there children, too?"

"He's gone," Dante insists.

I know he's right. Still, I deliver one last ruthless blow to his head.

Our sister, Trinity, was raped, brutally beaten, and left for dead by a sadistic monster, but she's not alone. For every Trinity, there are countless predators eager to unleash their worst.

My uncle's empire rises on the broken backs of these victims. Well, tearing it down, bit by bit, will become my favorite pastime.

My pulse quickens as anger shifts to a desperate need to set things right. But how?

I quickly scour his belongings for his phone. Dante shakes his head. "Facial recognition probably won't do the trick."

I deadpan. I press the dead man's broken finger against the phone. Instantly, it unlocks.

I hold up the unlocked phone. "Not my first rodeo," I quip.

Chapter Ten
KENNEDY

"WHY CAN'T YOU STAY?" Riley asks, her chocolate and Nutella gelato slowly dripping down the cone.

I take a leisurely lick of my *amarena* gelato, savoring the burst of cherries and creamy sweetness, as we enjoy an after-dinner stroll through the quaint Italian streets.

Last night, I cut my evening with Riley short to rush back for dinner with Enzo. A sumptuous spread of bruschetta, handmade pasta with a decadent cream sauce, and grilled sea bass drizzled with lemon and caper sauce I savored alone, since Enzo never showed.

So, to hell with him. I'm spending all the time in the world with Riley. Not that he would notice. Did I mention it's been over a day since I've seen his arrogant ass?

I shake it off as Truffles tugs me forward, his curiosity leading the way as we amble along. It's easy to forget I have only a few days left. Unless I can find a way out that guarantees both Riley and me stay safe.

I take a breath and ponder Riley's question as I admire the building ahead. The town wears its history like a cherished heirloom, each building adorned with trailing vines and vibrant bougainvillea.

The air hums with the melody of an accordion drifting from a nearby café, mingling with the tantalizing scents of freshly baked bread and rich espresso.

My steps slow, echoing on the cobblestones as I think up an answer.

Why can't I stay?

Hmm, let's see . . .

I'm trapped into repaying Jimmy Luciano's debt while Enzo and Andre tear me apart in a vicious tug-of-war for who can fuck me over the most.

With a resigned sigh, I decide to give her the only excuse that makes sense. Reaching into my bag, I pull out my phone and show Riley the screen.

My phone is filled with images of the girls from dance class. Their cute tutus and goofy poses make me smile as they all attempt adorable arabesques, cramming into the tiny screen. Like a band of wobbly toddler flamingos, they melt my heart every single time.

"Look at these," I say, scrolling through the gallery. "They've been bombarding me with these images several times a day." I shrug, telling her plainly, "Who could deny those faces?"

I flip through a few more, especially the pics with filters—dog ears and rainbow vomit, oversized glasses and flower crowns. Their eyes sparkle with playfulness, each photo a shot of sunshine and happiness. And innocence.

The only anchor truly dragging me back is the menacing shadow of Andre D'Angelo. If Enzo forces me to return and I run, I know what will happen. Andre will strike like a shark, tearing Riley from her life without mercy.

I'd rather die than go back to Andre or Rocco. But if anything happened to Riley, I'd never forgive myself. I promised *Da* I'd look after her, and I damn well will.

If Andre D'Angelo is hellbent on doing his worst to one of us, then it's decided.

It's me.

What happens to me doesn't matter. Keeping Riley safe is the only thing that counts.

"Is it because of your boyfriend?" she asks out of the blue.

My steps freeze. "What boyfriend?"

"That one there." She points at the screen, indicating the single picture someone managed to snap of Enzo. It's from before we left, when the girls were driving him nuts, surrounding him like he'd just sprouted a horn and turned into a glittery unicorn.

I can't help but laugh, the memory momentarily lifting the weight off my shoulders.

Then, I notice Riley, her brow arched, *definitely your boyfriend* written all over her face as if she's hit the nail on the head, dead center.

I finish off my cone. "He's not my boyfriend."

"But he's the reason you're here in Italy, isn't he? And the reason you have to go back?"

Wow. Riles is seriously batting a thousand here. "No," I say, gripping the half-truth like a vine in quicksand. Yes, I'm here because of him, but that doesn't make him my boyfriend.

Let's forget for a moment that he's a ruthless mob boss and a world-renowned player. The man only wants me for a week. That alone doesn't exactly scream *boyfriend material*.

She plants herself in front of me, stern-faced, pointing her cone right at my face. "Why. Can't. You. Stay?"

A wave of sorrow crashes over me as I remember a much younger version of myself asking *Da* the exact same question on the last night I saw him alive.

Did he know what might happen to him, the way I do now?

Channeling our sweet Da's words, I simply say, "Because I can't."

"*Booo*." She frowns, eyes narrowing as she angrily chomps down the last of her cone. Then, her brows shoot up. "Isn't that him?"

I spin around and there he is. Stubble grown out, wavy hair disheveled, and a suit that's seen better days. Even from across the street, he looks like he hasn't slept in a week—a complete walking disaster.

And yet, he's utterly gorgeous.

We watch as he slips on his sunglasses, glances at his watch, and scans the area. When his gaze shifts in our direction, Riles and I instinctively turn around.

"It is him, isn't it?" she whispers.

"No," I lie.

"Then why are we hiding?"

"We're not hiding," I say, feeling the sharp yank of the leash. Of course, Truffles wants to dart into open traffic to play with his pal Enzo.

Truffles whimpers and hops, desperate to give us away.

"Not now, little traitor," I mutter under my breath, quickly whisking him up into my arms to hide him, too.

Slowly, Riley turns around to check him out some more. "He's cute."

Only Riley would refer to a living, breathing god as *cute*. "If you say so," I reply, silently praying he doesn't see us.

"Who's that woman?"

What woman?

I whip around and see a beautiful woman in a form-fitting dress and painfully high heels rush into his arms, clinging to him like the last life raft on the Titanic.

He says something I can't make out, hands her what looks like a thick wad of cash, then unpeels her from him and swiftly ushers her into a waiting van.

Then, several more women emerge from a building, filing into the van in a steady stream. They don't all hug him or carry on like he's God's gift to women, but he hands each of each an equally large wad of cash.

"Did he just hand them all money?" Riley asks, as if reading my mind.

I can't reply. My chest feels like it's caving in, crushing my heart. Enzo makes me dry hump his leg, disappears for a day, and now he's here, handing a woman in a tight dress a wad of cash.

Did *she* beg for his dick? Did they all? Is that what's happening here?

Anyone can do the math. And by the look on Riley's face, she just did it too.

I'm almost relieved when my phone rings. Until I see that

it's the jerkface himself. I look up to find him suddenly seated at a café, facing away as a waiter brings him water and a menu.

"Who's that?" Riley asks, nosy as ever.

I ignore it and click it off. "No one important."

When it rings again, Riley grabs Truffles. "Looks like *Mr. No One Important* really wants to talk to you. Tell him if he breaks your heart, I'll kick him in the nuts. Repeatedly."

I smile because I know she really will.

Then she adds, "And I left a little something in your purse, but now that I've seen your *boyfriend*"—she exaggerates the word—"I doubt you'll need it."

Huh? I start digging through the tub-o-purse I lug around because I'm in a foreign country, and you never know when you'll need a raincoat. Or an adapter. And don't even get me started on the crap I carry around for Truffles.

I'm damn near tempted to dump it out right here on the sidewalk. If it's a bag of those little Italian almond cookies, I want to shove them all in my mouth right now. "What did you leave in my purse?"

She doesn't bother replying. She simply hugs me and flashes that evil smile of hers before skipping down the street, Truffles trotting after her, as they head towards the center of town.

Before I can rummage through my purse for whatever she stuffed in it, my phone rings again. I answer, "What do you want?"

"So many things, *Bella*," he says, all growly and rough. "Starting with, I want to know if you'll have dinner with me tonight."

"Funny, I thought we were having dinner last night. Since you didn't show, tonight I'll be having dinner with Riley."

His tone shifts, irritation rumbling beneath the surface. "You may not believe this, *Bella*, but there are aspects of my business that require my immediate attention."

Like prostitutes? I don't say it out loud, but the thought screams through my mind.

He sighs, "And as much as I'd like to spend every minute of this trip with you, the fact is I can't stay tonight. That's why we'll be having dinner promptly at six."

Am I the only one who noticed that he switched it from a question to a statement? I swear, the man is the living embodiment of frustration. "The answer is still no," I say firmly.

"It wasn't a request, *Bella*. We have a deal. You get time with your sister, and I get whatever the fuck I want. And tonight, I want dinner."

A small part of me is desperate to know why he's doing this. Collecting women like soccer trophies, yet still calling me.

And why his voice sounds so tired and worn. Though, with that many women fawning over him, I can probably guess.

Instead of telling him where he can shove dinner, I bite back the impulse and give in. "Fine," I say, keeping my voice steady. "Six o'clock."

"Six o'clock," he repeats then disconnects.

I should be ready to storm off and leave, but I can't. There's an unsettling allure in watching him when he doesn't know I'm here. It's like observing a magnificent, wild lion on safari, lazily surveying his domain.

I take a seat on a bench and stare like a stalker as he lights a cigar and makes several more calls.

An hour into it, a stunningly dressed woman approaches, clearly asking if the seat next to him is taken.

He presses the phone to his chest and says something to her that, judging by the look on her face, is both offensive and threatening.

Sheesh.

She bolts without a second glance, and he continues his call as if nothing happened.

With a sharp crack in the air, Enzo snaps his fingers, summoning the waiter. He hustles over, pad and pen at the ready. Enzo scribbles something quick and sharp, tossing the pen back like it's an afterthought. It's probably the bill.

A sleek black car glides to a halt at the curb, its timing impeccable. Enzo rises, smooth and purposeful, and strides towards the car, where the driver already holds the back door open.

It's then that for the briefest moment, his gaze locks onto mine.

Butterflies erupt in my gut, chaotic and relentless. The longer he stands there, the more my heart stutters, sending waves of heat crashing up my neck and cheeks, trapping me in my own skin—motionless, breathless.

Then, as if it was all in my head, he slips into the car without a moment's hesitation. The door shuts and the driver returns behind the wheel. When the car disappears around the corner, just like that, he's gone.

Why does this sting? Did I crave his attention? Is that why I'm still planted here?

"*Scusi,*" a voice interrupts my spiraling thoughts.

I glance up to see the waiter from the restaurant, handing me a small sheet of paper along with a menu.

The note reads:

Let the nice man know what you'd like for dinner.
See you tonight.

Chapter Eleven
KENNEDY

"What's going on?" Enzo's voice trails off, perplexed. It isn't the blustery boom I expected, not even the slightest bit irritated.

Just utterly dumbfounded.

Since I saw him this afternoon, he's somehow managed to clean himself up, transforming from something the cat dragged in to devastatingly claw-worthy.

His dark hair, now slicked back, accentuates the sharp angles of his face. And the unshaven mess from earlier is gone, replaced by neatly trimmed stubble that frames his chiseled jaw.

The rumpled blue shirt has been traded up for a crisp, tailored cream one that hugs his broad shoulders and tapers down to his sculpted waist.

My eyes linger a little too long, drinking in the sight of the top two buttons undone, revealing a tantalizing glimpse of tan skin and muscles that are pure torture to look away from.

The golden hue of his eyes is sharper now, framed by thick brows and dark lashes that make him even more devastating.

His scent—a heady mix of rich boy cologne and expensive cigars—fills the air, sending my pulse racing like a snare drum at a Queen B concert.

There are two dozen velvety red roses clutched in his hands that I try to ignore.

"I'm cooking," I declare with an authority that would be laughable if it weren't so pitiful. The most I've ever managed in the kitchen is an egg, and even that was a disaster. Charred rubber, anyone?

But here I am, with a pot of boiling water and a chaotic scene on the counter. Tomatoes, garlic, and onions are roughly chopped, their juices mingling into a sticky mess that's spreading like a crime scene. A jar of homemade sauce, the market vendor's pride and joy, has already been knocked over twice now. And meat.

A lot of meat.

He motions to the mounds of paper-wrapped ground chuck, pork, and veal. "How much did you buy?"

I shrug, trying to look nonchalant. "I'm not exactly a wizard at converting metric to standard, but judging by the weight, I'd say we're staring down the barrel of eight to ten pounds."

His brows arch in surprise. "Went for the traditional bowling ball portion, did we?" He scrutinizes the mountain of food laid out. "What happened to *Antonio's*?"

"Who?"

"The restaurant that gave you the menu."

Innocently, I shrug. "There's a lovely market just down from Riley's that had everything we'd need for a cozy meal. And I'm in Italy, the home of marinara. Plus, I've always dreamed of making a home-cooked meal in a lavish gourmet kitchen."

I gesture enthusiastically at the restaurant-quality space, only to knock over the jar of sauce for the third time. With an embarrassed smile, I quickly set it out of reach.

"Is that so?" he asks, shaking his head. "I really don't have time for this," he mutters, frustration seeping from every word.

"I'm almost done," I assure him, lying through my teeth.

"You are if my options are *E. coli* poisoning or death by beef."

"You should've worn your buffet pants."

With a huff, he sets down the flowers and rolls up his sleeves, brushing past me to head to the pantry. It's the size of a gas station convenience store, so God knows what he's grabbing.

"How long did you know I was across the street today? The whole time?" I holler into the pantry.

"Yes," he replies back, with the calm of a seasoned sniper. "The whole time."

"How?"

He reemerges with two black aprons, slipping one over his head and the other over mine. "Keeping an eye on you is my favorite pastime. I'm always watching."

Always? Of course he is. At least I'm not the only stalker.

Then, with a firm grip on my wrist, he drags me to the sink and starts washing my hands.

"What the—? I am not a toddler," I protest.

"No, you just cook like one." He pats my hands dry, tilts my chin up with a commanding finger, and presses a quick, possessive kiss to my lips. "Watch and learn, *Bella*."

And so, I do.

For the next hour, I watch my big, bad mob boss transform

into Julia Child. How being able to cook makes one of the sexiest men alive a million times hotter is beyond me. But as he lifts a wooden spoon of sauce to my lips, sweet baby Jesus, it sure as hell does.

"Mmm," I let out, savoring the flavor.

He suckles a drop of sauce off my lower lip, his brow furrowing in concentration. "It needs a little..."

He reaches for his phone and dials. It rings once. "*Si, signore.*"

"Chef, I need a bottle of Nebbiolo."

"Why?" The voice on the other end isn't the chef. It's his brother, Dante.

"No reason." Watching Enzo clam up in front of his brother is like watching the keeper of the Holy Grail withhold its location from the town crier.

Dante chuckles. "I know you're not making your world-famous pasta, or you would have invited me."

"World-famous pasta sauce?" I mouth.

I smile as Enzo's jaw tightens. "Just have the chef bring me the Nebbiolo," he demands sternly, then abruptly disconnects the call.

A few minutes later, the bell rings. Enzo's head is in the oven like he's evaluating a breach birth, so I hop off the counter and head towards the door. "I'll get it."

Playing house with Enzo is definitely surreal. But watching him go gray over whether the cannoli shells need another minute in the oven? It's like a mashup of *MasterChef*, *The Godfather*, and *The Twilight Zone*.

But before I even take two steps towards the hall, the door swings open. In comes Dante, Sin, Dory, Striker, a guard, another guard, and a man who looks suspiciously like the gardener.

The tray of hot cannoli shells hits the counter with a clang, and Enzo's murderous brow furrows in a murderous *what the fuck* expression.

The bodyguards cower behind Dante's mountainous frame as Dory holds up a bottle. "Someone ask for fancy wine?"

We begin ferrying portions of the lavish feast to a grand table, Dante pulling out my chair with a style that holds an old world charm. As we settle, Enzo's silent fury settles like mist.

But the storm that was brewing behind his eyes dissipates as everyone takes their seats. Dante leans in close to me, his voice a deep, reassuring rumble. "He can never stay mad for long."

I whisper, "How can you be so sure?"

Dante's blue eyes dance with delight. "Because he misses this shit. The chaos, the family. Sitting around a table, giving each other hell while we devour comfort food like it's the apocalypse."

Enzo arches a brow, clearly having overheard. "You can thank Kennedy for the spread. She made sure we had enough to feed an army."

Sin lifts his glass, a gentlemanly smile tugging at his lips. "To Kennedy."

They all follow suit as Enzo's glass clinks mine. "To Kennedy."

Within the first few bites, it's clear to see why Dante referred to it as *world famous*. The sauce is probably the best thing I've ever eaten.

Dante wipes sauce from his lips. "Come on, bro. This isn't just Nonna's recipe. What's the secret ingredient?"

"Crack cocaine," he teases with barely a grin.

It's strange to see him so at ease, as if the weight of the world has magically lifted from his broad shoulders.

"How was *salvataggio*?" Sin asks, and the room falls silent, everyone holding their breath.

"How was *what*?" I ask, sticking my nose right into the middle of what's probably something dangerous and very much none of my business.

Enzo's gaze sweeps across the table, lingering on each person before he sucks in a tired breath. "Fifty," he says, deflated.

Dory pats his hand with a surprising tenderness. "Fifty is good."

"Fifty is shit. It should've been five hundred." He yanks his hand away, and it hits me like a ton of bricks that I'm wading into a conversation where I don't belong.

I set down my napkin, latching onto the quickest escape route. "I'll just go grab the cannoli."

"I'll help," Dory offers kindly.

We make our way to the kitchen, giving me a chance to take a closer look at Dory. She's older, with brilliant red hair and the most outlandish, beautiful blue-framed glasses that make her look more like a rockstar manager than a personal assistant.

There's an air about her that's completely unafraid of Enzo. It makes me wonder how many people in the world can claim that.

Once we enter the kitchen, Dory inspects the counters and stove. "Spotless," she says, complimenting how nice and tidy everything is. "It's not how I cook," she teases.

"Me neither. If not for Enzo, you'd need a hazmat suit to

enter." I pull the full tray of cannoli out of the fridge, three dozen with assorted dipped ends: mini chocolate chips, pistachio and cherry, and crushed hazelnuts dusted with white chocolate.

"Enzo's always been like this," she says, smiling. "Total control is his superpower."

"You've known him a long time?" I ask, curious.

She shrugs a shoulder. "Not that he remembers, but yes."

That line throws me off. "Why wouldn't he remember?"

She pauses, her eyes flickering with old memories. "It was a very long time ago. And a lot has happened between now and then. But he always loved to cook. Something his Nonna taught him."

"Nonna?"

"Grandmother." Her smile turns wistful, almost sad. "They were very close. He wasn't always the ruthless monster that manages to make headlines."

It's hard to imagine all the layers that make up Enzo D'Angelo, or how far I'd have to drill down to find the real him.

I don't just want to know. I *need* to know. Savannah Whitaker warned me that Enzo had exactly one person that was important to him, and that was himself. She also said he hit on her and that Enzo is handing me back by the end of the week.

My head screams for caution, but my heart—the one that's been shattered so many times it can't take another blow—whispers that Enzo is worth the risk. A safe haven in a tumultuous sea. And deep down, a good man.

Which, admittedly, might be a stretch. Enzo is still a lethal mafia king notorious for everything from being a player to a psychotic murderer.

Seriously, no one wants to be on his bad side.

And the idea that Enzo deeply, truly cares for me might be my ridiculous heart living way too long in the cold and mistaking that first ray of sunlight for . . . love.

Still, when it comes to Enzo, I can't help it. My heart overflows with hope. How can it not? He rescued me from Andre and sent Riley halfway around the world just to keep her safe.

He didn't have to do either of those things. Yet, he did.

Plus, I'm pretty sure that whatever came out of Savannah's mouth was pretty much straight-up dog shit, but that's just a memo from my gut.

Like Alice in Wonderland, curiosity gets the better of me, and I dive in, headfirst, straight down the D'Angelo rabbit hole. "What's *salvataggio*?"

Dory's expression shifts slightly, a guarded look crossing her face. She eyes me for a moment, then grabs one of the cannolis—the white chocolate hazelnut one—and eats as she talks, keeping her voice down. "I think it means 'rescue' in Italian. But in Enzo's world, it's more complicated than that. It's about saving what's important, sometimes at great personal cost."

"Saving what?" I ask, nibbling on a chocolate chip one.

Dory leans in, her eyes darting around as if we're in a spy movie. "In case you didn't know," she whispers, "their uncle is a total a-hole."

Considering the man had me attacked and kidnapped while holding my douchebag stepfather's debt over my head like a guillotine, I wholeheartedly agree. "A-hole of the century."

Dory's expression darkens, her eyes narrowing with a mix of rage and resolve. "Apparently, one of Andre's latest monstrosities is trafficking women, and our boys here are determined to stop him. No matter the cost."

Our boys repeats in my head, but so does *no matter the cost.*

I think back to the woman at the van, how desperately she clung to Enzo. What if she was actually thanking him?

Realization hits me like a punch to the gut, sharp and unforgiving. Maybe Enzo isn't just a ruthless mafia overlord. Maybe, just maybe, he's risking everything to demolish his Uncle's human trafficking pipeline. Is that why he's been gone all this time? To save the lives of fifty women?

Because my big bad Enzo D'Angelo isn't just Satan incarnate, but an angel, too.

All the pieces start to fall into place, each revelation more staggering than the last.

His work with Dante.

Why he didn't want me to see any of the photos.

Moving Riley to the safest place on the planet he could find.

Risking his own life to rescue me.

"Keeping them all for yourselves?" Enzo's voice is a smooth rumble as he enters the room.

Dory, having inhaled her cannoli in a few ravenous bites, leaves me standing here like a greedy child caught red-handed, a tray of cannolis in one hand and a nibbled one in the other.

"It's not what it looks like," I stammer, my cheeks flushing with warmth.

"It looks like two women gossiping as if the world is their cannoli." Enzo steps closer, his presence overwhelming, and plucks the tray from my grip, handing it to Dory. "We'll join you in a minute."

Recognizing her cue, she exits with a subtle wink and a

sweet smile, biting into another cannoli as she leaves. When she's gone, his eyes lock onto mine. "What did she tell you?"

I don't want anyone to get in trouble. "Nothing. I mean, other than you've always been a control freak."

He sweeps my hair behind my shoulder, his gaze fixing on my heart-shaped freckle. "Lies," he whispers, his breath feathering my skin.

Goosebumps scatter across my arms, and the electricity between us could power all of Italy. When his eyes fall to my lips, I nibble them nervously.

Softly, he takes my hand, gently pulls the cannoli from my fingers, and devours most of it in one bite.

"Hey," I object, giggling as he chews.

"Are you kidding me? Those vultures will hoover them up in three minutes flat," he says, his words muffled by the mouthful of cannoli. Then, with surprising tenderness, he feeds me the last bite.

His expression shifts, a frown creasing his brow as he checks his watch again. "I need to leave."

"I know."

He doesn't pull away and neither do I. It's as if neither of us wants this fragile tether between us to break. Slowly, he begins to turn, heading for the door.

I can't let him leave like this, thinking some part of me is pissed at him when he's probably about to dive into something incredibly dangerous.

I can't let him leave like this, thinking I'm pissed at him when he's about to dive headfirst into a storm. Rescuing me from Andre was risky enough, but ripping countless innocent women from Andre's clutches? That's not just dangerous—he's asking for an all-out war.

"Enzo, wait."

The second he turns around, I kiss him, pouring all my desperation and fear into it. Then he's kissing me, fierce and unrestrained, totally losing control.

He slams me up against the wall, the impact sending a shiver down my spine. His hand cradles my neck, fingers threading through my hair, while the other tightens around my waist, pulling me flush against him, forcing me to feel every inch of his hard cock.

It's nothing but scorching heat—hunger and raw emotion colliding in a frenzy of everything we want to tell each other, but can't say.

My hands grip his shoulders, clinging to him as if he's my only anchor in a storm. Every touch, every kiss, feels so impossibly right.

His breath sears my skin as his mouth moves down my jaw, nipping and kissing, leaving a trail of fire in its wake.

My heart races, pounding damn near out of my chest as his hand makes its way to my breast. Instinctively, I wrap a leg around him, gripping his hair, wanting him so bad, I can hardly breathe.

Knock-knock. "Sir, it's time."

Enzo steps back from me in a rush, the fog of arousal dissipating like smoke. His eyes, now cold and distant, avoid mine entirely. "Yes. It's time." He clears his throat, the shift in his demeanor stark. "Is the jet ready?"

Jet? How far is he going?

The bodyguard nods. "The pilot is on standby. Your brother is in the car."

Enzo straightens, collecting himself with a swift, practiced efficiency. He pauses for only a second before saying, "Let's go."

No lingering gaze. No last look. As abruptly as snapping off a twig, he breaks away and leaves.

The molten mess of me crumbles as each fragment of my heart splinters with raw, jagged pain.

This is Enzo.

And this is how easy it is for him to walk away.

Chapter Twelve
KENNEDY

TWO IN THE MORNING.

And I'm still awake.

Eyes wide open, I follow the flickering moonlight as it filters through the wind-stirred trees. Shadows dance across the ceiling in a hypnotic ballet, each movement silent and sad.

When tossing and turning fails, I find myself reaching for my phone once more, a ritual I seem to repeat every ten minutes or so. It's gotten to the point the screen's bright glow doesn't even phase my eyes anymore.

Nothing.

Not a single message or missed call to let me know he's alright.

Ugh, can't the lethal idiot spare two minutes from his harrowing mob mission to let me know he's okay?

Or that he misses me.

Or hell, that he's even keeping an eye on me like a stalker.

Frustrated, I slam my eyes shut and will my body to sleep.

But I just want to hear from him, and it's driving me straight to the bowels of insomnia hell.

Not that I'm a stranger here. Nights have always been an anxious time for me.

After the night my *Da* was found dead, it's like my brain permanently short-circuited. Enzo just managed to ratchet it up a hundred notches. And not even the opulence of his bazillion-thread-count sheets or cloud made from sleep angels can save me now.

I toss and turn, as nervous energy pulses through my body like a live wire, thrumming for me to get up. If Truffles was here, he'd be whining for me to stay still. But even he has abandoned me to disappear off to who knows where.

Probably canoodling with Dory again.

Frustrated, I totally unleash on the innocent pillow next to me—Enzo's pillow—pummeling it with several harsh punches before resting my head against it again.

One whiff of his natural musky, earthy scent manages to soothe the low-grade fear that's been a constant companion since I was a girl, but not by much.

For a guy who wanted me all to himself for a week, he's playing hard to get like a champ.

Gah. It's impossible to get to sleep here. I inhale the pillow next to me again, and blow out a breath. I know what the problem is. It's the bed. It's *his* bed. The scent of him swirls all around, impossible to ignore.

Not his cologne, which is heavenly. Or his body wash, equally addictive. It's *him*. That sweet blend of hot-blooded Alpha male with just a hint of scotch and cigars.

When he's here, I sleep like a baby.

Yeah, because he usually fucks you into a coma.
Shut up.
And it's not like he does it with his dick. Which is weird, right?
I close my eyes. Instantly, solid muscles and ripped abs consume my thoughts before another thought enters the picture.
Oh, God. What if something happened to him?
I mean, he's a D'Angelo. His own father was one of the most powerful men in Chicago, and he vanished without a trace.
Wide awake, I stare at the ceiling and quietly whisper, "Look after him, *Da*." Which feels a little ridiculous . . . asking my deceased father to look after the notorious, psychotic kingpin.
Still, I do.
I check the phone again, then scroll to his contact information.
I flip to the internet, where my fingers suddenly scroll to all things Enzo D'Angelo. His unofficial fan page pops up first, a site created by and for fans of *Big Daddy D*.
Seriously? Does anyone actually call him that?
As soon as I go to click on a thread, a banner pops up requesting I subscribe to enter.
I roll my eyes, but who am I kidding? Of course I sign up.
And not just to see if I can find a dick pic, but because my mind is racing, wondering why I'm apparently the only woman in the northern hemisphere not to have sampled it.
I mean, make no mistake, he has one. A magnificently big one. I've felt it pressed up against my body many

times. I've just never seen the monster cock with my own eyes.

But from the feel of him, he's long enough to make me salivate, with just enough girth to make me the teensiest bit scared.

I find the latest string of comments on it. Several women rave about being, and I quote, "dangerously good." One fan even posted the following disclaimer:

> CAUTION!
> USE AT YOUR OWN RISK!
> SERIOUS CHOKE HAZARD.
> MASSIVE DICK MAY CAUSE HEART PALPITATIONS, SUDDEN FAINTING, AND A SEVERE ALLERGIC REACTION TO BUG-FUCKER DICKS.
> YOU HAVE BEEN WARNED.

I continue scrolling and laugh when I read one girl's testimonial:

> THE FACT THAT THE MAN CAN WALK UPRIGHT WITHOUT THE ASSISTANCE OF AN INDUSTRIAL, HEAVY-DUTY CRANE BLOWS MY MIND.

Then I see a comment that catches my attention:

Alert!! Where in the world is Horse Dick D'Angelo? If he switched teams, I will be crushed.

MIA? As in, he's missing. The message was months ago. Right around the time we met. I try not to make too much of it and read on. Message after message and months of women crying about the severity of their withdrawals and how much they miss Big Daddy, I choke back a bit of vomit and find this:

> *Keep hope alive ladies & check the map.*
> *Spotted getting into a PJ with a woman.*
> *Horse Dick Rides Again.*

Wait, what?

Did Enzo just hop on a jet and leave me for two other women?

What in the actual fuck?

I'm two seconds from calling him and giving him a piece of my mind when I pull up his contact and stare at his picture—a private moment of him having a bizarre stare down with Truffles.

My sleep-deprived brain suddenly kicks into overdrive, bombarded with random thoughts from out of freaking nowhere.

What if the woman in question is actually with Dante? I mean, he and Enzo did leave together. And he's got the same dark, wavy hair and panty-melting smile. And Dante seems, I don't know, a player in his own right.

Or, what if it isn't even Enzo or his jet at all? This could be up there with sightings of aliens and yetis. Just a bunch of sex-starved women clinging to the hope that Enzo the Sex God is skipping around like a wickedly bad Santa, ready to bestow his mighty Christmas stick to women near and far.

Or, what if this is one of the women he's actually rescuing? Like the ones I saw with my own eyes. It's easy to imagine Enzo as the king of the ruthless mobsters by day, and hot, dark hero by night.

That in his own special, maniacal way, he's doing what he can to right all the wrong's of the world.

Then again, there's one more option left. What if his legion of fans are actually right? I mean, they're spot on about the size of his obelisk of a dick, that's for sure.

God, why can't my hyperactive brain just shut down already?

Feeling deflated, I set down the phone and grab my purse. If Riles really did leave me cookies, they're about to get demolished.

I rummage through it in the dark because everyone knows there are no calories in the dark, and finally pull out the box. It's harder to open than I thought, and I pretty much tear it apart in my frustration.

That's when I notice it—a small red dot glowing from the corner of the ceiling.

What the hell is that?

I stare harder, trying to remember. Was that there earlier? Maybe. Who ever looks up at the ceiling?

Is it . . . it couldn't be . . . a *camera*?

And does the red light mean that thing is actually on?

I switch on the light, and there it is—a camera, clear as day. And in my hand? Definitely not cookies. Not even close.

It's the Titan 2000. The label reads:

Extra-long, Extra-thick,
Made for her Ultimate Pleasure
Engineered for maximum satisfaction with

LIFELIKE TEXTURE AND REVOLUTIONARY
TECHNOLOGY
20-SETTINGS PLUS HEAT

Below, in fine print, it boasts, "Waterproof, rechargeable, and guaranteed to deliver toe-curling ecstasy—or your money back."

Blech. Who takes back a vibrator?

And my baby sister found it, bought it, and stuffed it in my purse. I couldn't be prouder of her if I tried. How I didn't notice it earlier, considering it's roughly the size of Florida, is beyond me.

But I'm definitely noticing it now—along with the watchful eye of Enzo's spyware dangling from the ceiling.

Is he watching me?

Fondle a vibrator?

My pulse skyrockets at the thought of him spying on me, stalking me in my intimate, private moments. It should make me feel angry and violated, furious if I were even the slightest bit sane.

But it doesn't.

Of all the things I could feel right now, I feel bold. And definitely a little bit *naughty*.

And whether he's watching or not, my hand moves without permission. I know I shouldn't do this. I'm asking for trouble. And possibly a straight jacket.

I slide a finger along its length, delicately stroking every ridge, smoothing my hand up and down as if every move is for the pleasure of two golden eyes hiding in the dark.

I guess when I'm sleep deprived is when I become brave. Or

delirious. I look up at the small red dot and let out a ripe, delicious moan, "*Ahhh...*"

Nothing happens.

Hmm. I test the waters even more and shove aside the blankets, giving the light and whatever it's attached to in the ceiling full view of my body.

Then, I undress. Slowly so what's probably a smoke detector can catch every move. I slide the oversized cock between the valley of my breasts, down my stomach, and finally, to the delicate triangle of my thighs.

This wasn't about Enzo D'Angelo, though my nipples tightened at the thought of him, furious with rage at my disobedience, barging through the door, spreading my legs, and burying himself in me with one swift thrust.

And this wasn't even about getting myself to sleep, which, an orgasm usually does when I'm restless or anxious.

This was about me, reclaiming some small semblance of control, doing whatever the hell I want, whenever the hell I want.

And maybe Enzo isn't watching at all, but imagining he is makes me hot enough to keep going. My finger tracing circles along the base, ready to get off with the mother of all vibrators.

"Is this what you want, Mr. D'Angelo?" I ask no one at all.

When I press the button, the buzz is so loud, I jolt. It takes me a minute to figure out the settings—fast, slow, pulse, jackhammer.

I ease it back to something I'm used to. Then, I imagine what he would do, and dial it up the slightest bit.

Half of me screams, *What the fuck are you doing?* while the other half of me—the one controlling Titan—presses forth like the charging of the bulls.

"Are you watching?" I asked, my voice raspy to the empty room. Out of nowhere, I add, "This could be you, Enzo. Shoving that big cock of yours where you want."

Jeez. Who am I?

Propping up to my elbows, I smiled at the dark corner of the ceiling, lick my lips, and smile shyly. "Would you command me to spread my legs," I say to the ceiling, spreading my thighs just enough.

Confident that he isn't actually listening at all, I add, "Would you make me open up wider?"

Silence.

Well, except for the low hum enticing its way to my sweet little spot, as I prepare to go to absolute town on myself.

I suck my middle finger hard before slicing it down my body, ready to work in tandem with the toy. "Please, fuck me, Mr. D'Angelo," I beg. "Fuck me hard."

Chapter Thirteen

ENZO

I MENTALLY grapple with the question: How many can I actually take on at once?

Half a dozen? Maybe.

A dozen if I truly put everything I have into it.

This isn't bravado talking. It's my inner predator—the beast—the one that's been unleashed before and will come out again, without hesitation.

Growing impatient, I repeat, "How many?"

We have one shot at this—a single chance to storm the warehouse, annihilate every one of Andre's henchmen, and free hundreds of captive women. Simple.

Easy fucking peasy.

And that's not just the two bags of C4 at my feet talking; it's me betting everything on a team whose skill, brutality, and thirst for blood are unmatched in every way—including my own brother. The knot in my gut twists that much more thinking of Dante by my side.

I know this won't be a clean getaway. It'll be chaos. Full-blown Armageddon times ten. And with Dante here, if things go south, our family risks losing not one but two brothers.

We'll be battling our way out to the bitter end, which is why I need the numbers.

Ryder's voice crackles through my earpiece, husky and certain. "Boss, I count a dozen."

"Is that because that's as high as you can count?" Blaze fires back, sarcasm evident.

"Technically, I can count to twenty-one if I use my dick," Ryder responds, without missing a beat.

Bruno jumps in, amused. "At least it's good for something. More like twenty and a half."

Ryder refocuses, the mission at the forefront. "Again, I count twelve. But I'd bet my house, dog, and left ball we're looking at twice that many at least."

"No one wants your left ball," Diaz replies dryly, adding, "Least of all, your wife." We all chuckle, and part of me is vindicated.

The guys never wanted Diaz here. Not because they doubt her abilities. Badass Diaz is more than capable. And we needed a pilot. But they all worried it would hit too close to home.

Her release from the hospital was months ago, not years. Rushing from one brutal attack into the arms of battle? No one was sure she was ready.

No one but me.

When she looked at me with those ice-cold eyes and threatened to throw a Molotov cocktail at my onyx black Aston Martin if I even dreamed of stepping foot on the jet without her, it was clear she was ready.

And how could I say no? I just got that car.

Besides, I owe her—a debt not many can claim. It was Diaz who uncovered where Kennedy's kidnappers had taken her. Without her sharp instincts and relentless drive, who knows what might have happened.

We're more than a team. We're family. Most of us have known each other since grade school, and three tours in the sandbox only solidified the bond my men have. You couldn't separate us if you tried.

Some say trust is earned. In our world, real trust is forged through blood, sweat, and more near-death experiences than even Ryder can count.

These men would take a bullet for each other in a New York second. Giving each other shit is just our love language. The way Dante and I crucify each other to our faces while having each other's backs.

Every fucking time.

Still, even I know the risks of having my brother here. It's a double-edged sword. Constant fear churns in my gut like acid, a relentless reminder that our lives are always at risk.

Our father's disappearance taught me that much.

I hate it.

Hate wondering which of us will fall first: one of them or me.

Hate the way my chest tightens at the thought of staying away because it keeps them safe. Out of all of us, I've poked the biggest bears and have the largest targets on my back as a result.

But when everything's on the line, and the possibility of chopping the entry point to Uncle Andre's most sadistic operation at the knees, there's no one else I'd trust more than my brothers.

I cover Dante as he peers through a rear-facing window. We've had people scouting the area for twenty-four hours—cameras, mics, infrared sensors. But nothing beats firsthand surveillance.

That's how we knew the shipment was happening tonight. Two guys outside, smoking a joint, while one idiot brags to the other and calls dibs on the youngest of the incoming victims.

His intention is to break her, with everyone watching, by forcing her to count her toes while he shoves his dick up her ass.

My intention is to rid him of that dick permanently.

My men also heard that *J.* would be doing the delivery himself. Which means Jimmy Luciano's day of reckoning is today.

Do I trust my men to execute this mission with flawless precision and not fuck it all up to hell and back again?

With my life.

Do I want to be the one who demolishes the apex of my uncle's operation and be the last person Jimmy Luciano ever sees before I pour battery acid on his eyes?

So badly I can taste it.

Luciano somehow backed Kennedy into a corner, orchestrating some twisted scheme for my uncle that forced her to swallow his debt whole. A setup designed to make her choke on it, and I need to know why.

But that's not why his death will be epic.

The man will beg for death for the years of torment he carved into her beautiful body. And trust me, skinning him alive will be the highlight of my year.

So much so that, even though all I want is to tie *Bella* to the headboard and let my body crash into hers like a wrecking ball, I need to be here.

To do this.

For her.

My phone buzzes again. It's been doing that on and off for the past hour whenever a movement sets it off.

It's clear that my *Bella* can't sleep, tossing and turning restlessly, as if her very existence in my world is agony.

Maybe things would be better if I let her go. And I'm not just saying that because, once again, my prick of an uncle has sent me another anonymous text with a single number on it:

3

It's his way of reminding me I have three days left with her. What he can't get through that useless brain of his is that it's over with Kennedy when I say it's over.

But, *fuck*, what am I doing?

I mean, I know that having a camera on her is a gross violation of privacy—and felony voyeurism in some states. Though technically, we are in Italy.

And I'm not gonna lie. Seeing her on the screen soothes me in a way that a dozen armed guards and a twelve-foot-perimeter wall around the property never will.

Sure, from the outside, it seems like Kennedy is safe, but I need the extra assurance. Besides, nothing says *I care* better than round the clock surveillance.

While Dante maneuvers to another wall, when my phone buzzes again, I steal a glance at the screen.

My eyes widen, stunned, as I watch Kennedy beat the living shit out of my pillow like it owes her money.

What the actual fuck?

A second later, she finally calms down, and I try not to take it personally.

Who knows? Maybe I'm moving too fast for my sweet *Bella*. But bringing her here was . . . unavoidable. Andre's vultures are circling, and I'm not ready to toss her to the curb like a broken toy.

Not yet.

Her only way out is through me and it's better to keep her close. If dancing on the edge of a razor blade makes her a little unsettled, so be it.

When the notification buzzes again, I ignore it. It's time to tuck Kennedy back on her pedestal in the recesses of my mind while I focus on work.

Dante circles back, and I've gotten used to the fact that he never speaks when he's on direct surveillance—a job tailor-made for a guy whose superpower is sniffing out the truth.

Watching him in action, I'm convinced he was the best peeping tom in a past life.

It's also the only time he actually shuts up, so I breathe through it and savor the peace.

When he's this deep in enemy territory, even a whisper could get him shot. Instead of uttering a word, he holds up three fingers high in the air for all of us to see.

Fuck. I blow out a breath. "Looks like Ryder just lost his left testicle. We're not looking at twice as many men, but three times."

"I said at least," Ryder snaps back, then sighs. "What's the call, boss? Cut bait and bail, or storm in like Vikings?"

"When we're outmanned, outgunned, and out of our fucking minds, there's only one answer," I reply.

"Viking shit!" they all roar in unison, their voices echoing through my earpiece. The high-pitched noise is so intense, I'm pretty sure my eardrum has exploded. Leaving me high on adrenaline and completely deaf in my left ear.

I adjust my bluetooth, and Bruno's voice cuts through the chaos, clear and urgent. "Incoming. A heavy. Eighteen-wheeler. Two of them."

He didn't even need to say a word. The cries of women reach us, sharp and desperate. The sound is a cattle prod to my rage.

"Calm, boy. Ye must stay calm."

Oh, good. The Scotsman is back with his customary pep talk.

The sad truth is, I don't even want him gone. But how about a little less zen and a lot more blinding, psychotic fury, okay?

"Ready to storm in, boss?" Ryder's voice crackles through the earpiece, his impatience evident even in the static.

Then it hits me—the warning from the Scotsman. The trucks. The reason we can hear the women.

I rush a command. "Stand Down." From the corner of my eye, I catch Dante throwing his hands up, his expression screaming that I've lost my mind.

Calmly, I explain. "Those trucks are surrounded by a thin sheet of metal. If we charge in, guns blazing like a bunch of trigger-happy cowboys, stray bullets will rip through those trucks like pins through a voodoo doll."

Tension racks through Blaze's words, urgent and raw. "We can't wait for them to fall asleep because, one, they never do, and two, we'd be standing by, watching women get raped and tortured for hours. No one wants that. Least of all you, boss."

It only takes a heartbeat for me to decide when I see Jimmy Luciano directing the trucks toward a second warehouse. My gaze drops to my feet, where two bags brim with enough plastique to tunnel to the center of the Earth.

"Two of you, take the trucks. Now. You've got a minute to kill the drivers and get those trucks out of here. Dante and I will stay back with the rest, draw their fire, and turn Andre's little hideaway into a three-mile dumpster fire."

"But sir—"

"I said go!"

We move with the deadly grace of seasoned operatives—a necessity when you're carrying bags of volatile explosives, where one wrong move could end us all.

Sixty seconds. That's all it takes for us to lace their perimeter with plastique like it's lethal Christmas garland. Then, all hell breaks loose. A series of explosions go off, lighting up the night with deafening roars and blinding flashes.

My men have managed to do as I commanded, with the trucks down the road and far enough to be safe—at least, that's the hope.

An amateur might think these explosives could finish the job.

But experience has taught us that all the C-4 and Molotov cocktails in the world never kill all the roaches. There's always a few that scuttle away, hiding in the shadows, waiting to crawl back out and wreak havoc at the worst possible time.

Any second now, those idiots will start shooting blindly into the darkness, riddling the air with semi-automatic fire. Just as we planned, each of us carves out our territory, picking off Andre's men one by one as we revel in the bloodbath as if we're vampires.

In the midst of the chaos, I spot him—Jimmy Luciano. Panic-stricken, stumbling over his own feet, running for his miserable life.

My vision narrows, every ounce of my focus locking onto him. In that moment, nothing else matters.

In three giant leaps, I've got him by the collar. "If you're alive, Jimmy, then Kennedy has no debt," I spit, dragging him through the blaze, ready to present him like a pig on a spit to *Bella*.

His voice is garbled, probably because I've got him by the neck. "You're making a mistake," he chokes out. They all say that. But it's the next words that make me pause. "I don't know Jimmy."

I turn, and Luciano's face is gone, replaced by an equally vile shell of a human, but not him. Panic sets in, twisting my gut. "Please," he begs, desperation dripping from his voice. "Let me go, and I'll give you anything you want. You like girls? I've got a stash of them."

My blood runs cold as I look up at the building, flames licking at its walls. "Where?" I demand, my voice shaking with urgency.

"There's a locker inside," he stammers, eyes wide with fear.

"On it!" Dante's voice cuts through the chaos, sharp and

unwavering. I know he means it—he'll tear this place apart to save them or die trying. And that's exactly what settles in my gut like a lump of lead.

The warehouse is massive, engulfed in flames. Goddamnit, he needs a direction. I tighten my grip on the man's throat, his eyes bulging as I snarl, "Where's the locker?"

He gasps, his face turning a sickly shade of purple. "North corner," he wheezes, his voice a desperate rasp.

"Who else do you have in there?" When his eyes glaze over, I knock his head against a rock to jog his memory. "Answer me."

He sucks in a breath. "No. I hid them for me."

That's when Dante's voice crackles through the earpiece, choked with smoke. "I've got them," he coughs, the sound harsh and raw.

"And they're alive?" I ask, my heart pounding hard in my chest.

"Yes," he gasps out between coughs, and relief floods me. Losing my brother is not an option. Losing any of them would destroy me.

"Two girls," Dante continues, his voice ragged. "Kept in a fucking gym locker."

The guy who's not Jimmy decides he's got more to say. "You'll like them," he sneers, as if he and I live in the same twisted universe. "Come on, man. You have them. Give them a little bread and water, and they'll do anything you want. You can train them to drop to their knees and suck your dick on command."

At this point, reality blurs. Jimmy. Not Jimmy. It doesn't matter.

I slam his head against a rock so hard, his face morphs into a grotesque mask of blood and bone. It's just like Dante said. He could be anyone.

I don't mean to kill him, but the rage surges unbridled, and knocking his skull around until the bones rattle like pinballs inside seems almost instinctive now.

I know there's a fine line between justice and vengeance. Where it is, I have no idea. All I know is in this moment, brutality feels fucking great.

"Time to go, boy," The Scottish voice insists.

But I don't hear him. Rage pounds in my ears, a deafening roar that drowns out all reason. It's all too easy to lose myself in it, to surrender to the dark urges my brothers, Sin, and a battalion of corporate attorneys insist I keep chained away.

Then, a sound slices through the chaos.

It's like a pin dropping in a cathedral, echoing through the silence, sharp and clean.

When the whiz snaps past my ear, no pain registers. It's not until I feel warm liquid trickling down my hand that I realize what's happened.

Not even the ghost of a Scotsman can save me now.

Fuck.

I've been shot.

Chapter Fourteen
ENZO

"*Cazzo!*" I spew through gritted teeth.

"What does that mean?" the little girl asks, her accent thick, her brown eyes wide as I clench my jaw so hard, I damn near crack three teeth.

Bruno pours more antiseptic onto my wound like acid cleaning a rusty blade. The pain is instant and fierce, and so blinding that I nearly throw up.

But, I don't.

Instead I suck in a breath and simply hand a little girl back my cigar to hold while I exchange it for my scotch. I take a sip, the liquid burning down my throat, offering enough of a distraction from the fire in my arm I can answer her.

"It means *'ow'*," I say, managing a strained smile. Technically, it means *dick*, and as an expletive translates to *fuck*, but considering this little girl is five at the oldest, I try to keep it PG.

The hum of the jet's engines is a lull, almost comforting noise, but it doesn't mask the chaos we just left.

My arm aches like a mother, the pain so intense that

Bruno's semi-gentle touch as he crisscrosses my skin back together is almost numb in comparison. Each stitch he makes is methodical, a necessary evil, but all I can focus on is the other little girl—the sister—dabbing the blood so Bruno can see better where to jab.

"What the hell?" Dante asks, judgmental as shit.

"What?" I ask, pretending that I don't have a five-year-old holding a cigar like a pro, or a six- or seven-year-old deputized as a combat nurse.

"Dante, meet Sofia"—I point to the older one—"and Lili."

"Hi, Sofia. Lili," Dante says tenderly, his voice a gentle balm against the raw edge of their emotions.

He offers a warm smile to Sofia, who pointedly ignores him, then tries to coax little Lili into meeting his eyes with a small wave. She remains transfixed by the long ribbon of smoke curling from the cigar, her silence a fortress.

"I heard they weren't talking," he says, his brows knotting tight with concern.

"I have ways of making people talk. Ask anyone," I quip, a wry smile tugging at my lips. "Girls, this is my brother Dante, the man who saved your lives."

I know they understand but they still don't speak. Whatever horrific shit these kids have been through is evident in the shadows in their eyes.

Little Lili clams up, retreating into herself, while Sofia's silence is defiant, her need to hyper-focus on a task her only lifeline in the storm.

I point to Sofia. "This one started thrashing her fists at Bruno when he began," I say, taking another sip of Scotch before handing it back to Lili to hold. "Her tiny frame trembled with so much fury, Bruno actually took a step back."

"In my defense," Bruno adds, "the kid is stronger than she looks and came at me like she was possessed." He winks. Her eyes dart to the floor.

"Why would she do that?" Dante whispers, though we can all hear him.

I shrug, instantly regretting it as pain shoots from my arm to my neck.

Bruno smirks. "I think she thought I was hurting the big guy."

"*Cazzo?*" Lili asks, pronouncing the profanity with such cuteness that I can't help but pat her head.

"You're teaching them to swear?" Dante scolds, his eyebrows shooting to the sky.

"Yes, *cazzo*. That's right, *angioletta*," I say. She looks at me, curiosity shining in her eyes. "It means little angel."

Dante rolls his eyes as I simply nod and grin. Her tiny hand wriggles into mine as she repeats the word. "*Angioletta.*" Then, concerned, she points to her sister. "Sofia, too."

"Yes, Sofia too," I assure her, giving Sofia a gentle nod.

Sofia's hardened expression doesn't change, but some part of me knows she doesn't want to be left out. Just like I know she's swallowing so many emotions inside her, she's suffocating.

It's what happens when you have no control over a situation. When things are done to you, and you're defenseless to stop it. Becoming my combat nurse was the only thing that calmed her down.

It's a tragic irony that such a young life knows the rituals of survival so intimately.

Now, she stands resolute, her eyes hardened by experiences no child should endure. She presses my wound just a little too hard, waiting for my response.

"Easy, *diavoletta*," I seethe through a smile.

She barely peeks at me through the corners of her eyes, curiosity brimming to the surface.

"It means little devil." When she frowns and presses agonizingly harder, I add, "The devil has strength. And determination. It's a compliment," I wrench out, my voice strained.

Her eyes flicker to mine, giving me a small, almost imperceptible nod of approval. She needs this, a tether in the chaos.

And maybe, in some twisted way, so do I.

With barely a nod, the pressure finally eases up before I pass out.

Bruno's handiwork is pretty good, considering he's sweating from his own pain from two pieces of metal lodged in his leg. But he refused to tend to himself before taking care of me—an action both stupid and gracious.

And as much as I want to tear him a new one for doing this, I sure as hell wasn't doing it in front of the kids.

When he completes the last stitch, he announces, "Done," and holds out his hand for a high-five from Sofia. Bruno has four children—two his own and two adopted after fostering them for years. He knows how to break through, though Dante and I anxiously wait with bated breath to see if he will.

Nothing.

"C'mon, kid," Bruno coaxes. "Don't leave me hanging." When she still doesn't bite, he sweetens the offer. "Give me a high five, and I'll teach you how to stitch up my leg."

"Is that wise?" Dante asks, nervously.

Bruno doesn't miss a beat. "I'm betting *toughy* here has seen worse than this. Besides, we all crave control, don't we?"

No one can argue with that logic. Least of all me.

Sofia's eyes flicker with something—maybe curiosity, maybe the need for some semblance of power. Or maybe our little devil just relishes the idea of jabbing a man repeatedly like a sewing machine.

He holds up his hand again. "In or out, kid?"

She hesitates only for a second. Then, instead of a smack, she channels all her power into a punch straight to his palm. With an Oscar-worthy performance, Bruno staggers back, shaking out his hand. "You got a mean right hook on you there, kid."

The smallest smile crosses her lips.

Bruno grins, a glimmer of relief in his eyes, and Dante and I release the breaths we didn't realize we were holding. It feels like the first time Trinity did something normal after her attack, like smiling after a compliment, or laughing at one of our stupid jokes.

Small acts of normalcy aren't just moments. They're everything.

"'Atta girl," Bruno says, his voice filled with quiet pride. "Now, let's get to work."

Bruno nudges her away gently, and she looks long and hard at me. "I'll be right here, *diavoletta*," I assure her.

My eyes fall to Lili, who lingers behind.

"You too, *angioletta*." Fear and uncertainty flicker across her face. I lean in and whisper, "Bruno needs someone brave to hold his hand too."

It takes a moment before she finally pries her hand from

mine, but no one rushes her. Slowly, she steps away. But before Dante and I can say a word, she backtracks. My impatience nearly seeps through when she hands me back my drink.

Just what I needed. "*Grazie, angioletta*," I say with a grin. I'm trying not to play favorites, but bribing me with booze definitely tips the scales in her favor.

Dante takes a seat beside me, and as soon as they're out of earshot, I exhale a weary breath and slam back the rest of the scotch. "Since when did I become kid Velcro?" I murmur, genuinely perplexed.

"Probably since they managed to witness you flatten their assailant's brain like human scaloppine."

I glance at Sofia and Lili, their small frames almost swallowed by the oversized leather seats. Their eyes are still wide with adrenaline and fear, but there's a resilience there too, a strength that makes me feel both proud and guilty.

I dump my cigar in the glass and hang my head. "They shouldn't have seen that." I shake my head. "You nearly died while I wasted who knows how long smashing a man's brain in while two innocent children watched."

"Hey," Dante says, blowing out a breath. "If you hadn't grabbed him, those two girls would be s'more marshmallows. We had no idea they were in there. At all. What made you grab him?"

I don't tell him that I thought the guy was Jimmy. For the same reason I don't tell him that I'm constantly hearing the haunted voice of a dead Scotsman. "Instinct," is all I say.

He pats me on the back, a dark chuckle escaping his lips. "Glad to know those feral, psychotic instincts of yours are good for something." He points to the girls. "Your girlfriend is going to love this side of you."

"She's not my girlfriend."

"Oh, don't give me that shit. You're clearly seeing the woman at the villa. Kennedy," he sings, his smile turning dreamy. "Her name sounds like sunshine and spring." He bats his eyes, mocking me.

I need to keep Kennedy out of this mess. The fewer people that know we're connected, the better. Whoever shot me knows I was there. And if I'm wearing a target on my back, I'm wearing it alone.

"A convenience," I assure him. "She's here for the week, and then she's gone," I state, though the words taste like cigarette ash on my tongue.

"Lie to all the people you want, Enzo. Even to yourself. But I've seen the way you look at her. And that look means only one thing..."

"That your vision is worse than your poker face?"

"That you're speeding headfirst into the L-word, whether you like it or not."

Chapter Fifteen
ENZO

L-word?

As in... *love?*

I blink, deeply disturbed. What the fuck? I'm not in love.

Sadistic psychopaths don't fall in love. We maim, manipulate, torment, kill. We do not fall in love.

Ever.

Am I obsessed?

Perhaps.

Possessive?

Damned straight.

But in love?

Not a goddamned chance.

"Whatever gets you through the night," the Scottish brogue taunts.

Bite me.

Ignoring my mental snap, I jab Dante in the chest. "Listen here, asshole. Don't make me kill you in front of the kids. Accusations have consequences."

"Lying to my face has consequences, jackass." He cracks his neck. "You want a piece of me? Bring it on. But I'm in a take-no-prisoners mood."

Without warning, he flicks me right at my stitches. Pain explodes, sending stars dancing in my vision and a howl of agony echoing inside my skull. I suppress the scream, not wanting the girls to hear.

I shoot him a death glare, my eyes burning with fury.

He arches a brow, a smug grin playing on his lips, and curls his fingers toward me, Matrix style.

At this point, I give up. There's no point in arguing with Dante. Not unless I want us in an all-out brawl on the floor like eight-year-olds. And as his behavior clearly shows, he will take zero pity on me for the fact that I've been shot in the arm.

"Fine." I wave a hand in surrender, the weight of defeat settling on my shoulders. "You win. She means something to me. What, I have no idea. But this"—I motion to my arm—"was no accident. The only reason I'm still breathing is probably because of their lousy aim. So as far as anyone's concerned, I'm not seeing anyone."

The gravity of my words roll across Dante's face, his expression hardening. "What about us? Family. Or the guys," he tilts his chin toward Bruno. "We can help keep her safe."

"If Andre is gunning for me, no one is safe," I say, my voice a low growl.

"So, what are you going to do? Cut her loose?"

"I don't know," I admit, uncertainty gnawing at my gut.

"Our father would want you to follow your heart."

"And look where it got him," I scowl bitterly.

The familiar ache of unresolved grief tightens my chest. If

he were dead, at least we would know. But he's been missing for years, vanished without a trace.

It's like being trapped in a relentless torture chamber. Just when the wounds begin to scab over, the mere mention of him rips them open again, another raw lash of the whip.

Dante blows out a long, slow breath. "This doesn't feel right. You have feelings for her. I know you do."

"And if those feelings end up getting her hurt? Or killed? Does that feel right?" I slump against my seat. "That I'm seeing anyone at all stays between us. Agreed?"

He knows I'm right. With a resigned nod, he concedes. "Fine. It stays between us." He air quotes, "You're not seeing anyone." Then, with an annoyed shake of his head, he adds, "It still sucks big hairy donkey nuts."

I manage a weak smile. "What you do in your spare time is your business."

We stare off, watching as Sofia carefully stitches up Bruno under his guidance, while Lili has found the first aid kit and is wrapping his opposite ankle like a mummy. It's almost surreal, seeing this enormous hulk of a man so gentle and patient.

Bruno catches us watching and mouths, "Keeping them busy." Then, he points to Lili with a soft smile. "You missed the heel," he instructs tender.

"Did you get a hold of Father Marc?" I ask, knowing our friendly neighborhood priest will be able to find safe haven for these girls.

"About that," Dante grimaces. "There's a little speed bump with him taking the girls."

"For the six-figure donations I hand him, there shouldn't be as much as a hiccup."

"Nevertheless, he needs to speak with you."

Of course, he does. Because it's not enough that I give him truckloads of cash, he now demands my attention too.

I glance over at the girls, both seemingly content to turn Bruno into a zombie. At the rate they're going, they could probably keep bandaging him for another half hour.

Hmm. Whatever conversation I have with Father Marc needs to be private. But if I leave, I'm certain all hell will break loose with these two girls in less than sixty seconds.

And I can't risk them getting riled up.

I grab my cell and call, keeping it off speaker and trying to maintain a steady voice. It rings twice. Father Marc sounds frazzled from the moment he answers. "I can't do it."

"You. Have. To." My voice is tight, the coil of a king cobra as I smile and wave at the girls.

"You don't understand. Dante tells me they've become attached to you."

"So?"

"As horrified as I am to admit this, they need to stay with you, Enzo."

"What?"

My voice cuts through the room, louder than intended. Every eye swivels to me, suspicion brewing.

I force a broad smile and lower my tone.

"Hang on"—I press the phone to my chest—"I'm just going to use the bathroom."

A furrow of worry crosses both their brows. A second later, they're both front and center in front of me.

"I'll be back," I promise.

Lili bites her bottom lip, a gesture so reminiscent of *Bella* that I can't think straight. Would our kids look like this?

When her lower lip starts to quiver, my heart pinches so hard it feels like it's being lassoed by a crown of thorns. And every cell in my body chants, *make it stop, make it stop.*

I once considered myself a strong man. A torturer who could give as good as he got. And yet here I am, about to cower to two girls and beg for mercy just so I can go to the bathroom, talk openly with Father Marc, and hopefully not piss myself between here and there. "Five minutes," I plead.

Dante removes his watch and holds it out for the girls to see. "Look, this is the time now. When the hand reaches here, what happens?"

"Enzo comes back," Lili announces, her chest puffed up with pride at figuring it out. Sofia, however, remains unconvinced, her face a mask of doubt as she tightens her arms across her chest.

Dante leans in with a smirk. "Between her innate suspicion and impressive death glare, it's like looking into a mirror for you, isn't it?"

"Shut up."

I kneel down, bringing us eye to eye. "I will never lie to you."

She rolls her eyes, utterly underwhelmed.

I hold up my hand, spreading my fingers. "Five minutes. If I'm not back by then, you can punch my brother in the nuts."

"I heard that," he barks from behind me playfully.

A faint smile tugs at the corner of Sofia's mouth. *Finally.* It's enough of a pass, I take it.

Without a backward glance, I stand and bolt for the furthest bathroom.

"Enzo?" The voice crackles from the phone. "Are you still there?"

I slam the door behind me. "Two minutes."

"You told the girls five," Father Marc reminds me, his tone imbued with the pious indignation of *Thou Shalt Not Lie*.

"And I meant it. Two minutes for you, three to keep me from pissing myself. Stop wasting time. One minute, forty-five seconds left."

"They're in a vulnerable space, Enzo. If I had known there would be children, we would've had people on site."

"What about their parents?"

His long, drawn-out sigh tells me everything I need to know. "We spoke with some of the women you rescued. Both their parents were brutally killed. Apparently, they fought to the death to protect the girls."

Fire eats at my insides, but I stamp it out. Emotionless, I say, "One minute."

Father Marc races through his words. "After a traumatic experience like this, tearing them away from a new bond could have catastrophic psychological impacts."

No one needs to tell me about catastrophic impacts. After Trinity's attack, she didn't speak for four years. And she had us —five brothers—protecting her, tending to her every need and willing to go to hell and back for her.

I think of the two innocent faces, my heart splintering like shattered glass, and rub my temple, trying to stave off the growing headache.

Trinity had us. They have no one.

"What are you trying to say?" I ask, my patience fraying at the edges.

Father Marc's voice softens, brimming with compassion and hope. "I'm saying they need you, Enzo. Just like Kennedy needs you."

It takes a minute for his words to sink in, each one hitting me like tiny sledgehammers, determined to break through the empty tin shell of my heart.

With ten seconds left and my bladder about to burst, I snap. "Fine. They stay with me. *For now*," I add with a steely determination.

"You're doing God's work, Enzo."

"You say that now. When they turn into deranged ax murderers, don't come crying to me."

I hang up, do my business, and collect my composure. Father Marc's words replay over and over.

They need me? And what does he mean just like Kennedy?

With a minute to spare, her fiery eyes and breathtaking smile flash through my mind. I deliberately avoid thinking about her body and instead flip to my phone.

LAST VIDEO RECORDED: 97 MINUTES.

Huh?

A million thoughts bombard my brain like flaming arrows as my pulse ratchets up sky-high.

I run through the mental checklist:

- Hourly check-ins by security, verified.
- Entry points secured.

- Communication lines active.
- Backup generators, powered.
- Vehicle fleet, secured and accounted for.
- Weapon cache, fully stocked.

I'm not sure what the world did in the dark ages before wifi, but thank god for technology.

I glance back at the feed and the little green dot.

- Surveillance cameras, operational.

I open all ten live feeds and find *Bella* in the gym. It's equipped with state-of-the-art machines, free weights, and plenty of space for yoga. But of course, my *Bella* is enjoying the polished hardwood floors and full-length mirrors for dance.

I can tell she's partial to the pair of ballet slippers she brought along with her—old, worn, and likely her version of a security blanket. Undoubtedly, they fit her like a glove, but they're riddled with holes and so mangled I wouldn't be surprised if Truffles regularly uses them as chew toys.

Satisfaction beams from my smile as I watch her dance in the vibrant red shoes I had delivered today. Kennedy took an extra-long glance at them when she and Riley were at the market the other day.

They weren't an expensive pair by any means, but as she soars through the air, her form exquisite, her smile radiant, I know she likes them. And now, my *Bella* dances for me and only me.

In that ephemeral second, everything is perfect. She's fine. Everything's fine.

Hmm.

Ninety-seven minutes spirals through my head like a boomerang.

Unsettled, I switch back to the recording, and click to a random segment of the feed and . . .

Holy fuuuck.

"Is this what you want, Mr. D'Angelo?" the woman of my dreams purrs to the camera. Her luscious body is on full display like an eight course meal, and my cock instantly springs to attention.

I go to turn up the volume when a stampede of knocks barrages the door.

Fuck.

I pause the video and pry open the door. Two sets of eyes look up at me, eager and expectant.

"I still have eighteen seconds," I say, flustered, pointing to my watch. As if eighteen seconds will do anything for the raging hard-on in my pants.

Lili shrugs. "We ran out of bandages."

I glance over at Bruno, who looks like a house that's been TP'ed.

My eyes narrow at them. "I still have time."

"Not according to my watch," Dante says, amused with a smug-ass grin.

I level him with a ruthless glare.

Heartless bastard.

Chapter Sixteen

KENNEDY

For the second time this morning, my cell rings.

I watch it vibrate angrily with Caller Unknown, and let it ring out.

Whatever it is, it can definitely wait.

From the moment I tore open the bright gold box Enzo had delivered, nothing else mattered.

Not the baked cornetto with its light, flaky crust seducing me with a buttery interior and luscious apricot jam filling. Nor the thinly sliced prosciutto whose rich, savory flavors perfectly complemented the tangy pecorino cheese.

Not even the velvety espresso, with its heavenly aroma, hint of hazelnut, and silky crema—my usual morning go-to against homicidal urges—could compete. This gift transcended even breakfast, which is saying a lot.

The second Truffles was done with his morning business, I was here, in the most lavish gym I've ever seen in my life.

I relish every second of lacing up my elegant new dance slippers—a ruby red pair reminiscent of grand stages and seventy-piece orchestras.

Granted, I'm in my normal *dancing-for-the-hell-of-it* attire: leotard, sweatshirt, and messiest of messy buns. In the real world, I'd have no earthly reason to ever wear them. But today, oh, I'm wearing them.

For the next few hours, I'm wearing the shit out of these puppies.

The moment I lace up, I come alive.

My feet spring into a series of piqué turns, warming up as I circle the entire room. Almost instantly, I shed my sweatshirt, my body on absolute fire.

The polished hardwood floors and full-length mirrors urge me to push harder. Unlike the formidable grandeur of the grand Italian estate, this room and I are old childhood friends, our bond as familiar as a second skin.

I open Spotify and let it shuffle, the music setting the tone as I begin to move.

At first, it's a mix of pop and jazz, light and freeing. I lose myself in the rhythm, each step and pirouette shedding layers of stress and fear. Dancing is my sanctuary, where joy peers through like sunlight breaking through storm clouds. And for the first time in forever, I feel light and free and alive.

After hours of working my body to the brink of fatigue, when the soft, magical notes of "Dance of the Sugar Plum Fairy" fill the room, my heart skips a beat, memories flooding back, full force. Of *Da* clapping louder than anyone at the church recital, unapologetically and fiercely proud.

No one would ever suspect that a big, burly, towering lug of a man would be teary-eyed, whistling at the conclusion of my performance in "The Nutcracker" as if I were a Prima Ballerina at the Chicago Ballet Theater.

I close my eyes and let the music guide me across the floor, imagining his proud face in the audience, his rough hands coming together in applause. His deep voice cheering louder than anyone else's, a mix of pride and love that made me feel cherished and adored.

Tears blur my vision. *Ye did good, lass. Ye made yer Da proud.*

For my whole life, I danced for him, even after he'd gone. Twirling and leaping across the floor, each movement a tribute to the man who always believed in me. Because no matter where I went or what I did, I knew he was with me. So close, I could open my eyes, and almost see him there.

As the final notes play, I hold the last pose a moment longer, breathless and a little teary—not because *Da* isn't here, but because I feel his presence stronger than I have in years, and it's all because of Enzo. The thought tugs at my heart, a bittersweet ache.

I wish *Da* could've met him.

I'm still riding the high of floating on air when the music stops abruptly, and my phone rings again. Which is weird, considering it must be an ungodly hour in the States.

Caller Unknown is about to get an earful. I snatch it up. "Hello?" I bark.

"Kennedy?" the man asks. Great, just what I need—a telemarketer.

"Look, I don't have money for fake sheriff's fundraisers or timeshares in Florida, not that I don't believe in both worthy causes. I can't extend the warranty on my nonexistent car, and as much as I'd love to switch my energy provider, mostly because I'm three months behind on paying them, you might want to call someone who actually has cash. So if there's nothing else—"

"Kennedy, this is Agent Caleb Knox."

My ears perk up. First, he's hanging around Riley to weasel his way into Enzo's world, then he's coaxed Savannah Whitaker into becoming his spy.

I'm not exactly sure how the FBI does that with the Dog Trainer to the Stars, though it's definitely smart. I mean, what better way to get to know people than through their dogs?

"What do you want?"

"I'm just calling to see if you're alright."

There's enough concern in his voice that my interest is piqued. I retie the loosened ribbon from my shoe. "Why wouldn't I be alright?"

"You don't know?"

I don't like where this is going. If he tells me Enzo was with another woman last night, I'll be devastated. "Know what?"

He exhales sharply, frustration evident. "I know you're in a" —he struggles for the right word—"*thing* with Enzo D'Angelo."

Thing? Did he just call us a *thing*? Like we're what? Bad pasta or something. My pulse quickens, irritation bubbling to the surface.

Sure, maybe I can't neatly define my relationship with Enzo, but I loathe how he reduced it to a mere *thing*, as if it were something so trivial, it's distasteful. "My personal life is none of your concern, Agent Knox. So, if there's nothing else—"

"I have it on good authority he's been shot."

My legs buckle as the floor whips out from under me. The room spins to the point I can't breathe.

Shot?

Emotions crash over me in waves—fear, disbelief, shock. Words are floating through the phone—"Kennedy? Did you hear what I said?"—but my heart pounds so loudly I can't hear it.

Not again.

Not again.

Not again.

My fingers fumble as I disconnect the call and frantically dial Enzo's number. It rings and rings. Fucking voicemail again.

I hang up, and call again, claws of anxiety ripping apart my insides. "Pick up, pick up, pick up," I mutter, pacing like a caged animal, trapped in my own skin. "Damn it!" I shout, my voice cracking, echoing off the walls.

I can't stay here, not knowing.

Maybe the guards know. There's dozens of them circling the grounds. One of them has to know something.

I bolt for the door, not giving two shits that I'm practically in nothing but underwear and toe shoes.

Just as my hand reaches for the doorknob, it swings open. And I plow into the solid frame of Enzo himself, nearly knocking the mountain down.

A mix of concern and exhaustion are etched on his face. His eyes lock onto mine, and for a second, everything else falls away.

"Enzo!" I choke out through tears. The relief is overwhelming, a tidal wave that leaves me trembling and weak. I grab his face, cheeks, and run my hands along his shoulders. "You're okay?"

He doesn't answer.

Instead, he spins us, pinning me against the cold, unforgiving wall. His body, hot and unyielding against mine. "No. I'm not okay." His lips graze my ear, his breath a mix of raw emotion and heat.

His thumb gently wipes away my tears. "Why are you crying?"

"I heard you'd been shot."

Suspicion flickers in his eyes, then vanishes in an instant. "Yes."

Confused, I let my gaze roam over his body, sculpted with precision. His broad shoulders taper down to a chiseled chest and taut abs, every inch of him seemingly invincible.

His right bicep is slightly bulged more than the left, but I see no trace of injury. My voice wavers, disbelief coloring my word. "Where?"

He motions to his arm, the gesture almost nonchalant. "Here."

We lock eyes, a charged silence stretching between us. I don't know if I can do this. Open my heart only to watch it be torn apart again. The fear of losing another man, of enduring that pain, feels like a vise tightening around my chest.

I look away, desperate to avoid his gaze. "You could've died."

His fingers find my chin, lifting until I have no choice but to meet his eyes, now darkened with intensity. "How could I die when my sweet *Bella* begged me to fuck her?"

Oh, shit.

He saw that—saw me?

My heart races, the memory of last night flowing like molten lava beneath my skin.

Me. Making love to a camera like a porn star.

The look in his eyes, a fierce possession that steals my breath, is everything. I want to be owned by him—be his. Maybe more than I've ever wanted anything in my life.

I don't know if it's him kissing me or me kissing him, but holy hell, is it hot.

My fingers dive into his thick waves of hair, gripping tight, pulling him closer so I can lick, taste, and devour him at once. The groan he makes when I do is pure heaven, sending shivers down my spine and setting my entire body on absolute fire.

For a fleeting moment, his body trembles, hands braced against the wall, as if he's summoning every ounce of his strength to hold back the storm within.

I say one word. The only word I know he needs to hear me say. "Please," I gasp.

His arms wrap around me tight, pulling me forward until every hard inch of him is pressed against me, and it's a lot.

Then, with a swift motion, I'm lifted off the ground, hoisted into his arms. My legs wrap around him instinctively, clinging to him and climbing him like the solid Redwood he is.

There's this erotic flick of his tongue that makes me feel like I'm free-falling, dizzy and drunk with desire. He's done the same thing between my legs, and now, I can't breathe.

"Clothes. Off," he commands in a low, husky voice. God, the dominance of this man. He's not waiting for me to comply —I can already hear the fabric tearing as he rips the neckline of my leotard.

It's a good thing, too, since my fingers are fumbling with

the buttons on his shirt, desperate to expose the hard planes of his chest.

Would it kill him to wear a T-shirt just once?

The faint click of a door handle jerks us both from our frenzy. We freeze, hearts racing.

"Who's that?" I gasp, breathless.

"*Shh.*" He holds his breath, straining to hear. After a minute of silence, he adds, "I think they've gone."

"Enzo?" A small voice drifts through the door.

My eyes snap wide. Is that a kid?

Chapter Seventeen

KENNEDY

THE DOORKNOB JIGGLES AGAIN, more insistently this time. Whoever's on the other side clearly isn't giving up.

"Enzo," the little voice sings, a melody I know well. A signature blend of ceaseless energy and relentless tenacity bestowed in spades to kids under ten.

Especially when all you want are a few minutes of peace to think, eat, or pee.

"Is that a child?" I whisper.

"Yes," he murmurs, dropping his forehead to mine. "Who knew tiny humans could be the biggest dick deflators of the year."

"*Tsk, tsk, tsk*. The King of Chicago running from a child?" I tease, unable to contain a giggle as I shake my head.

The handle jiggles harder. "*Shh*." He deadpans and presses a finger to his lips. "If you stop moving those delicious lips of yours, maybe they'll go away," he whispers.

"They?" I ask so loud, a succession of little knocks pound on the door like a drum circle.

"We know you're in there," another voice says, unimpressed. This one sounds older and more confident.

"Your new boss?" I ask giggling.

His nostrils flare as he lowers me back to the floor, his voice steady despite the frantic jiggling of the door handle.

"It's a long story," he rushes through. "They've been through hell. Their parents are gone, and they've got nowhere to go . . ." His voice trails off, heavy with sadness.

"What are their names?" I ask softly, my heart going out to them, still stunned and filled with empathy.

"The older one is Sofia," he replies gently, pocketing a hand. "The younger one is called Lili, short for Eliana."

And he's taking them in. I melt like butter over toast. "It's good of you to keep them," I say softly, rubbing his hand.

"Temporarily," he asserts firmly, his fingers intertwining with mine. "Until Father Marc can make other arrangements."

"So, they're at Camp Week-o'-Enzo, too?" I quip lightly.

"Hopefully less," he grumbles.

"Harsh." I shove him aside and open the door, eager to meet them.

I throw on my sweatshirt and swing open the doors. Two cherubs with big eyes and long black hair blow past me, each latching on to one of Enzo's hands.

"I don't want to play hide and seek anymore," the youngest one complains, tugging at his hand for attention. "Play with us."

I glance up at his face and stifle a laugh. With one botched escape plan and all exits chopped off, his expression resembles a doberman trying to figure out quantum physics.

Then, his eyes lock onto mine. He mouths, "Help me."

With two kids shackled to his sides, it's more a command than a plea.

I kneel before them. Like Enzo, they both look like they just washed up, and their little dresses look brand new. I smile wide. "I'm Kennedy. How about I make us something to eat?"

"What?" Enzo asks, alarmed.

"Pizza?" Lili chirps.

"And what about you?" I ask Sofia cautiously. Her eyes, dark and hollow, remind me of a time long ago when I saw the same look in the mirror. She's present, but not ready to fully engage just yet. "Do you like pizza too?"

She gives a silent shrug. A small response, but it's something.

"My puppy likes pizza," I say, hoping to lure them in. "Well, he likes the bread and cheese."

I leave out the part about how the sauce gives him next-level gas. Seriously, the dog nearly killed me.

Sofia's expression softens, curiosity flickering in her eyes. "What's her name?"

"Truffles," I reply with a smile. "But he's a boy."

Sofia looks up at Enzo, confusion etched on her face. "She named a boy dog Truffles?" she asks, childlike and unfiltered, as if I'm not a foot from her face.

"I know, right?" Enzo says, chuckling.

A pang of longing fills the empty space in my heart. I want this—the everyday happiness that comes with sassy kids and a strong, protective man.

I blink away the fantasy and quickly add, "And after we eat, you can both play with him as much as you want. He's the sweetest little guy."

Finally, a hint of a smile tugs at Sofia's lips, a small victory that feels monumental.

Lili hops on both feet like I've just offered her a ride to the moon. I extend my hands to both girls, partly to pry them away from Enzo. "Ready?"

Both little faces frown, their hands clinging to Enzo as if he might float away if they let go.

His shoulders slump, and he lets out a sigh of defeat. "Fine. I'll have lunch with you. It's not as if I can trust any of you in the kitchen." His eyes lock onto mine, a mix of exasperation and amusement. "Especially you."

We all head out of the gym, and Sofia and Lili freeze the second they look down the hall, their eyes wide, their breaths held in.

Ruff-ruff!

Both girls' faces light up with pure delight as Truffles appears, front and center, as if delivered by Amazon. They squeal with excitement, their eyes sparkling with joy, and race toward him.

Enzo seizes the moment, grabbing my arm and pulling me close, his hot breath grazing my ear. "We still have unfinished business, *Bella*. And I'm taking care of it."

"When?"

"Tonight."

AFTER STUFFING OURSELVES WITH PIZZA AND AN assortment of cookies, Enzo watches as I teach Sofia and Lili a flurry of dance moves. The girls twirl and giggle, their faces lit with pure joy, their laughter echoing clear down the hall.

Enzo leans against the wall, arms crossed, a small, almost imperceptible smile playing on his lips as he watches us. Or rather, watches me.

I guide the girls through a few moves, my usual method to gauge a little dancer's potential and see if they've had some training. Then I join Enzo and watch with delight.

Sofia moves with stunning grace, her dark hair cascading like a dancer's veil, her steps infused with a melancholy exuberance. Every motion she makes is a blend of elegance and a quiet sorrow.

Lili, on the other hand, is a whirlwind of energy, her boundless enthusiasm radiating with every step. She mirrors each move her sister makes, infusing them with her unique flair, her curls bouncing wildly in sync with her exuberance.

"They're naturals," I remark, captivated by how effortlessly they execute each move. "Dance was always my escape. My safe space."

I sense Enzo's gaze before I meet his eyes. His golden eyes warm with barely a smile, sending a rush of warmth through me. "And now, you've given them a safe space."

In this moment of soft words and tender emotions, my heart swells with feelings for this man. Despite the thick sweatshirt and jeans I threw on before lunch, a shiver runs through me the instant his fingers brush mine.

By early evening, we retreat to an extravagant home theater I didn't even known existed, concealed in the lower level. *Sheesh*, how big is this place?

"We all need a safe space," Enzo says. And I suppose he's right. Enzo, his family, his team—they've carved out these pockets of sanctuary, ensuring safety when they're most vulnerable.

I feel closer to him. As trapped as I've felt, it's as if his entire existence is confined within one immense cage, squeezing tightly around his broad shoulders, leaving me wondering how he breathes through it all.

The plush seats and state-of-the-art sound system are definite perks, but it's the movie—an animated classic not yet in theaters—that seals the deal.

As the opening credits roll, the girls snuggle in under plush blankets, their eyes wide as they fight a flurry of yawns.

Truffles curls up at their feet, his tail thumping lazily.

Surprisingly, Enzo takes his place in the middle, his broad frame occupying more space than seems fair, creating a comforting barrier around him.

Sofia's eyelids flutter, Lili's head nods forward, and Truffles stretches out, surrendering to sleep. Even Enzo seems more relaxed than I've ever seen him, even with them all sticking to him like refrigerator magnets.

"I'll be back," I whisper, tiptoeing out of the room. I need to grab my phone and snap about a hundred shots of this. I'm in my room for only a moment when I see no less than a dozen calls from the ever-annoying Agent Knox.

"Everything alright?" Enzo's voice rumbles through the room, startling me. I quickly shove my phone into my bag. I don't want the epitome of a possessive Alpha male to know I'm being agitated by a Fed. Who knows what would happen?

I turn around, and my mouth falls open.

Here he is, Enzo Ares D'Angelo, displayed in all his magnificent glory like a tempting, unwrapped Christmas gift. His shirt hangs open and untucked, revealing a tantalizing trail of dark hair that leads down, down, down.

With his belt discarded, the dark band of his briefs peeking out, just one provocative glimpse has my pulse racing.

"Alright?" Hell yeah, it is. I swallow hard. "Everything's fine."

"You sure?" His warm hands cradle my cheeks, and I inhale deeply, his intoxicating scent enveloping me in a dizzying swirl. "You look flushed."

"Just"—*Stunned stupid? Horny?*—"wondering how you escaped being sandwiched."

"I tucked pillows against them. Trinity used to cling to me like superglue, too." He runs a hand through his tousled hair, a small smile playing at the corner of his lips. "There are three more movies in the queue, and Dory is keeping an eye on them."

"Oh?"

He shuts the door. The click of the lock sends heat licking up my neck.

Enzo strips off his shirt completely, and it's the first time I've seen him without one—though I'm not exactly sure how that's possible.

My eyes trace the contours of his body, each line more surreal than the last: olive skin draped over a powerful chest, tight nipples, and abs carved from stone.

"Say it, *Bella*." God, the growl of his voice.

I lick my lips. "Say what?"

"What you said the other night." He unzips, deliberately slow. "When you begged." He pushes his slacks to the floor, leaving him in nothing but a dark pair of briefs that only emphasize his size.

And up close and personal, the man is big.

His breath becomes rhythmic, his chest rising and falling, his nose flaring. "Say it." These words aren't just a demand. They're rough, yes—pure seduction wrapped in ironclad control.

But the second I do, I know there's no going back.

And then what? I wake up, and the beautiful dream is over?

When he removes the last of it—his boxers—and his cock springs free, I can't think.

My gaze is drawn down, the meaty girth of him, the weight of his balls. If I ever thought this man was gorgeous, I was wrong.

Enzo is a masterpiece.

Heat floods my system, lips quivering as I blink away a fog of doubt and sanity, until there's nothing before me but him.

He steps in front of me, invading my space like a roman soldier. Pressing into my belly. Fear and anticipation flutter in my gut and I clench.

With one finger, he tilts my face up, his lips brushing against mine like a whisper. "Say it," he murmurs, as my eyes flutter shut.

And I do. "Please," I whisper back, the word slipping out like a desperate prayer. "Please, fuck me, Mr. D'Angelo."

With a hand at my neck, he kisses me, and it's nothing like I imagined. It's soft, tender, his tongue licking and exploring with a sensual precision that makes my knees give. Have I mentioned the man can kiss? The man. Can. Kiss.

He takes my hand and guides it to stroke his length. Jesus

H., my fingers barely fit around it. It's like that moment when you eye a massive burger, wondering if it'll actually fit in your mouth...

With one more deep, mesmerizing kiss, his lips trail down my neck as he peels off my clothes, one by one. He lowers himself to his knees, and soon he's eating me out so good that I can barely stand.

I grab his hair. "Enzo, I—"

Two fingers invade me, forcing their way in and out, but he doesn't let up. That lethal tongue of his—licking, sucking, circling my clit until there's nothing stopping this runaway train. The orgasm is building so fast, the impulse to grind his face comes without warning.

Rough stubble, his slick, wet tongue, one, more, finger, and —*"Oh, God!"*

With one more hard suck of my clit, I see stars.

To the point that, I don't know how, but the next thing I know, my back hits the cold wall. His teeth graze my neck, his hands grip my ass, and the thick tip of him glides just past my entrance.

We're both panting, sheened in sweat, when before I can think or speak, and he's in, stretching me, pulling out, pushing in...

Thrusting...

Thrusting...

Thrusting...

And *God*. This man owns me. All of me.

"So fucking tight, *Bella*," he hisses through his teeth, pushing, shoving his way in with each breath, deeper and deeper.

My back arches, rocking with him in a painfully delicious

rhythm. Each thrust drives in, giving me breath, until I'm screaming his name. "Enzo!"

The orgasm slams through me, a riptide of pain and pleasure tearing me apart so intensely that I'm crying out, laughing deliriously, utterly drunk on sex.

"I can't hold back," he grunts, fucking me so fast and so hard, I have to spread my thighs wide—wider—"That's it, *Bella*. Take it all, good girl. Take. It. All. *Fuck!*"

The way he slams into me, nips my neck, cups my breast, and forces me to take him so deep, I'm not sure the wall will hold up. Or me.

And then I feel it—heat filling me up—as his body rocks and trembles hard, emptying everything he has. Long, deep thrusts push us both to the edge and beyond. "*Shit*," he groans, a raw intensity in his voice.

His head drops to my shoulder.

"What?" I whisper, laying kisses on his muscles and neck, my fingers tangling through his damp hair.

"I couldn't stop—I—" He blows out an angry breath, shaking his head. "No condom. It isn't like me."

I pant through a breathless laugh. "Really? Because there's an entire fan page dedicated to you that claims bareback is the only way you ride."

His full lips twist into a grin. "Now who's the stalker?"

Definitely me. Fangirl, too.

"I'm clean. I've never been without a condom, Kennedy. With anyone. I swear." His voice is earnest, eyes locked onto mine, with so much sincerity, my heart skips a beat.

I'm not sure which surprises me more: his confession or his

need to tell me, especially since I can still feel him pulse deep inside me.

"I'm on the pill," I say, as if that somehow makes it better. Me, not thinking at all about how many women he's been with. "So no baby D'Angelos anytime soon."

He frowns, then kisses me. "I know."

What? "How?" How would he know I'm on the pill?

He kisses my shoulder and neck, then trails his lips to my heart-shaped freckle. "I know everything about you, *Bella*. Your bra size. Your preferred speed of vibrator. That you have some really weird kinks."

"What?" Kinks? The lies.

"You and your werewolf porn."

I straighten my back, indignation flaring. "It's not porn."

He smirks, kissing me again. "I read chapter three." Another kiss, deeper this time. "Definitely porn."

I feel the length of him growing harder as his tongue lazily licks in and out. My body trembles, and I'm not sure I can handle round two, but I doubt either of us has the self-control to stop.

"What else do you know about me?" I whisper against his mouth.

His eyes darken, and he fists my hair. "That the next time you come, it'll be on your knees."

Chapter Eighteen
ENZO

Fuck.

I read the single number text, and it instantly pisses me off. Not good, given the circumstances.

2

My uncle's daily reminders—that I now have two days left with Kennedy—only fuel my imagination for destroying his empire in more creative ways.

I glance over, my eyes tracing the sensuous curve of Kennedy's hip, the dip to her waist, and up to the most breathtaking breasts I've ever seen.

A small whimper escapes her throat, her brow pinching tight as her entire body jolts. The more her monsters chase her, the more rage rises to the surface, burning holes through my restraint.

Until my hands encase both her wrists, flinging her arms over her head, my knees between her legs, prying them wide.

She wakes with a start, blinking away the fog of sleep, breathing hard. "Enzo?"

"Nightmares?"

Confused, she nods slowly, tears welling up. Her small arms struggle to free themselves from my grip. "What are you doing?"

I drag my cheek across her breast, letting my rough stubble scrape against her soft skin. Her back arches, and she fights so little that I know her mind is warring with her body. "Destroying them. The more they return, the harder your little body will endure my wrath."

"Wrath?" Panic flashes over her expression, and her struggle amps up, though not by much. "I can't control what I dream." Her hips thrust up, her resistance smearing wetness across my skin.

I nip her breast hard, eliciting a sound that is a perfect blend of a frightened cry and a breathless moan. "And I can't control how much pleasure I'll take in punishing you."

There's a fight in her eyes—a blazing fire. A decent man would want to extinguish it, smother it with gentle kisses and tender caresses. But me?

I wanted to douse it in kerosene and watch it burn.

The stiff peaks of her breasts are so tight, they can cut glass. A strangled cry escapes her lips as my teeth scrape against her perfect skin, marking her.

When her hips buck against me again, I flip her onto her stomach, resting my cock between her cheeks. Instantly, she freezes. And I know exactly what she's thinking. There's no chance in hell of fitting this into her tight little hole.

Slowly, I let that thought sink in, pressing my length against her, making sure she feels every inch of my cock rubbing up and down between her cheeks.

"Enzo?" Her voice comes out timid and full of fear.

I fist her hair, forcing her head to twist and face me. "My dirty girl's sweet little ass needs my wrath. Needs to be fucked. Doesn't it, *Bella*?"

A faint squeak escapes her throat. I know she can't take me. Not yet. Because of her nightmares—the men who break in and out of her mind against her will—I want a pound of flesh.

I need her on her knees.

I force her around, positioning her on all fours, head at my crotch, ass within arms reach. I wrap her hair around my fist as I slap her ass. "Doesn't it?"

"Yes," she gasps, breathless and trembling.

"With what?" I demand, rubbing her pussy and smearing wetness up to her hole. And fuck, she's drenched. "The choice of punishment is yours. How I punish you is mine."

I half expect her to say my finger—her smallest option by a long shot. So it surprises me when, out of those pouty little lips, comes a single word: "Titan."

Holy shit.

I lick the back of her neck. A shiver runs down her spine. "Will you take your punishment like a good girl? Take two big dicks at once?"

She hesitates, her mouth quivering in that shy way that tells me she's still fighting her own urges.

I spank her again, harder this time, and plunge two fingers deep inside her, thrusting in and out. "Answer me."

"Yes," she moans, and my brain explodes.

"Yes, what?" I demand.

"Please, Mr. D'Angelo. Please fuck my pussy and ass. Make me take two dicks at once."

I've never been this close to coming just from dirty talk and fingering a girl before, but holy fucking shit...

I finger fuck her at first, slow and rhythmic, letting her feel every deliberate thrust. "You need to suck my cock for that filthy fucking mouth."

I move into position, every part of me aching for relief, stroking as I line up my cock with her beautiful, parted lips. Her eyes widen at the sight of me hard and glistening with pre-cum.

I rub the tip along her open lips, savoring the moment. The first lash of her tongue sends my head falling back, and when her hot mouth envelops me, all the air floods from my lungs. *Fuck.* "Rub yourself, filthy girl. And take it down your throat."

When she starts rubbing, lavishing attention on her sweet pussy without fear or doubt—while taking more of my cock down her throat—this is the moment the truth crystallizes between us.

I own her.

The way her throat tightens around me, God, I feel it in every nerve of my body. And when those big eyes look up at me as I fuck her mouth, the edges of my control fray.

I'm lost. In this moment. In her. Kennedy. *Bella.* Nothing and no one else matters.

I indulge a few minutes more, savoring every second before I come up for air and remember what the hell I'm doing. Then I open the drawer and pull out the toy. Titan. Her punishment. Her wish.

I rip her mouth away from my cock and toss her like a rag doll exactly where I want her: crouched over me, ready.

I turn on the toy, her eyes widening, mesmerized by its hum. Her pussy slowly glides along my shaft, and I grab her hip, thrusting deep inside her.

"*Ahh*," my *Bella* moans.

Her eyes slam shut as she gasps, hissing through the pain of me spreading her so fast. I let her body adjust, the tightness easing into a rhythm that ratchets up to the pace she needs.

By the way she bites down on her lip and her entire body clenches, she's already close.

I twist her nipple, pulling her out of the mounting climax. "Did I say you could come?"

"No," she sighs.

Once I find the right setting, a hum of vibration that lights a spark in her eyes, I slide it around, teasing the tiny hole of her ass before forcing it in.

"Oh, God," she whimpers.

I give it to her in hard, relentless strokes—in and out—just fast enough that she slams onto my dick even faster and so much deeper.

"Please," she begs. "Please let me come."

But I don't want her to come. Because I'm a greedy bastard, and *Bella* brings out the best and worst in me all at once.

I crave this moment, prolonging the exquisite torture, feeling her so goddamned tight around my cock while another toy invades her ass. The intensity is unbearable, even for me.

As much as I want to remain trapped between heaven and hell, hovering at the edge of this abyss won't last.

"Are you ready to come on my cock?"

"Yes. Please. Yes."

Her whole body rides the pleasure, then stiffens in my arms, like the taut string of a harp I'm pulling back to the brink of breaking before letting go.

"Come," I command.

Instantly, her body clamps down, and I thrust so hard that when I squeeze her tight and her teeth sink into my shoulder, it's enough to send us both tumbling into nirvana.

As the waves of ecstasy subside, I ease the toy out of her, kissing her softly and caressing small circles along her back. But I don't pull out. Not yet.

Not when I'm still throbbing with the need to empty every last drop. Besides, I'm pretty sure her body would rip my dick right off like a vise if I tried.

For a long while, we lie there, catching our breaths. My fingers lazily feather through her hair as she plants small kisses along my chest.

Then my phone buzzes, snapping me out of the blissful haze. Annoyed, I glance over and see yet another text.

This time, my idiot uncle has sent me a time and a location. I grit my teeth, trying to control my body's response.

The irritation simmers just below the surface, but nothing will disturb *Bella* and the warmth of her afterglow.

My uncle never wants to meet, so it's either an ambush or a truce. An ambush makes more sense. But a truce . . .

My mind toys with the notion that Kennedy is mine, free and clear of my uncle.

"She is yours," the Scottish voice whispers, and for a fleeting moment, I almost believe the madman in my head.

Until the last text comes through.

It's a picture of Kennedy, dressed in a flowing, emerald-green dress that clings to her curves in all the right places. The neckline plunges just enough to tease, while the delicate lace sleeves add a touch of elegance.

The fact that my uncle is having her followed isn't a surprise; my men had already tipped me off.

But what grabs my attention is Riley, standing right in front of the townhouse I put her up in. It's more than just surveillance.

It's a message.

And it looks like no matter what, I'm getting fucked in the ass today, too.

Chapter Nineteen

ENZO

The ocean crashes against the rocky cliffside, each wave a thunderous reminder that power comes in many forms. In its rawest form, it's nature. In my form, it's a net worth that rivals half the free world and a small militia at my beck and call.

The beach sprawls out, an endless stretch of desolate sand and restless sea, the only movement a few seagulls circling above.

If one of them shits on my suit, I swear to God, I'll shoot them.

Andre finally rolls up, twenty minutes late. It baffles me that there was ever a time I considered him anything but pond scum. His crooked smile and perpetual smirk lock onto me, stirring a potent cocktail of anger and regret I've spent my life trying to bury.

Seeing him now, a fresh wave of bitter memories crashes over me. It's like bandaging a wound with barbed wire—brutal and excruciating, each thought ripping me apart all over again.

If I hadn't given him an ounce of respect back then, maybe

none of this would be happening. And no matter how I distance myself, I'm always drawn back in.

His web of destruction is vast, nearly invisible until you're trapped at the center of it. No matter how far I go, its strands are always floating around, their sticky presence constantly brushing against my skin.

Uncle Andre's brand-new car represents him to a T—sporty enough to broadcast his one-inch dick and expensive enough to make people fawn over it. Some might call it luxurious; I call it gaudy as fuck.

He exits and heads towards me. If I kill him on the spot, who would know?

But then I catch the glint of a sniper rifle reflected on a distant crag. From the angle, I know it's not one of my guys. Which means it's one of his, and they would definitely know. Probably take me out with a clean, precise bullet straight to the heart.

Killjoy.

"Having fun with the girl?" Uncle Andre sneers, his voice slicing through the tension like a blade.

There's a glint in his eyes that I can't quite read—sadism, pleasure, maybe both. Then he pulls out a vial, and I see it's just my coked-up uncle itching for a hit.

He dabs some onto his hand and takes a long, indulgent sniff—his twisted version of liquid courage. Normally, he'd offer me some, knowing I'd refuse. But today, there's no offer. Guess he's not feeling so charitable after I annihilated one of his choke points.

I don't bother with pleasantries. I shove both hands into my pockets, too exhausted for this conversation. "What do you want?" I spit, my patience as worn as the bad rug on his head.

"I want to know how your arm is," he says, motioning to the wound hidden beneath my shirt. "Consider it a warning shot. Mess with my operation again, and both your girl and her sister get sold to the highest bidder."

I pull out a cigar and light it, letting the smoke curl around my face. The slow drag is calming, though not as much as envisioning a clean, straight slice across his neck, just below the jaw but above the Adam's apple.

Or better yet, one swift stab through the artery, puncturing the esophagus and letting him drown in his own blood. At the very least, it would finally shut him up.

"You cost me a lot of money," he goes on, as if he isn't already a multi-millionaire several times over. But then again, he's not a billionaire, thanks to me.

"And?" I ask, blowing a long puff of smoke in his face.

"And you're going to make it up to me." He holds up two fingers, a sinister smile twisting his lips. "You have two days with her. Then, either you hand her back..."

"Or?" I ask, underwhelmed.

"Or you can take on two. In the ring." I swear, he's the only man who calls an MMA cage a ring. And the implication is clear: the men I'd be fighting, probably armed with tire irons, chains, and baseball bats, would bring my uncle eight figures. Maybe even nine.

And the small fact that I'd be a walking vegetable if I survived only sweetens the deal for him.

I smile and walk to his car. "I'll think about it," I lie, studying the sleek angles of his car. It's a flashy model I've never seen before.

"Do we have a deal?"

I don't answer and walk around the side, inspecting it from a different angle.

He loses patience the way he always does with me. "Debts will be honored, Enzo."

Mantra of our world. *Debts will be honored.* The entire reason Kennedy even made his radar. My heart kicks up a beat, remembering how she tastes when she comes—

"Are you even listening?" he asks. "Or is your brain already oatmeal?"

He would know. It was the matches I did for him that made my brain the lost cause that it is.

"I have two days," I repeat.

His laugh is cold and hollow, devoid of any real humor. "She must be one hell of a lay. I can't wait to find out for myself."

"You'll never touch her," I reply, my voice steady as I continue puffing my cigar calmly.

"And you and I both know your family will never support a war, and sure as hell not over a dime-a-dozen cunt." He smacks my cheek, the sting sharp. "Think about it. Do the fight. I'll even tell them to stay away from your face."

We're eye to eye. Or we would be if I didn't tower over his pathetic ass.

I smirk. "You and I both know it won't end there." I flick a bug from the top of the dash. "Is this a limited edition or vintage?" I wonder aloud.

A small flicker of pride lights in his eyes, and his grin widens. "It's a one-of-a-kind. Handcrafted." He brushes his stubby fingers along the paint.

"How much?"

"Two and a half million dollars."

"It's nice." I puff my cigar and turn to face him. I want to watch his expression as I shove the ash end of it on the hood.

It's almost slow motion, his reflexes. The wave of shock melts his fake-ass demeanor and reddens his face with rage.

The threats he makes as he bitches about the custom gold flecks that can't be reproduced in the destroyed paint. "You're fucking dead," and "I will end you." Blah, blah, blah.

Frankly, the color looks like some kid melted down gray, green, and orange crayons and added a bunch of sparkly shit to it. I'm doing him a favor.

He shoves a gun under my chin. I press my own piece against his gut, relishing the surge of adrenaline through my veins. "Let's fucking do this," I growl, eyes locked onto his. "Mutual annihilation. Right here. Right now."

The tension between us is an electric fence, primed to release a fatal surge with the slightest misstep.

"Your little bitch will pay for this," he vows, stepping back slowly until he feels all snug and safe in his butt-ugly car. He rolls down the window. "Two days," he spits. "And her ass is mine. And anyone else I care to rent her to."

His wheels spin out, and he drives away.

Getting into my own car is automatic. I drive aimlessly

through the narrow, winding streets, the shops and buildings passing by in a blur.

The car has a mind of its own, which is good, considering the pain in the base of my neck feels like a shank going from my spine and exiting out my eye.

I need to pull over and rest, but with the city crawling with Andre's spies, there's only one place I can go.

The brothel—the one the team and I rescued all those women from. And if I know my uncle, the fact that I sanitized it means it's nuclear waste to him.

I park in a hidden carport and find my way in. I need to rest, to think, before I face Kennedy. She can't see me like this—enraged. Broken.

I see a man—myself in the mirror. Between my pain, Andre's threats, and my own fucking reflection, I do what I do best.

My fist flies into it, dead center. It shatters, shards raining down like tiny, glinting daggers, each piece reflecting me in my fractured fucking state.

"You'll figure it out," the ghost of Mullvain says. For a figment of my imagination, he's strangely encouraging.

"I have two fucking days," I argue with no one at all, dropping onto a bed that would under any normal circumstances make me cringe and want to dive straight into bleach. But right now, I just need to close my eyes and think.

Chapter Twenty
ENZO

AS SOON AS I hear my uncle's voice, I run.

"Why the fuck did you tell him Enzo was here?" From behind the thick velvet curtains, my Uncle Andre's voice is a low growl, the kind of quiet threat that makes grown men tremble.

But not this man.

I peer out to find a giant of a figure, standing tall. "He deserves to know where his son is, boss. He's the boy's father. Yer brother. Family."

His broad back faces me, but I'd know that voice anywhere—deep, brogue, and unwavering. It's Mullvain, his prized fighter. Brute force personified, his presence is towering yet gentle, even from where I'm hiding.

"Family?" Uncle Andre's laugh is sharp and bitter. "I don't need a life coach, Mullvain. I need loyalty. Do you understand?"

Mullvain nods once, and my uncle stops pacing, turning to face him directly.

His eyes narrow into slits. "Someone's been barking up to the

Feds. You wouldn't happen to know anything about that, would you?"

"No, sir," he spits, clearly offended. "I handle me own battles. I'm no snitch."

"Good to know." Uncle Andre's voice drops to a low, feral growl, almost predatory. "You got kids, Mullvain?"

There's a heartbeat of silence. Then Mullvain shakes his head. "No," he says, with a casual shrug.

"Liar," I whisper before I can stop myself, panic flaring as the word slips out.

But no one notices.

I strain to hear, because I don't know everything about Mullvain, but I know he's lying. I once saw a picture on his phone—two girls, unmistakably his.

I hold my breath, my heart pounding so loudly I'm sure they'll hear it. My uncle is infamous for making examples of men who cross him, and lying ranks right up there with stealing and informing.

Through the crack in the drapes, I see Mullvain's clenched fists and the tight line of his jaw. It's the look he gets just before he turns someone into hamburger meat.

Not that I've seen it myself, but I know when he fights for my uncle, all the guards place their bets on him. I might have thrown in a few bets myself.

In this world, even a fifteen-year-old can place bets, and not because I'm a D'Angelo. It's because a C-note is a C-note, no matter whose hand it comes from.

Mullvain always wins. That's why my uncle has him teaching me to fight. Not to turn people into hamburger meat, but to protect myself and what's mine.

"Good," Andre says, his voice cold and calculated. "Because if you did, you'd have a hard time with this next fight."

"Why?" Mullvain asks, a wary edge creeping into his voice.

There's a pause before my uncle speaks, a smug grin forming on his lips as he considers his words. "So we all can see what you're made of. And to show that nephew of mine how our world works."

Mullvain's defiance falters. "Enzo is impressionable," he murmurs, almost to himself.

My uncle gathers his keys and heads out the door as I duck behind a massive oak cabinet. "That's what I'm counting on," he says, his voice cold and calculated.

With that, Uncle Andre and his henchmen blow past me, their footsteps heavy and rushed. Mullvain lingers behind, seething. "Fuck," he mutters under his breath.

"What's wrong?" I ask, stepping out from behind the cabinet and quietly shutting the door.

He sees me and forces a smile, the kind you give a three-year-old. "Nothing, boy. Ye shouldn't be here. Yer uncle's in a mood. Best ye stay out of sight."

I step closer, my curiosity burning. "Why would you tell my dad I was here?"

He blows out a breath. "Yer Da's worried about you. I would be, too, if I had a son camping out in a lion's den."

"Like you worry about your daughters?"

His face loses all its color, going pale. "How do ye know about them?"

"I saw the picture on your phone once. Two girls." When his frown deepens, I step even closer. "You can trust me. I won't say a word." I hold up my hand solemnly. "I swear. We have a pact. Like Fight Club?"

A cautious smile curls his lips. "Ye know the first rule of Fight Club."

"You do not talk about Fight Club," *I recite, puffed up and serious. He rubs my hair, and there's a closeness between us. A bond. A protectiveness I can feel emanating from him.*

He's protective of me—a great grizzly adopting a wolf. A protectiveness I adopt, too.

"Can I see them? Your girls?" *I ask, though it's really just the one girl I want to see.*

"Our secret?" *he asks, holding his hand up like he wants to arm wrestle.*

I latch onto it and grip it tight. "Our secret."

He opens his phone and scrolls to an image. There are two of them, but I can't take my eyes off the little freckled girl with dark hair and eyes like his. Her smile is slight, and my mind spins with all the ways I could make it wider. Cannoli? Or maybe by fighting as well as her dad. "She's pretty," *I blurt out, sounding like a dork.*

"Aye, they both are." *He throws me a mock stern look.* "Don't ye be getting any ideas. From what I've heard, her Da's a mean bugger." *He winks and goes to put the phone away.*

Before I can stop myself, my hand shoots out to his. "Is there another picture of her?"

"Maybe. Ye been practicing the series of jabs I showed ya?"

His question instantly flips a switch. He lights a cigar as I run through the moves, pushing power and force with each punch, ending in a tornado kick I've been itching to show off.

He chuckles when I fumble the landing but still applauds. "All right, young Jedi." *He pats me on the chest.* "One more picture, then it's back to practice."

Bzzz.

Bzzz-bzzz.

What feels like a second after I closed my eyes, my phone rings.

My eyes adjust to the brightness of the screen as the name SMOKE cuts through the haze. My pain-in-the-ass older brother, probably ready to lecture me on starting a war with Andre.

I answer, groggy and irritated. "What?"

"Just calling to make sure you're still coming to my wedding."

His wedding . . . *fuck*, when is that again? "Of course, I'm coming. I said I would, so I will."

"Oh, good. I wasn't sure, considering I just heard you'd been shot."

"Do not tell Trinity," I order, my voice firm.

"Then stop getting shot," he fires back. "But since you're not dead, I guess there's no reason to say anything to our baby sister. Other than you're an idiot." He huffs. "A fucking idiot."

"Are you almost done?"

His voice rises so loud that the sound warning goes off on my phone. "It's just like you to pull a dangerous stunt like this, days before my wedding, without at least clueing me in."

When he finally takes a breath, I cut in, "You sound like a nag."

"And you sound suicidal!" he shouts. "Butting heads with Andre? Are you out of your fucking mind?"

I hold the phone away to avoid my eardrum bursting. I let

Smoke vent; he probably needs it with the wedding jitters and all. Finally, he calms down. "So, you got yourself shot. Where? In the ass?"

"In the arm." I sit up, wincing as pain radiates from both my arm and head. "Just a graze," I mutter, trying to blink my eyes open and realizing it's pitch black. How long have I been out? I shake off the grogginess and squint at the time.

Past midnight.

Fuck.

I fumble around the abandoned building as Smoke's voice booms through the phone, giving me more shit. "From the way you've been going after Andre, I was sure you'd been shot in the head. What else could explain Mr. Reckless Behavior other than something close to a lobotomy?" He blows out a long, meditative breath. "Are you okay?"

"I'm"—fucked six ways to Sunday—"fine."

"So, my man of honor is still coming to the wedding?"

"Yes."

"Good. Because you know it's in about thirty hours."

What? Thirty hours can't be right. "It's in three days," I argue, pretty sure the groom should at least know the right day he's getting married. "Sunday."

"That's right, genius. Sunday. And today's Friday. Do the math."

"I know that." I totally forgot.

I trip over something in the dark, swearing up a storm as some furry, screeching Chupacabra darts over my foot and across the room, scaring the living shit out of me.

"What was that?" Smoke obviously hears the commotion,

and maybe even the unholy hissing from a demonic rat from hell. "Where are you?" he asks.

My brain finally kicks in, and I use the flashlight on my phone to meander the rest of the way out of the building.

Hmm.

One glance around what remains of the brothel, and I seriously wish I didn't need the light.

The place is a living nightmare: moldy walls peeling like old scabs, stained mattresses strewn about, and the unmistakable stench of decay hanging in the air. It's the kind of place luminal would make light up like the Vatican City at Christmas.

I shake my head. "Trust me, it's better that you don't know." I finally make it to the street, disoriented for only a second before remembering where I parked. "I need to go."

"Don't get killed."

"Don't fuck up your vows. Seriously, women hold onto that shit forever."

WEARY AND WORN AND NEARLY AN HOUR LATER, I finally make it home. The house is bathed in silence, and as exhausted as I am, my hand still wraps around my Glock.

I peer into the guest room and find Sofia and Lili snuggled together in front of the fire, with Truffles at their feet.

I don't know what it is about the warm glow of flickering flames and everyone cuddled under blankets, but it tugs at heartstrings I didn't even know I had. The sense of satisfaction and peace that comes over me is eerie as fuck.

Shit. Is this what it's like to be tamed and domesticated like a fucking house cat? Oblivious to the world and happy for it?

Maybe there's a pill for this.

Or some miracle cure like electroshock therapy.

From the corner of the room, a floorboard creaks. I'm already zeroing the barrel of my gun at Dory's head before I realize it's her.

She's in a recliner, fast asleep, with her glasses still perched on her nose and a copy of *Matilda* resting on her lap, open to the part where the evil hag is scouring the house for the precocious child. What's her name? Punchbowl?

Now, Miss Honey—that's a name I remember. The woman with the pretty face and light brown hair was the only highlight of my reading this book to Trinity. All eighteen million times.

My lips twitch into a smile, picturing Dory leaving the girls on a cliffhanger before bed. Who knew she had a dark side?

She rustles slightly, and I pocket my gun before carefully removing her glasses and setting the book aside. Then I drape a blanket over her.

There's something endearing about her serene expression, though I know the crick in her neck will be a bitch in the morning.

By the time I reach *Bella*'s room, my phone buzzes again. I know I should ignore it, but what if it's Smoke or Dante? What if something's wrong?

I glance at the screen and read the text. He spells out the date, along with a message.

Debt Due

8:00 p.m.

D'Angelo Estate

In his own special way, my uncle is letting me know he's aware of my every move. The thinly veiled threat is evident: Either I hand my *Bella* over, or we turn Smoke's wedding into a bloodbath.

And considering the bride's family is as bloodthirsty as we are, it should make for an interesting reception.

"Sure, Uncle Andre. I'll hand Kennedy right over to you. How about tied up and naked on a silver platter," I scoff, shaking my head. Anger fuels my long, deliberate strides from the hall to the nearest guest room. "Over my dead fucking body."

I need to see Kennedy so badly, my body thrums with a deep, aching pain. A live wire sparking just beneath my skin.

But I can't. Not yet.

First, I need to shower in a firehose of bleach and clear my head. I'm too edgy and riled up, and if I fuck her when I'm this emotionally charged, the girl's vagina will combust.

Then, I need to text Smoke.

I detour to the nearest guest room, stripping off my clothes and vowing to burn them. With one step into the shower, I meditate beneath a cascade of scalding hot water that nearly melts my skin off. The heat sears away the grime and tension, but not the anger.

My uncle wants a war? He's got one.

I dry off and shoot Smoke a text.

ME
About the wedding . . .
I'll need a plus one.

Chapter Twenty-One
KENNEDY

AFTER A FUN-FILLED day at the beach with the girls and Truffles, I find myself tossing and turning again. We all missed Enzo, and his absence gnaws at me.

The clock blinks extra bright now, telling me that it's one in the morning, and the whole world is pitch black.

Where is he?

I mean, after last night, I wasn't exactly expecting a marriage proposal, but he seems distant.

And if anyone should be distant, it should be me. Highly guarded, fleeing with my sanity intact. He doesn't understand I've had walls up my entire life. When *Da* died, so many parts of me died with him. It's a wonder anything is left.

Enzo going MIA is triggering as fuck, and goddamnit, why doesn't he call?

When my phone pings, I grab it in a rush, my heart fluttering with the hope that it's him.

But it's not. Surprise, surprise, it's Agent Caleb Knox.

Again.

Can't this guy take a hint?

> **C.K.**
> Are you okay?

ME
> For the thousandth time, yes.
>
> Why do you keep asking me this?

He sends several texts—photos of Enzo going in and coming out of a building, with timestamps and all.

I squint at the images, trying to place the location. Why does that building look familiar? I feel like I know it.

Then it hits me. The building the women came out of. The local brothel.

But I thought he shut that down.

No. That can't be. I frown and scan the images again and again. And again. Expanding them to make sure it's not a trick. Some Italian doppelgänger or pod person.

But it is him. Same shirt. Same face.

Same butthead. Different day.

My heart squeezes so hard, it feels like it's being slowly carved out of my chest.

> **C.K.**
> He was in there for 5 hours.

Wait. What?

ME
> 5 hours??

>   C.K.
> He's a wild card, Kennedy.
> You need to be careful.
> I can help.

My heart sinks into a messy cauldron of confusion, anger, and hurt. Why would Enzo be at a brothel for five hours? My mind races, trying to find any possible explanation that makes sense.

Don't be an idiot. There's only one reason a man goes to a brothel, and it's not for the ambiance.

I sit up in bed, the weight of it all crashing down on me. The words of Savannah Whitaker replay in my head. *"Then he gives you back."*

Tears burn my eyes as panic begins to slowly set in. Churning in the pit of my gut.

He's giving me back? Then what happens to Riley? To the girls? Even the thought of brave little Truffles being pitched to the side of the road makes me sob.

This can't be happening.

I'm hyperventilating myself into a frenzy, trying to think of what to do. I can't leave Riley or the girls. And there's no way I'm leaving Truffles.

"Breathe, darlin'." My father's words burst in like fresh air after a dust cloud. *"Don't panic."*

He said them before every show. I'd be puking in a trash can, and he'd be rubbing my back, whispering in my ear.

Why would Enzo bring me here—bring *us* here? All of us. He didn't have to. He could've just as easily been lounging at the brothel twenty-four seven.

I can't shake the feeling that something is off.

That, or I'm grasping at straws, unable to hold it together without fantasizing that he's the good guy. Even when he's dumping me off the side of the Titanic just to keep the big, cushy lifeboat all to himself.

Agent Knox's offer hangs in the air, like a carrot from a really long stick. He has his own agenda. I know he does. He's the FBI. The words CONFIDENTIAL INFORMANT come to mind, and they're not exactly known for their supreme life expectancy.

But he also has photos and an escape plan. Maybe for all of us.

Ugh, I need to know the truth. Part of me—the stupid part—feels like if I don't hear it from Enzo's own lips, I won't believe it.

The smarter part of me wonders if it'll take an action shot of him fucking another girl—or girls—to get it through my thick head that no matter how nice he seems or how good he looks or how good he is in bed, the man's a prick.

Just as I'm about to do the unthinkable and call him, I hear rustling in the hall. It's all I can do not to rip open the door, pound his chest, and demand . . . what? He be straight with me?

My fingers hover on the doorknob, more tears breaking through. I screw up my face and swipe my tears. I just want the truth.

But then I hear him from the other side of the door. "Sure, Uncle Andre. I'll hand Kennedy right over to you. How about tied up and naked on a silver platter."

My blood runs cold. He's really going to do it. Hand me to those monsters.

Some small, brave voice inside me thinks I could do that. Not run in terror, but let it happen so that Riley is safe. Sofia, Lili, Truffles. What happens when I'm gone?

My knees give out, and my back slides to the floor as I look to *Da* for help. "What do I do, *Da*?"

"Follow yer heart, darlin'."

I screw up my face in tears, defeated. "I can't," I whisper, my voice sounding strangled and small. "He's going to send me back to Andre, and I . . . love him."

God, I'm a fucking mess.

Stop thinking of him, I scream in my head. Think of you. *Think of all of you.*

My body moves on autopilot.

I grab the phone.

I call.

He picks up. "Well?" Is all he says.

I step away from the door and lower my voice. "Well, Agent Knox. If you'll protect all of us—"

"You have my word."

"Then," I blow out a slow, decisive breath and ignore the big, gaping hole in my heart. "Then tell me what I have to do."

Chapter Twenty-Two

KENNEDY

Moonlight slices through the gloom and darkness, casting a silver path that Enzo follows with unnerving ease.

The man moves like a panther, silent and assured, and his presence is instant. It fills the room to the point I'm suffocating.

I turn under the covers and curl on my side, cocooning myself against everything that's wrong between us. The last thing I want is to see his face, to feel his touch. Plus, if he catches sight of my tears, he'll know something's off.

I'm breaking, and I can't let it show.

He slides under the sheets, and two big, warm arms wrap around me. My body shivers involuntarily, and his grip tightens in response, pulling me closer.

I bite my lip, struggling to hold back the sob that's clawing its way up my throat. But the tears are relentless, brimming at all my tattered edges.

"Hey," he murmurs against my hair, pressing a tender kiss to it. "What's wrong? Whatever it is that's making you cry, I swear I'll kill it with my bare hands."

I turn to face him in total disbelief. For a fleeting second, I actually picture him strangling himself until he's blue in the face and unconscious on the floor.

Then, my eyes meet his, and oh, God. In the dim light, I search his dark golden gaze, desperate to find something to despise. Instead, I feel myself unraveling, my carefully constructed resolve dissolving to mush.

Warm fingers brush the tears from my cheeks and tuck the stray strands of hair behind my ear. "Want to talk about it?" His voice is a deep rumble, a lure. A trap I'll fall into if I'm not careful, because no matter how much I want to hate him, I can't.

Tenderness is my kryptonite. I don't know how to fight that. Why does he have to be this? Warm and comforting.

You're an asshole. Fucking act like it, okay?

"No," I whisper, hating myself for how much truth is in that single word.

He keeps his arms around me, caressing my back, laying soft kisses along my cheeks and neck. "I need to make you feel better."

He moves so slowly that my body responds instinctively, all defenses down. I try to fight it—the need to follow his lead as every touch ignites a response.

"So tense," he whispers. "Did you like the beach?" he asks, his lips brushing against my heart-shaped freckle. Goose bumps erupt in its wake, sending shivers across my skin.

"What?" I ask, caught off guard.

"The beach. You went there today. It's a private stretch of land we own. Did you like it?"

Fuck. Of course, he's watching me. He's always watching.

Does he know about my texts with Agent Knox? Does he

know that I know he's handing me to his uncle? Naked on a silver fucking platter?

I'm stunned, and the anger bubbles up. "No. I didn't much care for it, actually. I'd much prefer"—I think of the one I saw on a postcard in the market that flew to the top of my bucket list—"Elafonisi Beach."

"Elafonisi?" he murmurs against my breast. "Where is that?" he asks, his kisses trailing down my stomach.

He's going to go down on me. *Fuck*. I mentally brace myself, knowing I have to let him do this if I want to get us all out of this. Me, Riley, the girls, and Truffles.

But when it comes to my feelings, not the ones between my legs but the ones in my heart, where the fuck is the off switch?

And it's not like my body has an issue with it. It responds instinctively, my back arching to his touch, my legs parting as his rough stubble grazes my skin. His hot tongue—

"Crete," I blurt out. Stay in control. *Stay. In. Control.*

"Greece," he growls into my core, letting the word vibrate through me before chasing it with a smooth, long lick. "What's so special about Elafonisi Beach?"

By this point, I'm riding his face, both hands tangled in his hair. And why the hell not? Men have always taken from me. Maybe this is me taking something from him. Yes. Absolutely. Fuck him, for once.

"It's"—I moan—"the sand." God, this feels so good. "It's pink," I cry.

I come in a rush, panting and heaving as he finishes me off like the last bit of chocolate syrup when a sundae is done.

He makes his way back up my body, kissing me slow and deep. "Pink sand?" he murmurs against my lips, still nibbling as he lines himself up at my entrance. "Say the word, *Bella*, and I'll give you anything you want."

I want this ache in my heart to stop.

I want you out of my life.

I want to feel nothing for you but hate.

I want to be free.

A tidal wave of tears threatens to spill over, and I can't let him see them. So, I hold his body close. So close. And I tell him the one thing I want—and the one thing I hate myself for most.

"I want you to fuck me, Mr. D'Angelo."

Chapter Twenty-Three
KENNEDY

BREAKFAST IS a mix of chatter and giggles as the girls delight in feeding Truffles small bits of prosciutto. The little dog snuffles happily, his tail wagging with each morsel.

Enzo, on the other hand, seems more distant than ever, buried in his phone. "You're not eating," he says without looking up.

"I'm . . ." Furious? Heartbroken? "Not hungry." Then I notice his untouched plate. "You're also not eating."

"I'm . . ." he searches for the right word just as I did. "Preoccupied. Unfortunately, we need to get back. I've arranged for the jet to be ready."

What's he talking about? "Back?"

He stands and checks his watch. "Two hours," he says suddenly, shattering the morning's tranquility.

"Wait. Are you saying we need to be at the airport in two hours?" My heart skips frantically. Panicked, my mind races and keeps circling back to Riley. "But I thought we had one more day."

His sigh is sharp, but his words are even. "We don't."

The girls' excitement ramps up instantly. "We're going on a plane?" they squeal in unison, riling Truffles up to insane barking.

"All of us?" I ask, a tremor in my voice, trying to catch Enzo's eye.

"All of us," he replies, distracted, his attention already elsewhere. Panic grips me as the reality sets in. There's no time to prepare.

"What about Riley?" I ask. My voice is frail and desperate.

"I've already made the arrangements. She'll be joining us later," he says absently, his phone buzzing nonstop. Before I can process this abrupt change, he rises to his feet. "I need to take this. Can you help them pack?"

And with three hasty strides, he's out the door. I'd be less stunned if he'd handed me a shovel and said, "Pick a nice plot, then dig your grave."

I look at the girls, their faces bright with excitement, completely unaware of what's to come. Hell, *I'm* unaware of what's to come.

I bite my lower lip until I taste blood. Do we bolt? Get into the nearest cab and . . . go where? I have no money, no passport, and the girls don't even have IDs.

And I need to warn Riley.

A riptide of emotions threaten to tear me apart, the urge to curl up in the fetal position and sob overwhelming. Tiny hands tug at mine, chanting, "Help us pack! Help us pack!" as Truffles bounces around us like a buoy, adding to the chaos.

They drag me to their bedroom and rush into the closet. I

frantically dial Riley's number. Voicemail. "You need to call me. Now, Riley," I hiss into the phone.

I call six more times and send a dozen frantic texts.

Nothing.

Desperation claws at my insides as I throw clothes into suitcases, my mind spinning with fear and uncertainty. The girls chatter away, blissfully ignorant of the storm brewing around us. And it's all I can do to fight to keep my hands steady and keep my mind from spiraling.

I need to figure out our next move.

Dory pops her head into the room, witnessing the complete pandemonium of brand-new clothes flying into designer suitcases that apparently Enzo pulled out of his ass.

Sofie and Lili are jumping on the bed, giddy and laughing, while I wrestle with the knots tightening in my stomach. I want the girls to soak up the fun while they can. They deserve it.

My hands tremble as I try to fold the clothes, and Dory gently takes a shirt from my grasp.

"Enzo told me about your fear of flying. Do you want a sedative? I'm not a fan of flying either. It can help."

Part of me wants to take it. Just close my eyes, pop a pill, and say, *"Wake me up when it's over."* But then I catch the smiles on Sofie and Lili's faces, and I know I have to do this. I have to be strong for them.

The way *Da* always was for me.

"I'm fine," I say, forcing a smile as I continue packing, steadily reminding myself to hold it together.

The blur of events from boarding the plane to being in the air barely registers. My fear of flying is nonexistent. It's the fear of landing and not knowing what's going to happen the minute we do that's shredding my last nerve.

Enzo's been scarce, holed up in the ridiculous bedroom while the girls revel in their sparkly headsets and endless entertainment. At first, they loved having their own monitors, where they could each watch their own shows.

But now, they're watching the exact same thing, giggling in unison. They remind me so much of Riles and me at that age; it's a bittersweet ache in my chest.

"Another drink?" the flight attendant offers. It's the same one from the flight over. She's been so nice, always checking on the girls. And damnit, I'm trying not to get attached to the idea of this being my life.

Trying, and failing miserably.

A double should help. "Yes, thank you." What I really want to say is, *Leave the bottle*, but frankly, I'm not sure it's what I need right now. I'm so close to confronting his fucking face that being a little less drunk and a little more restrained might be in my best interest.

It's like I've adopted a wolf and wonder why it attacks me. I need to remember he's a dangerous, ruthless kingpin, fueled by primal urges and lethal instincts. He has no heart. Only cold, calculated precision.

As soon as the flight attendant—*Gail*, I remind myself—sets the glass in my hand, I down it in one go.

By my fifth glass of liquid courage, I'm braver than shit. The girls are asleep, Truffles is sprawled next to Lili, and my give-a-fuck has flown right out the window.

Fine, maybe he's handing me over to his uncle. Imagining

all the ways he and his thugs will defile me sends chills down my spine. But, goddamn him, he can't do this to Riley. Or to the girls.

You don't throw someone a lifeline just to tow them to the sharks.

I have half a mind to tell him I'm on to him. I'm on to you, fucker. And so are the Feds.

In a huff, I stumble to the back of the plane, past the conked-out kids, frustrated that my tequila legs won't cooperate.

I mentally will them to walk straight, and they sort of do.

I slam through the door like a bat out of hell—a bat who's really fucked up from the booze—and crash inelegantly on the bed.

Big, bad D'Angelo looks down at me and speaks into his phone. "I'll have to call you back."

"Who was that?" I spit out. His mistress? Or maybe he's cozying up to his uncle again, swapping tips on how to handle me. Bastard.

He smirks, a sinister glint in his eye. "You'll find out soon enough."

"When you sell me off?"

He raises one brow—the sexy one—and studies me for so long that I have to look away. I'm getting emotional again, drowning in those rich, golden eyes. "And here I thought I cured you of your fear of flying. How much have you had to drink?"

"Not enough," I snap, glaring at him through a haze of disappointment and hurt. "Riley," I utter.

"What about her?" he asks, his tone annoyingly calm.

"You swore you'd protect her. As well as your own sister." My hand shakes as I point to the door. "And what about the girls? Or"—fuck. What the hell is my dog's name again?

"I'm taking care of it," he says so solemnly that I shiver.

"Tonight?" I utter, irritation bubbling up. "When you serve me up on a platter?" When he just sits there watching me, I blurt out, "And what if I call the cops?"

"No, *Bella*, you won't. Because cops can't help. And you're speaking to the man with half the force in his pocket."

God, he's so smug. My big, fat mouth gets ahead of me, ready to teach him a lesson. "Then the Feds will save us," I slur defiantly.

He kisses my lips. Why do his lips have to feel so good? I swear, I feel his stubble all the way between my legs. "Your only savior is me, *Bella*. And you will worship me," he whispers, his fingers tracing my lower lip. "The way I will worship you."

The world spins as he lifts me into his arms, places me in the center of the bed and begins removing my clothes. Like a total asshole. Being all nice and shit.

I want to resist, but my clothes feel like they're burning my skin. And I just want them off.

When I'm finally naked and vulnerable, shooting daggers at him with my eyes, he begins to undress. As his shirt falls away, I'm staring straight down the barrel of chiseled abs and a sculpted chest, every muscle defined and taut.

His broad shoulders and inked skin make him a masterpiece, raw and powerful, cold and precise. He moves like hot steel yielding to an inferno. I lick my lips. "A friend of mine, Ricardo, will pick you up from the airport."

Panic flares, my brow pinching hard. "What about the girls?"

"Dory will see to them," he says, stroking my head as my lids grow heavy. "The only person you need to worry about is you."

"I. Hate. You," I remind him and myself, each word laced with venom.

"Hate?" he asks, brushing several strands of hair out of my eyes. When a tear breaks free, he kisses it. "I promise you, there's so much more of me to hate."

My eyes close, and I say it again, mostly in my head. "I hate you..."

"If you hate me now, *Bella*, you'll hate me even more tonight." Hot lips press against mine, and I shudder, feeling his body slide against mine, spreading my legs, his thick length gliding along my entrance.

My treacherous body wraps around him, betraying my resolve. He plunges in with such force that I gasp for air, struggling to take all of him.

His thrusts start slow, agonizingly slow, and I bite back a moan. I need more, but I'm sure as hell not begging for it. I refuse to give him the satisfaction.

With a swift move, he rolls to his back, propping me on top of him, forcing my legs to spread wide in a squat. Holy hell, he's deep.

He pumps into me, his hips driving into mine, shoving his monster cock in and out, in and out. Each thrust shreds away every last thread of control as pain and pleasure rip me wide, leaving me wet. So wet.

"Now, fuck me, *Bella*. Show me just how much your sweet pussy hates me," he growls.

His hands fondle my breasts, then glide over my ass, urging me to pick up the pace.

Oh, my pussy hates him all right.

And she hates him a lot.

Chapter Twenty-Four
KENNEDY

I STARE at the array of clothes around the room, my head pounding.

I vaguely remember a driver bringing me here. Correction—a driver and a bodyguard, both as mountainous as Enzo. Fucker probably knows I was thinking of running.

Not that I could run anywhere, considering Enzo had to carry me to the car.

Me, my shoes—because if the bastard is shoving me off to Andre D'Angelo, it won't be in six-inch come-fuck-me heels made by Jimmy fucking Choo.

This guy, Ricardo, fusses with my hair, sweeping it up, then letting it fall, before his hands brushing along my waist and across my back. Not in a sensual way. More like he's sizing me up.

For the slaughter.

I'm pretty sure if I wasn't so hungover, I'd be a freaking out by now. But with this much alcohol pumping through my veins, it's a wonder I'm still standing up.

Ricardo holds one gown against me, then another, and yet another. "Your body is exquisite," he says, his accent vaguely French. He gestures flamboyantly. "You'll look good in absolutely anything."

"Thank you," I say, annoyed. I'm seriously not sure what all the fuss is about. Is this some kind of weird rich-people kink? Playing with me like I'm his favorite Barbie?

"Any preference for color?" he asks, his eyes sparkling.

My shoulders rise and fall, deflated. "Got something that matches a silver platter?"

He laughs so hard he nearly shoots champagne through his nose. The sound of laughter is boisterous and genuine, infectious in its warmth. Despite myself, a smile tugs at my lips, breaking through the heavy weight holding it down.

Ricardo taps my chin with the crook of his finger. "Remove your clothes."

All traces of a smile vanish, replaced by a jolt of fear. "What?"

"Just to your bra and panties. For now." He waggles his brows.

My fingers dig into the fabric of my blouse, clutching it closed. I don't care how the man seems; it's just not happening.

When I hesitate, he spins me around to face the mirror. "You're pretty, eh?"

Okay, now he's just pissing me off. Like he's not so sure if I'm pretty. Then I catch my full-length reflection in the mirror, and now I'm not so sure, either.

My clothes are in shambles, I've got makeup smeared across one eye like a raccoon's mask, and my hair is such a tangled disaster that not even rats would nest in it.

When I frown, he leans in, the voice of reassurance. "But when I'm done with you, you'll be irresistible enough to eat."

"Like Little Red Riding Hood."

He bats my nose playfully. "Exactly," he says and disappears into a back room.

I'm about to grab my bag and run for the hills when my phone rings. Loudly.

The name RILES flashes across the screen, accompanied by the ringtone, "Who Let the Dogs Out?" because she's been messing with my phone again.

"*Shh!*" I press the volume down until my thumbprint feels permanent. I answer and rush into—well, I'm not even sure what. A sewing room?

Three sewing machines sit quietly, along with half a dozen ironing boards, irons and steamers, and a mannequin that looks eerily like me, hair and all.

Except for the fact that she's already naked.

Lace litters the room like a fabric bomb exploded. To my right, a board catches my eye. There's a photo of me from the beach yesterday pinned to its center, surrounded by sketches of dresses, each one signed with an extravagant flourish.

"What the fuck?"

"What the fuck is right! Oh, my God, Kenni, your boyfriend has his own private jet?"

Her words snap me back to the call. "You're on his jet?"

"And headed right for you. Did you know they'll serve me any drink I want? And food. And they even have—"

"You need to call Agent Knox," I cut in. "Tell him where you're landing. Make sure he picks you up."

"Why?" she asks, confused and wanting answers. "What's going on?"

"There's no time to explain." My heart pounds as I glance around the room, paranoia creeping in. My fingers clutch the phone so tightly it hurts. "Make sure he meets your plane and takes you somewhere safe."

"But—" she starts to protest.

"But nothing," I interrupt, gripping the phone tighter. "Don't ask questions. Just trust me, okay?" Footsteps echo down the hall, coming way too fast. "I have to go," I whisper urgently. "I love you, Riley." I disconnect the call.

The door slams shut, and I whip around.

Ricardo stands there, studying me with a cold, hard expression. "*Tsk-tsk-tsk*. Sneaking off. Discovering my lair," he chides, leaning in, his voice a low, sing-song whisper. "It rubs the lotion on the skin, or else it gets the hose again."

Horrified, I flinch. "What?"

"Oh, my gosh. I've always wanted to say that." Ricardo chuckles dismissively while I'm busy scouting the room for exits. "But seriously, darling, if you don't do exactly as you're told, I won't be able to finish in time. And we wouldn't want that, would we?"

I don't know. Is there a deadline? Like being a few minutes late will ruin the big reveal? News flash: Andre D'Angelo already knows what I look like. I mean, when a grizzly bear rips apart a lone hiker for breakfast, does he give two shits what they're wearing?

Ricardo's fingers are unexpectedly gentle as he brushes my hair behind one ear. "Make my year and tell me you're not attached to it."

I gulp. "Attached to it?" I squeak out, my throat suddenly dry.

"Attached to the length."

He toys with it some more, and I take a long, hard look at him. There's something unnervingly familiar about him. How do I know him?

I rub my temple. Is he a mass murderer? Top 10 on the FBI's most wanted list? My stomach churns. "I think I'm going to be sick."

He takes a deep, meditative breath, his hand gripping mine. "No, no. You can't be sick. You must be brave. Brave and daring, darling," he says, tossing back the last of his drink.

He sets down the glass and pulls out a straight razor, the blade glinting menacingly in the light. "Brave and daring?" I ask, my eyes wide, voice trembling.

"I'm going to make Enzo D'Angelo wish he'd never given me free rein over you," he smirks. "Don't worry. The first cut's always the worst."

My gasp is so loud he stops. He gives me a sympathetic look, patting my hair once more.

"Sometimes, if you close your eyes, it's easier, darling," he murmurs, his voice smooth as spun silk and eerily convincing.

After a brief hesitation and with no exits in sight, I shut my eyes, while my heart is pounding wildly in my chest.

"Trust me, you won't feel a thing."

That's just it. I'm feeling everything.

Fear.

Heartbreak.

Regret.

But then I think of *Da* and square my shoulders, standing tall and brave.

If I'm going down, I'm going down like a Mullvain.

Chapter Twenty-Five

KENNEDY

"You can remove the blindfold now."

I do, blinking against the sudden brightness. After an hour in darkness, it takes a moment for my eyes to adjust.

I guess I should be grateful. The last time I was blindfolded and snatched against my will, my mode of transportation was the cramped space of a trunk.

At least this time, I'm upright, in an actual seat.

"The precautions are for your protection, Ms. Mullvain," the driver says, his tone flat and devoid of emotion.

"Oh, is that why I don't have my phone? For my protection?" Only a total prick would keep my phone. Shit, what if Enzo unlocked it? Saw all the calls to Knox?

He shrugs helplessly as we pull up to a tall gate.

The driver rolls down the window and addresses the guards. "Mr. D'Angelo is expecting her."

A hornet's nest erupts in my chest. He's expecting me. Panic surges through me, and my fingers twitch toward the door handle. As soon as I try it, the driver turns around, his eyes cold. "Mr. D'Angelo wanted me to let you know the doors are locked."

"Let me guess. That's for my protection, too," I mutter. My eyes land on a stone plaque lodged in the guardhouse that reads, "D'Angelo Estate." I slump back in my seat, seeing my fate carved in stone.

The driver nods, and the tall gates swing open with a heavy, metallic clang.

I cast another glance at the driver, a stranger whose face I haven't seen before. Come to think of it, most of the people I've encountered, I've only seen once and then never again.

Why is that?

Are they part of some exclusive subscription service, where heavily armed guards and drivers are delivered monthly like craft beer and book boxes? Or do they simply vanish because they piss off their boss?

Who knows what measures he takes for their "protection."

The car rolls to a stop at a roundabout, and my heart rate spikes. Someone opens my door with practiced precision, revealing a man who looks more like a valet than a thug. His polite demeanor does little to ease my nerves, especially considering he also has a gun.

He takes my hand and helps me out of the car. "Mr. D'Angelo is waiting for you, Ms. Mullvain," he announces as I'm guided out.

How do they know my name? A knot twists tight in my gut as I watch the car glide away, along with the last escape plan I dreamed up during the hour-long ride.

The place is swarming with guards, each one more

imposing than the last, armed to the teeth and built like tanks. It might as well be a thug convention.

My chances of outrunning or evading them are about as good as winning the lottery, and pretty much guarantee I'll be shot. Multiple times.

Two men stand at the top of wide stone steps, looking like they stepped out of a *Men in Black* catalog. They're thugs, too, but clearly outrank the others with their tailored suits and gold Ray-Bans. As soon as I take two steps up, they open a grand set of double doors.

"He's waiting for you on the lawn. Straight down the hall," one of them says.

My feet freeze, doubt anchoring me in place. But then, *Da*'s voice cuts through my fear, clear as a bell and so loud, I swear he's right here with me. "*What are you waiting for? Do it.*"

And I do.

The grand double doors lead to a lavish foyer, the polished marble floors reflecting the glow of enormous crystal chandeliers above, all in a row.

Mirrored walls on either side catch my reflection, and I steal a glance at myself, surprised. Ricardo managed to transform me from a haggard mouse to a sultry temptress.

My already full lips are amplified by pouty lipstick. And the black dress I declined twice hugs every curve like a glove, yet comes off as flattering and sophisticated, a far departure from the stripperesque look I imagined from the sketch.

Ricardo was right—the first cut was the hardest. But once the initial shock passed, the straight razor left my hair with just enough length to be full and enough edge to be whimsical and fun.

Thank God he's actually a world-famous fashion designer and not a maniacal ax murderer. When a box was delivered to Mr. Ricardo Ricci, I finally caught on. Though by his obsession with blade maintenance, he might be both.

"This way, Ms. Mullvain," a man's voice echoes from down the hall, as he opens another door.

The instant I step through, I'm hit with the thick scent of roses and the mouth-watering aroma of food. My stomach rumbles in response, a stark reminder that I can't remember the last time I ate.

Soft music drifts through the air, mingling with laughter and murmured conversations—a symphony of opulence and wealth and rich people living it up.

If this is one of those virgin auctions I've read about in my latest shifter romance, these fuckers are in for a rude awakening.

I spot Enzo huddled with a group of men who all bear a striking resemblance to him. Same dark hair, same dominant stance. They seem deep in conversation, and I'm relieved when Enzo doesn't immediately notice me.

Before I can gather my thoughts, a man approaches me with a tray of champagne. He offers me one.

"No thanks."

"Take the glass, Kennedy." It takes me a moment to recognize him—Agent Knox, dressed like the waitstaff and sporting a gun.

"What are you doing here?" I ask, keeping my voice low.

"What am *I* doing here? I'm undercover. We received intel about a big event—a meeting between two rival factions. Something that could shake up the entire Chicago syndicate."

"What?"

"I have no clue. I just got here, grabbed a tray, and spotted you. Barely recognized you." His eyes flick across my body, lingering for a moment before shifting to the glass. I take it to avoid suspicion. "What are *you* doing here, Kennedy? Riley has been freaked out of her fucking mind."

"Where is she?"

"Somewhere safe."

"Where?" I press with enough urgency that it's all I can do not to grab him by the collar.

He rolls his eyes. "My place, okay?"

"Your place?" Protective alarms blare, and I narrow my eyes. His eyes dart away from mine, unable to hold my gaze. A flicker of unease crosses his face, like he's guilty as sin and doesn't want to admit it. "It's fine," he says, but the lack of conviction in his voice betrays him. "I think of her as a kid sister."

Sure, he does.

His gaze sweeps over me, lingering on every detail of my dress and hair. "Are you trying to get more of D'Angelo's attention?"

"No," I say quickly, though I shamefully wonder if I would.

A guard breezes by us, and my pulse kicks up. Nervously, I glance around, suddenly aware that I'm in the middle of enemy territory, talking to a fed. "Aren't you worried about what happens if they find you here?"

He smirks, his gaze darting among the guards. "The good thing about places like this? The help is invisible."

His response does little to reassure me, and I feel a surge of anxiety. "Can you get me out of here?"

"I can't," he bites out through clenched teeth.

"Why not?"

"Because Enzo D'Angelo is staring at you like you're a shiny new Bugatti." I down my champagne and glance back at Enzo and the men I assume are his brothers, feeling a knot form in my stomach.

Knox leans in. "I don't know what's going on with you and Enzo D'Angelo," he hesitates, "but does this have anything to do with your father?"

Stunned, my eyes snap to his. My father's death changed the trajectory of mine and Riley's entire world, and not just because he died. He was killed. Murdered in cold blood, his body turning up like a slab of beef at the medical examiner's office. "Why would it have anything to do with my father?"

"Shit. I—" he cuts himself off. "Just be careful. Enzo is a wild animal in a three-piece suit, and he's giving me a death glare. I have to go."

Panic grips my chest. "You can't go."

"Kennedy, listen to me. I'll be keeping an eye on you. If you need help, two fingers. If you're fine, one. Got it?"

"Yes," I squeak out.

With a subtle motion toward the tray, I realize he's offering me his card. "Take it, Kennedy," he urges, his expression grave and nonnegotiable.

Reluctantly, and without telling him I don't have a phone, I slip it under a napkin and take it as I return the empty glass. Knox heads off in the opposite direction, and I feel the weight of Enzo's gaze on me.

Heat flares along my skin. Buzzed on champagne, I head his way, and straight to the mouth of hell.

Chapter Twenty-Six

ENZO

Two Hours was all the text said. The last text from my uncle. The twelfth I received and ignored.

Today is not about him. It's about my brother, Smoke. It's the happiest day of his life. His wedding day. With more pomp and circumstance than an inaugural ball and more firepower than the Mossad.

"Just wait. There's a woman for each of you out there who will bring you to your knees." Smoke chuckles. Or threatens.

"As long as she's in six-inch heels," Dante says, toasting the air.

"And brings a friend," Dillon adds. "The more, the merrier."

Mateo crosses his arms. "The only way you got a woman to marry you was to kidnap her."

Smoke shakes his head. "Rescue. The term is *rescue*. Get it right."

I catch a glance across the vast lawn and see her arrival. Her new haircut is ravishing, and her body . . .

I indulge in lingering on her body. But before I get too far ahead of myself and fuck her right in front of all of Smoke's wedding guests, I make a decision. "I'm getting married," I announce as I take a long sip of my brut.

Horrified, every one of their faces falls.

Mateo's elbow nudges mine. "Let me guess. The Feds have caught up. You found some smoking hot baroness who's willing to make you her 90-day fiancé. Granted, she's still figuring out how to deal with all your fetishes."

I clink my glass to his. "I assure you, Mateo, this girl has no money or status at all. And I'll give her my fetishes the way I give her my dick: slowly. One painful pleasure at a time."

They all gag.

Dumbfounded, Dillon blinks. "You're serious."

"I am."

"But-b . . ." Dante stammers for a beat. "You haven't been seeing anyone." His face is murderous, repeating the exact words I told him to say.

I smirk. "So?" Before any of them says a word, I point my glass across the grounds.

Kennedy. My *Bella*. She downed a glass of champagne already. I can think of a million better ways to calm her nerves. All pornographic.

In a dazzling black dress, she makes her way toward us. I hand her the bride's untouched glass of champagne. "Hello, Kennedy."

Her pout is crimped. "Hello."

Those full lips are too fuckable for her own good. I ignore them for the moment and make brief introductions. "Kennedy, these are my brothers. Everyone, this is Kennedy."

Politely, they exchange nods.

Kennedy wilts beneath their stares and downs her drink. I offer mine. The poor girl is going to need it.

Smoke quirks a brow. "I know you from somewhere."

Her sheepish words come out. "I served you the court filings from Mr. Andre D'Angelo."

Smoke's death glare returns. "What?"

A flash of fear crosses her face. I don't like it. Protectively, I pull her body to mine and intervene. "Smoke *you* more than anyone knows that *what we do* and *who we are* are two very different things."

His expression softens with an agreeable nod.

The tension in her shoulders relax, but I don't let her go. Foolish little Kennedy. She should've never crossed my path.

See, I collect beautiful things. And unlucky for her, Kennedy is the most beautiful thing I've ever seen.

She was meant to be owned.

I was meant to undo her.

To have her. Possess her.

Own her.

Smoke raises his glass. "Then, a toast, to the bride-to-be."

Kennedy's wide eyes dart to mine, furious and sexy as fuck. "The what?"

"Didn't I tell you?" I ask. "We're getting married."

Before she can protest or freak out or run, my lips crush hers. Her fight is meager at best. Probably because she's about to kick me in the balls. Or is preoccupied with plotting my death.

Whatever's going on in that fiery head of hers, one thing is clear—Kennedy is giving me the best kiss of my life.

Chapter Twenty-Seven
KENNEDY

We're getting married.

Three little words never sounded so bizarre. They replay in my mind on an endless loop, and my what-the-fuck meter rockets off the charts.

Married?

In what twisted universe are we getting married?

Enzo is many things. Lethal. Ruthless. A notorious kingpin with a staggering body count—both in the psychotic killer way and the sexual way.

But marriage material?

No way. Not a fucking chance.

My heart pounds erratically as this chaotic whirlwind hits me in waves. One minute, he's handing me to his uncle. The next, he's marrying me?

This man is one big clusterfuck of mixed signals, that's for sure.

But then there's the way he's kissing me, and it isn't even a question. He wants to marry me. All signs point to yes. Especially his whopper of a cock. And the deeper his kiss goes, searching, needing, taking, the easier it is to convince myself he's serious.

Because, dear God, the man can kiss. Hands down, it's the best kiss of my life.

But the second Enzo pulls me against him like he's about to drill me into the nearest tree, I snap back to reality with a rock-solid thud. Heat flares, and in a rush, I break away.

With so many eyes on me, I might as well be a billboard.

"I'm not marrying you," I blurt out, loud and defiant.

A hush falls across the lawn of, oh, I don't know, two hundred people. As I take it all in, every puzzle piece falls into place.

Black tuxes.

Champagne overflowing.

A ten-tier cake that's bigger than my apartment.

My eyes bulge. "Are we at a wedding?" I manage to eke out, desperately trying to tamp down my dizzying hyperventilation.

The man who was ready to strangle me two seconds ago raises his hand. "You're at my wedding." He motions across the way, and I see a beautiful woman in a white gown that ombres to pink. "That's my bride."

All the air releases from my lungs in a whoosh.

His brother, Dante, strides over, grinning as he kisses me on both cheeks. "It's good to see you again, Kennedy. In case you're having second thoughts, let me reinforce that you'd be marrying the dark lord of the underworld, Satan himself." He smirks.

"My *Bella* knows me better than anyone."

Do I?

Knox is not-so-subtly trying to get my attention from the entryway, motioning with his hand as he mouths, "One or two."

Subtly, I use one finger to sweep the bangs from my face. I'm fine already. Plus, he's outnumbered by a billion to one, and I don't want him getting shot.

Knox looks confused, flashing two fingers in a V for verification.

I hold up a finger again. "One," I say out loud, quickly backtracking with, "minute. I just need one long minute with my, eh, fiancé," I say helplessly.

Smoke nods. "Why don't we leave the two lovebirds alone." He kisses me on the cheek. "Good luck."

They all depart, leaving Enzo and me alone. Enzo steps forward, a hand slipping into his pocket. I only half listen, keeping my eye glued to his pocket, waiting for a gun. My hand stays fisted, ready to flash two.

He clears his throat. "I was on the phone with our family jeweler when you barged in on me during our flight, all drunk and disorderly."

Normally, I'm way too practical to be bucketed as the hopeless romantic type, but when he pulls out a velvet box and presents a ring, I gasp.

Did I say ring?

It's more like a star, catching the light in the most mesmerizing ways. A single diamond is in the center, set in a vintage band surrounded by equally stunning stones.

Big? Absolutely. But with an old-world elegance and grace that makes it timelessly beautiful.

"It's breathtaking," I whisper, unable to tear my eyes away.

"It reminds me of you. Simple yet elegant. Dazzling even when you try to hide from the light."

"Did you just call me simple?" I snark.

He slips it onto my finger—a perfect fit. "The original ring was my mother's. I had the stones around it added for you," he says softly, his voice taking on a rare, tender note. I'm left speechless, studying him. "Smoke's bride had a family heirloom, so I knew he wouldn't mind that this becomes yours."

My heart stumbles in my chest, the weight of the ring so tangible and real. It's insane, but I can't deny the rush of emotions it stirs in me.

I glance up at Enzo, his eyes a deepening gold. So much so that I'm not sure if I should run or just linger in his darkness and lose myself completely.

For a split second, I see a different side of him. Maybe even a life with him. But then I remember who he is—a D'Angelo—and an unsettling feeling claws its way up from the pit of my gut.

I nibble my lower lip, uncertain. "Can I think about it?"

"No."

I throw my hands up in the air. "For all I know, you've just taken out a hefty life insurance policy on me, and everyone knows it's the overinsured who have the shortest life expectancies." I bow up to him. "Just to be clear, I want to live."

"It wasn't a question, Kennedy. You will marry me."

Suddenly, Knox's words come crashing through my brain, flooding my thoughts and squeezing everything else out. *Does this have anything to do with your father?*

A tightness grips my chest, each breath a struggle. Do the D'Angelos know what happened to my father?

With a deep breath, I step back. "I can't."

Enzo moves into my space, crowding me against the tree. His expression is dark, intense. He lifts my chin, forcing my eyes to meet his. "Unfortunately for you, *Bella*, you don't have a choice."

Chapter Twenty-Eight
ENZO

"What do you mean I don't have a choice?"

Her words come out flustered and upset. And, God, *Bella* is absolutely delectable when she's outraged. The temptation to keep her is one I could never deny myself.

"It's the only way to get you away from my uncle alive." The fact that it basically fucks my uncle in the ass is just a perk.

Panicked, she gasps. "What do you mean?"

I press my body against hers, inhaling the intoxicating mix of citrus shampoo and fear, whispering against her lips. "My uncle expects me to hand-deliver you to him, like I'm fucking DoorDash. He has no intention of letting me keep you, and I have no intention of letting you go. Being a D'Angelo will shield you from him."

"There has to be another way."

"There isn't." I shrug, repeating her own words back to her. "You're the one who, and I quote, wants to live. So, you have two options: me or him. Take your pick."

She takes an extra long time to process my words. Frankly, it pisses me off that she hasn't already chosen me over my douchebag uncle, but I'll punish her for that later.

Slowly, like prying her exhausted fingers from the edge of a cliff, she gives in. "When?"

"Tonight."

Her eyes widen in fear, then flit to that dipshit Knox, and I realize she needs convincing. "Signal him all you want, Kennedy. Agent Knox is an anchovy floating mindlessly in a sea of sharks. Whatever fingers you signal him with, I assure you, I'll take bolt cutters to before shoving them down his throat."

Terror flashes across her face, assuring me that what I'm doing is more than just a little fucked up, but I'm a psychopath. What does she expect?

She shakes her head, tears welling in her eyes as she trembles. "I don't want this."

I kiss her neck, and her body shivers. "What you want is irrelevant. What you need is two slow hours of me ruining you for life." I move my lips to her ear. "You think I don't know about your texts and calls to your friendly neighborhood Fed? Or that he has your sister holed up at his apartment?"

"Are you jealous?" she sneers. Always a fight with this one.

I smirk, tracing a finger down her cheek. "Does he look dead?"

Her heart pounds wildly against my chest, like a little bird suddenly desperate to escape her cage. "Enzo, please—"

"Please, what? Please take you to the church, or please drop you off at the nearest human trafficking ring?"

Her tears flow freely now, and I can see she's finally coming around. She takes a shaky breath. "Will you at least honor my father's wishes for my wedding day?"

"What wishes?"

"They were in his will," she says. "He didn't have money to leave me and Riley. He left us his wishes instead."

My mind races, speculating on what a man would want for his daughter's wedding.

Yeah, I got nothing.

But considering I have more money and power than half the countries in the world, it shouldn't be an issue. "Agreed." I kiss her. "Be my wife, *Bella*, and I vow to give you anything you want. Or die trying."

My darling Kennedy,

There will come a day when the man of your dreams will want to whisk you away, and if you're reading this, it means I'm not there to pound sense into the two of you myself. But from up above, I'll be looking down on you, and I swear if I could, I'd move heaven and earth to be there for you, lass.

Remember, darling, you're a Mullvain, and we Scots abide by our family traditions. Pre-cana. Devotion. Attire.

I know you'll make me proud.

My love, forever and always,

Da

With my brothers all gathered in the library, we get to work. Even though I told Smoke he didn't have to stick around, considering he has a honeymoon to jet off to, he's here.

Despite our differences, stepping over his wedding was never on my to-do list. Yet, here we are, and since Mr. "I'll believe it when I see it" insisted on witnessing the world's most notorious bachelor tie the knot, well, here he stands. With all of us.

The stark truth that we'll never know when it'll be safe for us all to be in the same room again cuts through my heart like a serrated knife. Though I'll never admit it to these buttheads.

"Where's the blushing bride?" Dillon quips, plucking a book from the shelf and flipping it open. "I'm surprised she hasn't run for the hills yet."

"And I'm surprised you can read," I retort back, eyeing the book in his hands, "though it doesn't shock me you grabbed historical romance. Dark romance, bro. Trust me on this."

"She's being fitted for her dress," Sin interjects as he strides in.

Ricardo has already delivered all three gowns, along with a battalion of seamstresses. He's spent the last thirty hours sketching for my approval, and they've been sewing like the wind.

Here's the thing: I know everything about Kennedy—her cup size, style preferences, even her favorite fabrics. Could I have picked out a dress she'd love with my eyes closed? Sure.

But today is her wedding day. Not that she knew it when she rolled out of bed this morning. The least I can do is give her one choice in the matter.

Having Sin by her side is a dowry of sorts. And not just for today. Knowing Sin, he'll embrace her as one of us no matter how much of a dickhead I am. And Kennedy needs that.

Having someone paternal and reassuring will ease what's to come. No one pulls off being a father figure better than Bryce Jacob Sinclair, Esquire. Sin. My father's best man and best friend for years. And a confidant to me.

No one is better suited to give my bride away. Thank fuck he agreed.

"She said yes?" I ask.

Sin nods. "She did."

"To everything?" I ask, the weight of the question pressing on me. This small point had become an insurmountable wall I couldn't scale alone. Meeting her dead father's wishes is important to her, which makes it important to me.

But only Kennedy could determine if all his conditions were met, putting the ball squarely in her court.

Sin nods again. "Father Marc is on his way, with reinforcements. I've also assured her that once you are legally wed, she becomes a D'Angelo, with all the resources and protections that title affords."

Dante pats me on the back. "What's the rush? Are you pregnant?"

"I have my reasons. Primarily, Uncle Andre." Just saying his name makes the vein in my forehead throb.

Mateo straightens his tie in the mirror. "So, instead of you two treating her like a wishbone, you're bringing all of us in to go full-blown tug-of-war, *Squid Games*-style?"

"Yes." That, and they'd never agree to go to war over a woman unless I was serious. And nothing screams serious like *till death do us part.*

Father Marc sweeps into the room like his robe is on fire, followed by another man lugging bolts of green and red fabric. "Okay, Enzo, I believe we have everything you need." He glances around, eyes wide with urgency. "Where's the bride?"

"Getting dressed."

"So, when do we see her?"

"When she walks down the aisle." Normally, Father Marc is the epitome of calm in Catholic tradition, but right now, I'm not so sure.

He blinks. "I need to see her now. Her and you."

"Why?"

He pulls up the will on his phone and points to the screen. "Pre-Cana. Devotion. Attire."

"And?"

"What's Pre-Cana?" Smoke asks, quirking a brow.

Dillon shrugs. "Sounds kinky."

Father Marc pinches the bridge of his nose, likely wondering if any of us can truly be saved. Then he collects himself. "Pre-Cana is pre-marital counseling. I meet with the couple weekly for about twelve weeks, discussing the gravity of choosing a lifelong partner and the principles of honesty and loyalty. It gives them time to let these concepts truly sink in. Twelve weeks is standard, though I've cut it back to six."

Honesty.

Loyalty.

And a migraine that's about to split my skull.

"Can't I just give a girl a big diamond ring and say I do?" I stare at him like he just jerked off in front of us. Six to twelve weeks, my ass.

He catches my look and nervously tugs at his collar. "How much time do we have?"

"About an hour."

"An hour?" He gulps, glancing upward as if doing mental calculations. "Fine. Okay. An hour."

The funny little man he entered with unrolls bolts of fabric at my feet. "What's this?"

"Well, I cover Pre-Cana and devotion," Father Marc explains, pointing to himself, then to the man. "And Hamish here"—Hamish waves—"has you covered for attire."

I point to my tux. "I'm wearing my attire. We all are. We blew through one wedding and are on to the next."

Hamish steps forward, hand to his chest, standing all stout and proud. "I'm yer kiltmaker, sir."

My face drops. "My what?"

A roar of laughter erupts from my brothers, especially when Hamish starts draping fabric across my loins.

I'm about to totally lose my shit when Father Marc shoves his phone in my face, and the handwritten document from Ewan Mullvain stares me down.

The man's dying wishes for his daughter. My wife-to-be. "Fuck. Fine. Whatever." I stare them all down. "And you'll all be wearing them too, dickheads."

That shut them up.

The man raises a hand nervously. "It was a bear findin' all this Mullvain tartan. Sorry, did you say I need to make kilts fer everyone? I've only got two hands." He holds up his hands as if to drive the point home. "I'm a stitch-tician, not a magician."

Dillon slaps his hand. "My man. Busting out the *Star Trek*."

My head falls into my hands. I'm pretty sure Hamish here has waited his whole life to drop that line.

Sin adjusts his glasses and speed-dials Ricardo. "We need seamstresses over here right away. Can you spare any?"

"What for?" Ricardo asks, sounding distracted.

"All the men are getting fitted for kilts." Sin barely gets the words out when loud squeals blast through the phone.

Mateo arches a brow, crossing his arms. "What was that?"

Ricardo laughs. "Those are my seamstresses stampeding out of the room and heading your way. The thought of stripping down the D'Angelos is like shouting *shirtless firefighters* to them. Will you be going regimental?"

Regi-what? By this point, I've had enough. "What about Kennedy's dress?" I snap, because she's definitely more important than my idiot brothers prancing around with the fabric. Is the style to her liking? What about the veil? All I manage to bark out is, "Take care of it."

"Don't worry. I'll be taking extra good care of your bride." He's just saying that to rile me up, and it's working.

I know Kennedy is right there, standing next to him, listening to every word, and she hasn't said a damn thing. The silent treatment? It's driving me out of my goddamn mind, and I hate that it does.

It also bothers me that Ricardo has probably seen her naked, and if I gouge out his eyes, who will make her exquisite couture clothes?

"Just take care of her," I bark.

"Definitely," he purrs. Fucker.

We disconnect just as Hamish circles me like a hawk, sizing me up. "So, we'll keep yer top. And I've got enough fabric for the kilts and fly plaids, but what about yer dress sporran? Or kilt hose? Or yer Ghillie Brogues?"

Fuck, my Ghillie what?

I place a firm hand on his shoulder. "You've got a dozen seamstresses, an unlimited budget, and an extra hundred-thou if everything you just said magically falls into place in under an hour. Can you be a magician now?"

He salutes sharply. "Aye-aye, captain." If this guy's full of Scotty quotes, I'm gonna need booze.

Mateo holds a strip of fabric across his waist, grinning. "What did Ricardo mean by going regimental?"

Hamish snorts. "I believe you know it as going commando."

Sin's face turns crimson. "You mean without a shred of underwear?"

Dillon perks up. "No boxers or briefs?"

"Buck-fucking-naked?" Dante asks in total disbelief.

"Naught more than what the good Lord gave ye," Hamish replies with a wink as a flood of women rush in, giggling and fawning. Not that Dante, Dillon, or Mateo mind at all—this is probably just a typical Saturday night for them.

But Smoke's head is practically steaming. He just tied the knot, and the last thing he wants is his wife's, or her family's, wrath all over his ass.

As for me, none of these women interest me. At all. My dick has been spoiled on an exclusive diet of *Bella's* mouth and pussy. Anything less, and he'd rather starve.

Hamish quiets the room. "Ladies, please. We're professionals. No ogling the steers. Each of you has very little time to cover these fine gentlemen's gibly-bits. The men will strip down, but only to their boxers."

A resounding boo echoes through the room. I tap Hamish on the shoulder. "While you're working miracles, I've got one more request."

Chapter Twenty-Nine
KENNEDY

"Why the frown, *bellissima*?" Ricardo asks.

There isn't a square inch of me that hasn't been fussed over, primped, and polished to perfection, and all I want to do is rip it all off, grab a tub of Ben and Jerry's, and lock myself in my crappy little apartment for three days, pretending none of this is happening.

But it is happening.

This is my wedding day. I know because there's a line of lace trailing from my hair to the floor, a ring the size of Mt. Everest weighing down my finger, and creamy vanilla silk wrapping me like a glove.

Or a shroud.

Honestly, I'm in too much shock to truly take in all of Ricardo's hard work. If he and his seamstresses hadn't worked me over like a pit crew, I'm pretty sure I'd be getting married in yoga pants.

What happened to something old, new, borrowed, and blue?

To soaking in the warmth of family and friends?

To the exhilarating sprint out of the church, while onlookers showered you in rose petals or biodegradable confetti or whatever the hell else we do to save the birds?

And what about love?

Am I the only lunatic left in a world gone cynical, believing that the cornerstone of marriage is love?

But the man has worked long and hard, and I will not shit all over his stunning creation. I force a smile, the kind that doesn't reach my eyes. "It's perfect," I say, my heart clenching as I miss *Da* more than ever.

He scrutinizes me, shaking his head—a gesture I've come to both dread and expect. It usually leads to more fussing. And hair shears are never off the table. "It's missing something," he mutters, lost in his creative thought.

Gee, could it be a bride who actually wants to get married?

"Ah, I've got it!" He claps his hands with dramatic flair.

And . . . nothing.

I'm pretty sure if he were summoning his band of seamstresses, they'd be too busy drooling over my husband-to-be and his insanely hot brothers. Someone's definitely getting a bachelor party, and yes, it bugs the crap out of me.

Then Ricardo does it again. Flamboyant clap, words repeated. "Ah, I know!" he hollers louder.

The doors burst open, and in fly Sofie and Lili, a rush of pillowy soft skirts and cascading curls. My smile widens as they dart toward me, my two lively pixies.

They swarm me with giggles and exuberant hugs, and I fight back the surge of tears.

"Are you really marrying the prince?" Little Lili asks, her smile so radiant it threatens to split her cheeks.

Their words hit me like a lead weight. Am I really marrying Enzo?

"Yes," I say, my voice betraying a sliver of hope. I don't correct her, though I should. I'm pretty sure fairy tales don't involve the sweet prince proposing with the ever romantic, *"Marry me, or else."*

"Here," Sofie says, her grin stretching wider than I've ever seen. She hands me a little gold box, and I open it carefully, puzzled when I see what's inside.

I recognize this tartan instantly. It's *Da*'s. The Mullvain one, rich red with its green and gold stripes. The very one I thought I'd never see again after Jimmy tossed out all of *Da*'s precious Scottish heirlooms.

Tears blur my vision, streaming down as I pull it out. "A tie?" I blubber, a little confused.

"Something new," Lili cheers, her voice bright and innocent.

"They wanted you to do the honors," Ricardo says with a grin. Then he lets out the loudest whistle, and on cue, Truffles bursts into the room.

My little dog, Truffles, is decked out in the most adorable black vest, standing perfectly still as I clip the bow tie on him. But the second it's secured, he's off, dashing around in wild circles, barking like a maniac. The girls erupt into squeals of delight, their laughter filling the room.

It's mayhem. And I love it.

Dory enters with another woman, a blonde, stunning in a deep midnight-blue dress that makes her crystal blue eyes shine.

She looks familiar, a memory tugging at the edges of my mind. Her hug is so tight, it drags me out of my wallow and slams me straight into the present.

"So, you're the woman who tamed my beast of a brother?" she says, her voice warm and kind.

Her brother?

This must be Trinity. I've only glimpsed her briefly on a video call, and Enzo rarely speaks of her. But the few times he does, there's a shadow in his eyes, a sorrow so profound it seems to consume him. It makes me wonder if his drive to rescue women somehow ties back to her.

"This is for you," she says, a wide smile lighting up her face as she hands me a small, neatly wrapped gift.

I tug at the bow and unravel the tissue paper. What the—

"Is this... *um*, Superman?"

It's a small scrap of cloth, frayed at the edges, as if it's been cut from an old bed sheet. In the middle, Superman stands poised, larger than life. I'm at a loss for words, so I manage a simple, "Thank you."

"This was a piece of Enzo's childhood blanket," Trinity explains, brimming with nostalgia. "I kept it because no matter how big and blustery my brother gets, I know that deep down, he's still that little boy, prancing around in his underwear, dreaming of saving the day."

Her eyes glisten, and for a moment, the depth of their connection is apparent, a memory that binds them tightly. One she's now sharing with me.

My heart clenches, a tender ache spreading through my chest because she's right. Beneath Enzo's gruff exterior and his relentless control freak ways, he's always trying to save the day, isn't he?

"Something blue," she says softly. Then, she lifts my hand between us, her fingers tracing the delicate lines of the ring. "Something old," she continues, sentimental as she admires the way it shines. "Enzo poured his heart into reimagining this ring. It looks perfect on you."

I lean in, my voice barely a whisper. "Shouldn't it be yours?"

She shakes her head with a gentle certainty. "No," she murmurs sweetly. "It was always meant for you."

By the time Dory steps over, Trinity and I are both teary-eyed, enough for her to pause. I hug her heartily. "Thank you for taking care of the girls."

"Oh, they're so easy. Angels, really." Her eyes sweep the room as she nods. "So that takes care of it. Something old, something new, something blue. And Enzo said he's taking care of something borrowed."

Is he? What's he up to?

I guess I'll know soon enough as little hands drag me out of the room and into a waiting limo. Laughter bubbles up as the girls press every button in the car and belt out Taylor Swift songs at full blast.

Even the driver, the biggest, burliest one yet, with piercings through his neck and knuckles, bops his head to the tune, grinning from ear to ear.

With the sunroof open, my eyes fly up as the car rolls to a stop before the church. The sky is clear, not a single cloud, just a blanket of stars. "I wish you were here, *Da*," I whisper, blinking through the tears.

Suddenly, Sofia cries out, "A shooting star! Make a wish! Make a wish!"

Absolutely everyone shuts their eyes, even Spike, our driver. I squeeze my eyes shut, my heart full of longing, and make my wish.

And when I get out, it comes true.

Riley is here. How? I have no idea, and I don't care. The thought of getting married without her was suffocating me, but now that she's here, I can finally breathe again.

Her emerald gown is stunning, her hair elegantly swept up, and she's holding a big bouquet of cream peonies. "Seriously?" she asks, one hand on her hip, blocking the door like a linebacker. "Getting hitched without me?"

I grab her so hard and tight she gasps. "You're smashing your bouquet," she laughs, but she hugs me back just as fiercely.

"I don't care," I say, my voice thick with emotion. "I'm so glad you're here. How did you even get here?"

"I have no idea. All I know is a guy said you needed me."

"What guy?"

Totally ignoring me, she continues. "They took my phone, blindfolded me, handed me a dress, and now I'm here. Are you marrying royalty or something?" she rattles off, as if being abducted and dressed by strangers is totally okay. Which, for the record, it's not.

I'll be giving Enzo hell for it. And definitely chastising her later, but for now, I'm too elated to say anything other than, "Or something."

Arm in arm, we enter the church, and it's the most beautiful thing I've ever seen. The moment I step inside, I'm overwhelmed by the glow of candlelight. St. Michael's is transformed, overflowing with white roses and peonies.

It's decked out like Jesus Christ himself is visiting, and suddenly, I'm nervous.

A flurry of butterflies kicks up in my chest as Father Marc and all the men take their places at the front—like a wall of Calvin Klein models... in kilts.

"Which brother is mine?" Riley whispers, her eyes scanning the guys.

"Absolutely none of them," I reply firmly. No player is getting his hooks, or anything else, into my sister. Not now, not ever.

"What's good fer the goose, darlin'..." My father's words haunt me from beyond, and I roll my eyes.

Sin steps beside me, addressing everyone else with a calm authority. "Like we rehearsed."

They rehearsed? When did they do that?

He extends his arm with a suave flourish. "Ready, my dear?"

Ha! Not even close. I'm still waiting for someone to wake me the hell up.

I take his arm, feeling the steady warmth of his support, as Riley shoves the bouquet into my hands. "You're going to go ape when you see what's in the church. They told me it was 'something borrowed,'" she whispers.

She pecks my cheek, and then she's gone, rushing off to join the others. They're all lined up ahead of me, ready to go, when I see him.

Enzo moves into position like a wolf through the pack, his gaze locked onto mine.

He's tall, dark, and sinfully built, with more raw magnetism than all the men in Chicago combined. And seeing him decked out in Scottish regalia makes my heart somersault like a Chinese gymnast.

I'm not exactly sure how the kilt manages to make him look a million times hotter, but damn, it definitely does.

Like a blowtorch firing off between my legs, the man is a danger to my sanity, my composure, and my panties. All at once.

Between that and my heart's amped-up jackhammering, it takes me a minute to register that the music I'm hearing is coming from bagpipes.

Is that the something borrowed? I mean, who actually owns bagpipes?

God, Riley was right. Little girl Kennedy is going ape, freaking out like it's a Fourth of July parade, ecstatic and beaming and I hate to admit it, touched.

Enzo is plucking every last one of my heartstrings, one after the other, until all I can feel is him. So why is that nagging little doubt still clawing at my gut?

By the time I meet him face to face, every last one of the peonies' stems has been properly strangled. Sin hands me off to my soon-to-be husband, and Father Marc carries out the ceremony devotional just as *Da* would've wanted.

When he gets to the, "Do you, Kennedy, take Enzo Ares D'Angelo, to be your lawfully wedded husband?" you can hear a pin drop.

But as much as this runaway train is all full steam ahead, I can't say it.

I try. I open my mouth, but all that comes out is a small, pathetic squeak.

Everything is perfect, and I still can't marry him.

But then, I don't have to.

The doors burst open, and Andre D'Angelo storms in, bringing everything to a complete cluster of a halt.

Chapter Thirty
KENNEDY

ANDRE D'ANGELO STROLLS IN ALONE. His face is icy, cold, and unreadable. Two armed guards rush him, frisk him, and then, as if hell itself has frozen over, they offer him a seat.

My eyes widen. He moves slowly and methodically, assessing my outfit, then Enzo's, understandably pausing at his kilt before he finally sits down in the very last pew.

"What's he doing here?" I whisper, hating how just one look from the man makes my pulse frantic and my lizard brain take over. Fight or flight. Survival mode.

My feet are ready to move, to grab the girls and Riley and run. Run as fast and as far as I can when Enzo's warm hand squeezes mine, grounding me.

It's as if he knows exactly what I'm thinking the moment I think it.

It's as if he really is a prince.

That is, until he isn't.

Calmly, quietly, his words hit me like a wrecking ball. "I invited him."

"You what?" The initial wave of panic subsides into a murky lull of disbelief. "Why?"

"I already told you. It's me or him, *Bella*. I'm not sitting around for months with my thumb up my ass while you think it through. We do this now or not at all." He motions to the door, his golden eyes dark. "Uncle Andre's chariot awaits."

He's forcing my hand the only way he knows how—decisive and cutthroat. There's nothing to argue. Either I'm doing this, or I'm just one more weight anchoring him down.

In his own special asshole way, the choice is mine.

"Enzo," Dante's low voice cut in, the voice of reason slicing through the tension. "This wasn't part of the plan."

"This was exactly the plan."

"One you didn't bother including us in," Smoke fires back, his anger bottled up in a whisper.

Trinity stands to my left, her expression, a clear *what-the-actual-fuck*, while Dory looks half a second from grabbing the girls and fleeing.

Free-spirited Riley, on the other hand, looks around with a patient smile, oblivious to the dumpster fire happening right in front of her face, and stifles a yawn.

With the calm authority of a man who's seen it all, Father Marc speaks up. "Please, everyone is welcome in the house of the Lord."

Yes, of course. Where demons can waltz in to witness Satan himself getting hitched.

Enzo locks eyes with Father Marc, and just like that, the ceremony resumes. "Do you, Kennedy, take Enzo Ares D'Angelo, to be your lawfully wedded husband?"

I knot my arms tightly, feeling my husband-to-be pushing

me to the boiling point. "I'm thinking." Yup. I'm thinking about what an asshole you are.

"I suggest you think faster," Enzo growls, his voice gravelly.

I tap my chin, irritation bubbling up. "*Hmm*. Death or Enzo, death or Enzo . . ."

Make no mistake. I know better than to poke the bear. It's a lesson I've learned many times over. And somewhere in my stubborn head, I know I'm putting Riley, the girls, and even Truffles at risk.

But goddamnit, I'm pissed. If the fuckface is backing me into a corner and strong-arming me into matrimony, then I'm taking my sweet time coming around.

He leans in, his breath hot against my ear. "Tick-tock, *Bella*."

I look up at Father Marc. "I'm sorry, can you repeat the question?"

By this point, I can feel the vibrations of Enzo's head about to explode. Father Marc's face quirks like a puppy seeking permission. To which Enzo cracks his knuckles. "Ask away."

And for the third time, Father Marc recites the words, each syllable dragging like molasses. "Do you, Kennedy, take Enzo Ares D'Angelo"—he tugs at his collar—"to be your lawfully wedded husband?"

I can't even look at Enzo. "Sure. Fine. Why not?"

A unanimous sigh of relief sweeps across the church.

Father Marc turns to Enzo. "Do you, Enzo, take Kennedy Luciano, to be your lawfully wedded wife?"

"I do."

I try to remind myself that Father Marc is only going by every legal document Jimmy Luciano ever changed. But when that name hits my ears, the rubber band holding my sanity together snaps.

"Mullvain." My eyes lock onto Father Marc's, my voice steady and firm. "My name is Kennedy Mullvain."

"Wrong," Enzo insists. He slips the wedding band onto my finger, locking it in place like a noose. "Your name is Kennedy Mullvain D'Angelo."

Without warning, his arms pull me in, forcing me against the solid planes of his chest. His lips crush mine.

Possessing me.

Owning me.

Devouring me and demanding more of me in that moment than in all the moments before.

It almost feels like he's proving a point, though what point that is becomes completely lost.

I'm dizzy and dazed in the slow, languid sweeps of his tongue and his soft, full lips. This is Enzo, a potent concoction of rage and white-hot desire that lifts me to my toes and brings me to my knees all at once.

His heart thunders against mine, and I can't tell if the rush sweeping me away is floating or falling.

I barely register the door slam.

Or the explosion of cheers and applause.

Or even the bagpipes roaring out a triumphant, time-honored melody.

All I can hear is Enzo's whisper against my lips.

"*Air a thagràdh*," he murmurs against my lips. I didn't know much Gaelic, but this I knew.

Claimed.

Chapter Thirty-One
KENNEDY

"Did you get married?" the children all holler as I walk into the dance studio, their voices boisterous and sweet. They huddle around me, all tutus and ballet slippers, each trying to outdo the other with a barrage of questions. It's clear that learning dance steps is the last thing on anyone's mind.

I scurry them to the center of the room, and we all form a circle, criss-cross, apple-sauce.

"What's it like being married?" one of the kids asks, her eyes wide with curiosity.

Weird.

Frustrating.

A master class in compromise.

"Like a roller coaster ride," I say honestly, the words barely scratching the surface of what being married to Enzo is like.

It isn't that I want to spread the news. Frankly, I'd be happy keeping it under lock and key, tucked away in a safe, and tossed into the middle of the ocean.

But the local media has other ideas. They swarmed like

vultures, forcing Enzo to amp up security for the dance school and secure private transportation for all the kids.

And let's not forget the full-time security detail shadowing our every move. Though it's been nice to see regulars like Spike, who despite his terrifyingly pierced exterior, is really quite sweet.

At first, the parents were a little alarmed, but now they know that Spike wouldn't hurt anyone. Unless, of course, someone touched a hair on any one of these kids' heads. Then, he'd really fuck someone up.

For the past few weeks, revamping the dance school has consumed me. Every corner, every barre, and every mirror reflects the all-expenses-paid renovation, a lavish gift, courtesy of Enzo's limitless resources.

"Where's Zo?" Addie asks, her wide eyes brimming with curiosity.

Question of the month.

For whatever reason, my tiny dancers have adopted him, turning him into their unlikely mascot.

But despite the grandeur of our wedding and his bold declaration—that I'm *claimed*—Enzo has been gone, and I feel his absence everywhere.

At first, I thought him being distant would be a relief, a chance to breathe. But it's not. It's isolating and lonely.

Each night, he sends a text. Nothing sweet or sentimental. Just the most random photos of buildings and sunsets.

Are they places he's at? Dozens of pics that all look like Italy. And the more I'm carried away under the subtle haze of his aftershave and the lingering scent of cigars hovering around our bed, I find myself missing him more than I'll ever admit to his smug face.

So, I grab Titan and give the camera a show. Each and every time. I know, I know. Pathetic attempts to show him exactly what he's missing, but fuck him, it feels better.

Then, just yesterday, a postcard arrived from Elafonisi Beach. *Wish you were here* was preprinted in big, bold letters across the front, with no return address on the back.

It's a small consolation to know he actually listens when I speak, but damnit, *I* wanted to go to Elafonisi Beach.

He's probably lounging in the sun, puffing on a cigar, his bare feet sinking into all the pink sand he can find. That's my pink sand. My idea. Knowing he's there, without me, is just cruel.

Suddenly, the door flies open, and Riley bursts into the classroom, red-eyed and urgent. "I need to talk to you."

I jump to my feet and quickly throw on my playlist. Riley should be back in Italy. If some bastard broke her heart, I'll sic the D'Angelos on him.

What's the point of marrying into the mob if you can't wield power against assholes?

I cue up a new viral song that's PG enough for the kids, and they instantly jump around like it's the dance party of the century. "I'll be back," I tell them, slipping out the door.

I barely make it into the hallway before Riley grabs my arm and drags me further down, her eyes darting around to make sure we're alone. "You married him," she cries, her voice a mix of shock and urgency.

For the record, I didn't exactly have a choice. But that's neither here nor there.

Rubbing her arms, I try to calm her down. "Yes. I married him. You were there." I take a step back, confused. "Shouldn't you be in Ita—"

"He killed *Da*." Her guttural words are an arrow to my heart, hitting me so hard I take a step back, my breath catching in my throat.

"Who did?" The question slips out, but I already know the answer. The truth is written in every line of her face, stark and undeniable.

"Enzo."

It feels like the ground has fallen away, ripped from under my feet, and I'm left grappling for something to hold on to.

"Yes." We both whip our heads down the hall. Enzo strides toward us, his presence instantly filling the space.

Tall and dark, with a lethal grace, his eyes are a storm of emotions, but his words come out the way they always come out. Even and in total control. "What's wrong?"

By this point, Riley is trembling hard. Her hand slips from mine, and no matter how much I call her, she runs.

Panic surges through me, and I'm about to chase after her when two strong hands lock around my shoulders. "Let her go. My men will catch up to her."

My mind races. And then what? Enzo always knows everything. Does he know this? That Riley believes he killed our father?

Did he kill *Da*?

"You and I need to talk, *Bella*."

I face him, searching his eyes.

Maybe it's because I want him to leave Riley alone. And the

kids. Or maybe it's because I can't believe Enzo could have done this. Or that I could have married him if he did.

But I don't fight.

I don't argue.

I don't scream.

Probably because I've gone numb, my mind reeling from the shock.

But when he kisses me and says, "I'll get your coat and have someone take your class. I'll take you anywhere you want to go, but we need to talk."

My reply is instant. "Let's go home."

Chapter Thirty-Two
ENZO

THE HIT IS swift and blinding, a brutal impact that slams straight into my chest. I'd be impressed if it didn't hurt so damn much.

The clamor of the crowd is deafening, but not enough to drown out the sickening crack of my rib. As long as the Goliath keeps circling me like a crazed jackrabbit and exhausting himself, I'm good.

Deep breath in, punctured wound out.

"You're weak, D'Angelo." His thick Albanian accent cuts through the chaos. It's almost refreshing—it means he's avoided my face entirely, and I'm not blacking out.

Weak? Maybe. Because nothing screams pussy-whipped more than marrying a girl, right?

By doing so, my brothers had no choice. Protect Kennedy and her sister at all costs. If necessary, with their lives. The creed of the D'Angelos.

La Familia Prima. Family First.

And yes, it was a dick move to force their hand by inviting

our uncle to the wedding, but time was of the essence, and the last thing I needed was a lengthy debate.

Especially with Dante. That fucker's half-lethal killer, half-incessant nag.

But the bigger dick move was forcing Kennedy into matrimonial bliss. My *Bella* doesn't understand the lengths I'll go to for her. But she soon will.

"Tell me what I want to know." My demand seems reasonable, even as I'm doubled over, gasping for air.

He laughs an evil fucking laugh. "What do you want to know, pretty boy?" Never mind that he's still chasing me like the giant from Jack and the Beanstalk. I'm not sure I'm comfortable with the way he called me *pretty boy*.

But I need answers, so I do what I always do. I strike a deal. "The photos. He has photos of girls. Not digital. Real. Give me the name of Andre's supplier, and I'll let you live."

Head cocked, he looks at me, confused. "Is this a joke?"

"Tell me what I need to know, and I promise to end this quickly."

That makes him laugh so hard, now he's doubled over.

Originally, I thought my uncle was just a low-life cockroach, peddling flesh because he wasn't smart enough for a more sophisticated racket.

But, and I hate to admit this, I was wrong.

After chopping Uncle Andre at the knees in Italy, photos began showing up, delivered to me wherever I was. Sometimes by professional couriers, sometimes by whoever will do it for a buck. Always of *Bella*.

Kennedy, younger and younger, posed in different outfits.

Dresses chosen by sick shits and predators to make her look like a doll.

Every single photo makes me want to lurch up whatever I'd eaten that day or kill someone with my bare hands.

Hence, my little interaction with Kreshnik here. No one's more connected in human trafficking than the Albanians, and Kreshnik has all the answers.

Every pinch point, every vulnerability. So, if my uncle thought I'd back off once he started leveraging my wife, he's dead fucking wrong.

When I zig and should've zagged, Kreshnik lands a direct hit. My body slams into the fencing, pain flaring in my side.

Dante's voice cuts through the crowd with his usual pep talk, "Only morons go in alone."

Groaning, I force myself up on my hands and knees, every movement sending fresh waves of agony through my body. Then I look up at him from inside of the cage. "Since when do you need an engraved invitation?"

"You sent me a text. 'Going to war with Uncle Cocksucker. See you there.' No place. No time. I had to track my own goddamn jet like I'd lost my phone." He looks up and switches gears. "Incoming."

I brace myself. As Kreshnik lunges to kick me in the gut, I catch his foot and twist until I hear a snap. He crashes to the floor with a satisfying thud.

Without missing a beat, I grab his other foot, rinse and repeat. He writhes in pain, howling like a wounded animal.

The crowd roars again, and someone tosses a heavy-duty chain into the center of the ring—the kind that can break bones with a single strike.

My sadistic streak kicks into high gear when Kreshnik starts army-crawling toward it. I stride over and kick it to the other side of the cage.

The rules are cutthroat. When weapons are tossed in, whoever touches it with their hands keeps it.

That's why hands are usually the first casualties. Broken, smashed up, ripped right off—whatever it takes.

But me, I go for the feet. Give the mouse a sliver of hope, and they'll race through your maze all damn day.

I snatch the chain just before his fingers are able to graze it and whip him once across the back. "The supplier," I demand.

Kreshnik's a beast—300 pounds, six foot seven. He fights at first, enraged and in pain. But after a few brutal hits to his arms, shoulders, and head, his fierce defiance crumbles.

His curses dissolve into mumbled groans. "You—" he gasps, struggling for breath.

I think he's about to call me another name, when he spits, "You're the supplier."

I stumble back, stunned. "I'm the supplier?" I glance at Dante, who just shrugs. I'm about to press for more when the referee declares me the winner, shoving my hand high in the air, which is a bitch on my ribs.

I rush to Kreshnik, delivering a sharp slap to his face. "Explain yourself!" I hit him again. "Wake up!"

Then the buzzer blares, signaling the end of the match.

I look up at the ref. "I need more time."

"Too late. A debt has been called. That trumps your little spar. We need the cage." He kicks Kreshnik's lifeless form. "He's dead. It's over."

I should be rejoicing over one less flesh peddler, but unease settles over me like tar.

Two of Andre's men, both naming me as the puppet master with their dying breath. And I need to know who's pulling the strings.

"DON'T BE SO HARD ON YOURSELF." DANTE HANDS ME a scotch and collapses onto the seat beside me, defeated.

I toss back the glass of scotch, hoping to numb the gnawing dread that my uncle has the upper hand. I know it doesn't work when a second later, I send the glass flying across the jet with enough force to shatter and bust a hole in the panel.

I can feel Dante's glare without looking at him. "First, you buy a jet with my Black Card, and then you destroy it?"

My lips twist into a grin. Yeah, I feel a little bad about that.

When I ignore him, Dante punches me in the arm—the one I was previously shot in. I suck in a wince. "Your rib next," he threatens. "Talk."

I blow out a breath. "Uncle Andre's setting me up."

"How do you know?"

"The dance school is a front. I've cleaned it up, but there are dozens of fronts with my name on them. So, I've been taking them over. Cleaning them, then holding them. But I doubt I've accounted for all of them. Hell, I'm not even sure I'm at half."

"Why would Andre do that?"

"Because I'm his biggest threat. He doesn't want me dead; otherwise, he wouldn't have had me shot in the arm. I run

D'Angelo Holdings. To the world, I'm at the helm. If I'm under his thumb, he owns it, too."

Dante leans back, considering. "Fine. You step down. One of us takes over."

The weight of the idea has merit. But between targeting me or one of my brothers, I'd rather be his target practice. "Not yet." I say it to placate him, avoiding a long, drawn-out argument.

Dante switches the monitor from a soccer game to a FaceTime call. Oh, for fuck's sake.

When Smoke, Dillon, and Mateo's faces light up the screen, I roll my eyes.

"You found him," Smoke says. "And alive. Which means Dillon owes me twenty bucks."

"You bet on whether I was dead or alive? For twenty bucks?" I snap, offended.

Smoke shrugs. "At least I bet you'd stay alive."

"What?" Dillon retorts, pointing at me. "Tell me you wouldn't have done the same if you were me."

Point taken.

"You look like hell, man." Mateo smirks, taking in my disheveled state. "Lady troubles? I've got a bottle of blue pills with your name on it."

"Keep them, bro. With that, you've got a marginal shot at actually satisfying women. Two-inch dick and all."

"Is there a point to this conversation?" Smoke grumbles. "Because I've got shit to do."

Dante elbows me hard in the arm—ow—and I huff out a breath, forcing myself to stay calm. "Kennedy is being targeted by Andre. But I know what he really wants

—me. I need to take him down before he takes me down."

"Correction," Dante interjects with his usual *quit fucking around* voice. "*We* need to take him down."

I shake my head, the weight of involving my brothers pressing on me like a hot iron. "I'm only telling you this because you need to shield yourselves. Keep your distance from me, and, as a favor to me, protect my wife."

None of them hesitates, but Smoke is the first to speak. "You're an idiot."

"Moron," Dillon chimes in.

"Totally brainless," Mateo adds, shaking his head.

I blink, confused, then turn to Dante. "What the fuck is going on?"

Dante grins. "We're telling you we've got your back, dumbass. Just tell us what you need done."

After a few tedious conversations and wandering aimlessly for several blocks, I'm finally in front of the dance studio.

The building buzzes with activity, bricklayers and construction workers weaving in and out of the guards. Safety precautions for the dance studio are nearly complete, and the former money laundering operation is gone.

I can appreciate washing money as much as the next guy, but a kids' dance studio? Not on my fucking watch.

I step inside and spot my *Bella* down the hall. It's been weeks since I've seen her—beyond the surveillance cameras, that is. The ache to touch her, to hold her, to absolutely consume her, hasn't let up one bit. And my dirty little girl hasn't helped.

I've sent her texts. Nothing overly sentimental. Just enough to let her know I'm thinking of her without actually saying as much because when she's riled up, she turns to Titan. And it's the most binge-worthy thing I've seen in my life.

Watching her is one thing.

But knowing that I own her—that no other man touches her without his hand feeding a meat grinder—is everything. It's kick-started my lump of a heart, and there is no going back.

Kennedy will be protected.

And I have to show her these fucked-up photos of her and find out what she knows. There's a piece I'm missing. Something that's staring me right in the face that I just can't see.

I'd rather toss back battery acid than do this, but I have no choice.

Pain is the only way I'm dragging her from an inferno, and no matter how much it burns, it's her only way out.

"Who did?" Kennedy's voice snaps me back to reality, cutting through my thoughts.

I move closer, catching Riley's answer. "Enzo."

"Yes." They both pivot toward me, and I catch Riley's face.

I didn't mind Riley staying here after the wedding. It's easier to keep a close eye on her this way. But her being under Knox's watchful eye—I'm not sure what I make about that.

If that asshole hurt her, which seems likely judging by her tear-streaked eyes and trembling form, then the bastard will pay. And making him pay will be my pleasure.

The moment Riley spots me, she bolts. I blow out a breath. Teenagers.

Kennedy moves to chase after her when I grab her arm. "Let her go," I say firmly. "My men will catch up to her."

Holding her like this, feeling her tremble in my arms, is more intimate than we've been in weeks. I can't bear to let her go—not now, not when she's about to be swept away like a leaf in the wind.

I hate that I'm about to shatter Kennedy's world, but I will build her back up. Shape her into the queen she was always destined to be.

"You and I need to talk, *Bella*."

For a lingering moment, I study her face, contemplating what it will take to mend her after I devastate her with these photos. How much time it will take? How many men will I destroy?

Then, I kiss her.

A slow, tender kiss that reassures her of the depth of my commitment.

I am hers.

Judge, jury, and executioner. "I'll get your coat and have someone take your class. I'll take you anywhere you want to go, but we need to talk."

"Let's go home."

Chapter Thirty-Three
KENNEDY

"Is there anything you need?" Enzo murmurs as we step through the door.

But I don't respond. Not to the way his hands trace up and down my arms, the warmth of his breath on my neck, or his kiss on that heart-shaped freckle he's so fixated on—I should feel something for him.

But I don't.

Is Riley right? Is he responsible for our father's death?

I do need something. Answers. It's the only reason I'm letting him touch me, be with me like this. "No," I whisper, my heart pounding so hard and fast it feels like it might burst from my chest.

He kisses me again, and my chest tightens. Can a kiss taste like regret? "There's something I haven't told you, *Bella*. Something that will change us. Change everything. But—"

I nod, understanding he's right. "But what?"

It surprises me when my hand rises to his chest without

permission, a primal reaction to the tremor running through his frame.

Instantly, his arms wrap around me, his lips kissing, nipping, licking, losing himself completely. A surge of desire crashes over us so hard that there's no stopping him now.

And in that moment, a sensation washes over me, cool to the touch, numbing my thoughts.

He gently removes my clothes, placing tender kisses on my shoulders and breasts, completely adoring my body before shedding all his clothes.

"What did you need to tell me?" I ask, absentmindedly stroking his hair.

I need to hear it: the truth. And if he's responsible for our father's death, I need one more thing. Something gut-wrenching. Something absolute.

Revenge.

And with every touch, every moment of pleasure he gives me, I repeat to myself, *"He will pay."*

The more he works me, making my body yield to him, wet and craving, teetering on the edge, the more I accept it.

I let myself do it—I come and fall from grace so willingly that a Bible verse echoes in my mind. *"An eye for an eye, a tooth for a tooth... But I tell you, do not resist an evil person."*

He crawls over me, plunging in deep and fast, and my body yields as it always does. Defenseless. The quicker his thrusts, the tighter I cling, arms around his shoulders, legs wrapped around his waist.

I hate myself for it now but vow to forgive myself for it later.

When the full force of him crashes into me—deep, shuddering, both of us crying out—my heart shatters to dust.

He whispers, "I'd do anything for you, *Bella*."

I say nothing, panting through my thoughts.

I wonder, would he die for me?

WHEN THE SHOWER STARTS, I THROW ON A ROBE AND charge into his office. With a flick of the lights, I tear through every drawer, searching in a rush until I find one that's locked.

I nearly break a letter opener, but the lock pops open.

What I find is horrifying. Photos of women. Girls. I flip through so many at once, to the point nausea shoves its way up my throat so fast, I nearly puke.

My eyes snag on another image, and all the air rushes from my lungs. Trinity.

Even through the blur of tears, it's her. Trinity. His sister. My thoughts trip over the vivid image, coming to a jarring halt.

Something's not right.

I've come to know Enzo as many things—cold, ruthless, a torturer, a killer—he freely admits to them all. But a sick, sadistic bastard who would do this to his own sister?

No.

Deep down, I know this isn't him. I can't explain how, but I know it to my bones, my core.

My soul.

I try another drawer, another locked one. This time, the letter opener snaps in two as it forces the lock, but the drawer opens. Inside, there's a very large gun and pictures of . . . me?

The photos are unsettling and twisted, and why don't I remember any of them? I'm pretty sure I'd remember being dressed up in baby doll dresses with lots of bows.

I flip through them again and again, trying to jog my memory. But each time I look, I feel detached, like watching a crime show with gory images, able to dissect every detail because none of it is personal. It isn't me.

Except it is me. I shake my head, sensing that something's off. Something—

"I wish you hadn't found those." Enzo's voice cuts like ice, his eyes darkening until the gold melts into black. "I wanted to speak with you first."

He stands there dripping wet, the towel around his waist barely covering his exposed form. A large black-and-blue bruise marks his lower ribs, and he shows no sign of a weapon.

Before I can second-guess myself, cold metal meets my palm, aimed squarely at his chest. "The only thing I want to hear from you is the truth." Determined, I tighten my grip on the gun, fighting back the sting of tears. "Did you kill my father?"

There's a desk between us. Not that it stops his presence from dominating the entire room.

He moves like a wild panther, the rise and fall of his broad, chiseled chest steady and hypnotic. His eyes hold a myriad of emotions yet remain void of any at all.

And I'm frozen.

Enzo takes another step, and I lift the heavy gun higher. It trembles as I struggle to keep it steady. "Answer me!"

His next few steps are silent, almost surreal, until the barrel is inches from his chest. A strangled sound escapes my throat, and fresh tears burn as they trail down my face. "Don't make me shoot you."

My voice trembles with a pleading note. He cocks his head, recognizing the desperation.

When his fingers brush against mine, my finger tightens on the trigger, just a fraction, before he murmurs, "If you want it to hurt, move it here." He slides the gun below the bruised stain on his ribs, down to his gut.

I force the words out, stammering, "Tell me."

"Or," he continues, sliding the gun to another spot on his skin, "here."

At this point, I'm blinking through the haze, tears blurring my vision, my heart lodged in my throat. "Enzo, please."

So many emotions swim behind his glassy eyes, a turbulent sea, deep and dark. His words land softly between us—my father's words. Tenderly, Enzo whispers, "What are you waiting for? Do it."

The gun lowers, and my heart constricts with tight, sharp pain. I blink. "What did you say?"

Suddenly, the door opens, and all the men file in—his brothers and Sin. Protective and ready to draw their own weapons, to finish me before I finish him.

Sin shuts the door behind him. "Put down the gun, Kennedy," he says, voice steady, words calm.

"No!" Enzo commands, throwing himself between his trigger-ready brothers and me.

The bewilderment on their faces mirrors my own.

"Get out of the way," Dillon demands.

When he doesn't move, Sin tries to reason with him. "We just need to get the gun."

Enzo pushes back. "I didn't call you here to stop her. I called you here to protect her."

"What?" they all say in unison, echoing my own shock.

Here I am, gun aimed at my husband's back. It would be so easy to shoot him. Why can't I do it?

"Because he's savin' you, darlin'." It's as if *Da* is whispering in my ear, and the tears won't stop.

"You will protect my wife."

"I'm not sure the woman with the gun needs protecting," Mateo says, motioning to me.

But Enzo doesn't let up. "The arrangements have been made. My wife will inherit my wealth, and I brought all of you here because she will need witnesses."

Smoke shakes his head. "Witnesses for what?"

"To verify it was self-defense, and"—Enzo sucks in a sharp breath—"to say goodbye."

Smoke steps forward, the blood draining from his face. "You can't be saying what I think you're saying. You can't—" He chokes on his words.

Did Enzo plan this? To sacrifice himself at my hand?

And then what?

Save me from jail? The wrath of his brothers?

Enzo turns to face me, his expression full of sorrow. "I wanted more time to figure out what was going on. But . . ." His sorrowful eyes shift to Dante. "My brother will have to find the answers I couldn't."

Dillon steps closer, defiant and looking damn near ready to tackle his brother. "I will not stand by and watch this."

"None of us will," Mateo adds, his words razor-sharp.

Enzo's smile isn't forced; it's genuine. "This gets Andre off our back and protects my wife. And settles a sin I've spent a lifetime trying to erase."

It's as if he's already made peace with the inevitability of this—of his death—of me killing him. And now, we're all here to come to grips with it, too.

"Come on," he says softly, almost tenderly. "We all knew if one of us was next, I was the sure bet. And besides, this isn't like our father. This way, at least we get to say goodbye."

"And what about Trinity?" Smoke's voice, now almost pleading, is laced with deep, unspeakable pain.

Enzo shakes his head, a haunted look in his eyes. "Tell her I love her. I failed her, too."

"Failed her?" I mumble, shock muddling my thoughts, making it hard to process his words.

Dante's eyes well with tears. They all do.

Then Enzo drops to his knees. His voice is chillingly calm as he moves the gun to his heart. "Here, *Bella*. If you want it over quickly."

Sobbing, I shake my head, unable to believe this is me, about to kill my husband. Or him, about to let me. "What are you doing?"

"Giving you what you want. If I could've traded places with your father, I would have. His death deserves vengeance. You're his heart. You both are."

My hand lands on my freckle. The heart-shaped one. *Da* said it to me every night. *You're my heart. You both are.* But, how?

Enzo's breath shudders. "Kennedy Mullvain D'Angelo, the day you agreed to marry me, I vowed to give you anything you want or die trying." His hand holds the gun firmly against his chest. "If this is what you want, then I want this, too. I love you."

The deafening crack shatters the room. My heart stops.

Chapter Thirty-Four
KENNEDY

"Freeze!" a man's voice shouts.

In the aftermath, my eyes snap to Enzo. He's still in one piece, not shot.

Relief floods through me so intense my knees nearly give way.

Then I see the entryway: the door frame mangled, the door swinging wildly from being kicked in. The source of the crack.

Agent Knox charges in, flanked by half a dozen men in FBI jackets, weapons drawn and pointed straight at me.

Once again, Enzo jumps between us, his half-naked, still-dripping-wet body ready to take a bullet for me.

"Get out of the way, Enzo," Knox orders, his voice taut with authority.

Enzo stands firm. "You're not touching my wife."

Knox raises an eyebrow. "Enzo, you might be a loose cannon who belongs in a psych ward as much as the pedophiles you chase down, but I can't just stand by and let you get shot. It's called law and order. Try looking it up."

Dante steps in beside his brother. "And you can't do anything to stop it."

Mateo moves in, too. All three of them, a barricade of D'Angelo strength. "It's a little something called the Second Amendment. The members of this house can carry weapons. Try looking it up."

Knox rolls his eyes. "For the last time, drop the weapon, Kennedy," he says, his gaze flicking to me.

"Oh, for fuck's sake," Enzo growls, snatching the gun from my hands. "Don't look at her; look at me. The man aiming a gun at your head. Now, you can shoot me in self-defense, or I can shoot you."

"No one is shooting anyone," Smoke commands, his voice laced with don't-fuck-with-me authority. "Enzo, put the gun down." Enzo grudgingly obeys, and before an agent can slap cuffs on him, Smoke turns to Knox. "Now, show me your warrant."

Knox's eyes flit to the other agents, then back to Smoke. "I don't need a warrant. She had a gun. At his head. Probable fucking cause."

"Actually," Sin in all his esquire glory points out, "it was his chest, and it doesn't constitute probable cause."

Flustered, Knox glares. "The hell it doesn't."

Dillon throws an arm around Enzo's shoulders. "What these two lovebirds do in the privacy of their own home isn't probable cause. And D'Angelo homes are strict, no-judgment zones."

Knox glares at him, disbelief etched into every word. "So, this is gunplay?"

Nonchalantly, Sin cleans his glasses with his tie. "Gunplay

might be kinky and a bit taboo, but it's not illegal in Illinois as long as it doesn't cross public indecency thresholds."

Smoke gestures around the room, drawing attention to the house. "They're in the privacy of their own home."

Enzo crosses his arms. "My home, my wife, where we have an expectation of privacy. If you have a warrant, arrest someone. Otherwise, get out."

Clearly out of his depth, Knox holsters his weapon and signals the others to do the same. His men file out.

"Fine. Whatever. If Enzo wants to play Russian roulette with the wifey, that's their business." Then Knox turns to me, his gaze softening. "You're not under arrest, Kennedy, but I'm offering you a way out. You can come with me now. No questions asked."

Chapter Thirty-Five
KENNEDY

"Where are you staying, Kennedy?" Father Marc asks as we stroll along the quiet path, Truffles trotting beside us.

He's been my rock, my sounding board, ever since my entire life went to hell.

I glance down at Truffles, watching as he discovers the first fallen leaves of the season rustling in the breeze. "A friend's place. It's temporary."

I don't mention it's Knox's place.

He's suddenly out of town on assignment and offered me a safe spot to hunker down as I lick my wounds and figure out my next move.

When Riley vanished, he promised to keep tabs on her, too. But he's become Fort Knox lately because he won't say where she is or what she's doing. Only that she's safe and protected. Knowing that she might turn up at Knox's place, I wanted to be here if she did.

"How are the girls holding up?" he asks, glancing at Sofie

and Lili with a fond smile as they make faces at the shiny surface of *Cloud Gate*.

For years, I wondered why an artist would create a giant metal bean and plop it in the center of Millennium Park. Obviously, it was so little girls could have the time of their lives making silly faces and giggling like maniacs.

"Sofia and Lili have been having a blast at Camp Dory's. Neutral territory. She's a natural with them, and they love it there. They build sheet tents and pretend they're at Hogwarts. Dory's even turned her kitchen into a mini cooking school."

"Is it as idyllic as it sounds?"

I exhale with a deep sigh. "It helps them sleep. They don't like beds." I pause, struggling to get the words out. "And Dory . . . she manages to soothe them better than Enzo and I ever could. Even when they wake up crying."

"It's hard," he nods, deeply sympathetic.

"Cries are easier. When they wake up screaming, it rips our hearts right out of our chests. For whatever reason, they always go rushing to Dory."

"I know it's hard." He sounds more than compassionate, like he's lived it.

I shake my head. "It's a relief. At least one of us can bring them comfort."

"You're all bringing them comfort in your own ways."

I shrug. "We're trying to make it work."

"No," Father Marc says calmly. "You *are* making it work, Kennedy. Working through trauma is like digging out of a tunnel with a spoon. Some days, you make great strides. Other days, it feels like you're stuck in the same place. They're lucky to have you all."

"Especially Enzo." My smile warms. "He reads to them every night, whether he's here or not, though lately, mostly not. The miracle of FaceTime."

For some reason, knowing he reads them all the *Harry Potter* books and does every last voice feels like a sliver of hope blooming in my chest.

I pause, feeling the weight of Father Marc's gaze on me. He teeters into the subject carefully. "Did he ever respond to your message?"

He's referring to my *Can we talk?* message. Shame and regret twist inside me like a knife. "Not a word," is all I say.

Some days, I think he'll text or call, and other days, he doesn't. And then there are days when my finger hovers just over his name on the phone, but before I can dial, a riptide of guilt drags me under, instantly killing all my courage.

Father Marc nods, his eyes full of understanding. "It's important to give yourself grace and time to heal, Kennedy. You've been through so much."

"I held a gun to my husband while he defended me." I shake my head, the memory stabbing at my insides. "I can't face him."

His elbow nudges me gently. "You're braver than you think."

The breeze kicks up, and I pull my sweater tighter and shiver. "Thank God Knox barged in when he did. I don't know what would've happened if he hadn't."

Hands clutched behind his back, Father Marc stays quiet and contemplative. He has to be around Enzo's age—maybe even younger.

Yet, there's an air of wisdom about him—a depth that's impossible to ignore. It's as if he's seen the darkest corners of the world and carries the weight of secrets and sins with a haunting grace, no matter how heavy the burden or how it torments him.

Truffles tugs on the leash, but my mind stays elsewhere. "What I don't get is how Knox knew to barge in right when he did. Until the gun was in my hand, I didn't even know."

His expression shifts, a flicker of something familiar. Could it be... guilt?

Why would a man of the cloth feel guilty? He's a living, breathing sanctuary of trust.

Sanctuary of trust...

The phrase lingers, gnawing at my thoughts. The church. A stronghold that weaves together the dark, dangerous threads of men who despise each other. Like Enzo and Knox.

I know Caleb Knox goes there, his St. Michael's pendant conspicuously dangling from his neck when he's not buttoned up to the chin. Which I only noticed it because when he left town, for once, he wore a T-shirt and jeans.

And Knox is nice and all, but he's no Enzo.

Frankly, no one is.

But the church represents a safe haven to monsters like Andre, who had me deliver a ridiculous wad of cash to Father Marc.

I might be slow on the uptake, but eventually, I connect the dots between these three men and a priest who looks guilty as sin. "Confession," I say aloud.

Father Marc nods. "Sure. Anytime you want. I'm happy to take your confession."

"I'm sure you are. Just like you're ready to take everyone's confessions. With the world going to hell in a handbasket, business must be booming, right? Sinners swarming in to get every sin absolved—Feds and mob kings alike."

He looks away, the conflict in his eyes unmistakable. "Kennedy, if you're asking what I think you're asking, I wish I could help, but—"

"You can."

"I can't. The seal of confession is sacred."

"Sacred enough to hide the truth?"

He blows out a long, tired breath. "Breaking that seal would not only violate the trust placed in me, but it could also cost me my priesthood. It's immediate grounds for excommunication."

"What if it prevents a crime? Or saves a life?"

"What kind of world would it be if people couldn't safely confess every last sin, seek forgiveness, and be absolved? It would violate the sacred trust placed in me by everyone—rich, poor, old, young, cop or criminal."

He's in an impossible position. I get that. But so am I, and I'm not backing down. I lock eyes with him, refusing to let him look away. "My father was killed."

His head drops. "I know."

"I blamed Enzo, almost killed him for it, and he just took it. Didn't argue. Didn't even fight back. And Knox, who can't stand him, dove in headfirst to save his life." I press my temple, feeling like I'm losing my mind. "Please, I'm begging you, Father, what am I missing?"

His gaze meets mine, regret and compassion battling in his eyes. "I know how confusing it must be from your vantage point. And if it's any consolation, it's probably just as baffling for everyone involved."

"Except you," I snide.

"I wish there were another way. But the answers you seek can't come from me."

Frustrated, I explode. "You're getting cash from Enzo and Andre, and you're what? Switzerland?"

He hushes me, glancing around nervously. "Yes, my child, I am. Andre's money keeps the lights on, pays for day-to-day operations. Enzo's money goes to . . ."

"Free the very women Andre enslaves?"

Stunned, he asks, "Enzo told you?"

Okay, here's the thing. It was just a hunch. But I'm pulling on this thread like it's a marlin. Even if it is a lie. "Of course, he did. Why wouldn't he? I'm his wife."

Great, Kennedy. You just lied to a man of the cloth. Exactly how many Hail Marys do I need to avoid burning in hell for all eternity?

He stays silent, and our tense little walk stretches on, him lost in thought, me on the verge of shoving my hand down his throat and ripping every last secret from his chest. I mean, if I'm already going to hell anyway.

"You could at least give me a hint," I mumble under my breath.

"A hint?" He considers it, his steps slowing to a stop. He glances at me, then down at the truffles underfoot. Truffles sneezes at him.

Then, as if by some divine intervention, a glimmer sparks in his dark brown eyes. His smile broadens so wide that I finally get why priest romance is a thing.

"Well, you're staying with *a friend*, right?"

"Right." I'm not sure where this is going.

"Sometimes the answers we seek are right in front of our face."

"Knox?"

He lowers his voice, leaning in. "More like his desk." He winks and walks ahead, smiling like the cat who swallowed three canaries.

I rush to catch up, bewildered. "Hang on. I never mentioned the friend I'm staying with was Knox."

A knowing smile plays on his lips. "It's like you said, Kennedy. I take confessions from everyone. And yes, business is indeed booming."

Chapter Thirty-Six
ENZO

Two steps into the diner, and I instantly regret it. This place makes me want to bathe in disinfectant and gargle with straight bleach.

I slide into the booth opposite the man I've been hunting for, and for a long, tense beat, we just sit there.

"Can I get you something to eat?" the waitress asks, her voice grating against the dive bar's bad lighting and crusty food.

Frankly, I don't need to be here. I have a million things to do. Kill my uncle. Destroy his empire. Find a world-class therapist for the kids. Perfect my *Snape* voice because Lili is completely unconvinced and thinks I sound like a princess. And protect what's mine. My wife. *Bella*. Even if she is pissing me off right now.

But to do that, I have to deal with this piece of shit.

So here I am, at midnight, taking care of business by committing a Class 3 felony—holding a gun to a Fed.

"Nothing for me," I reply, gripping the gun under the table. Yeah, seriously, not even water from this rat infested hellhole.

"Coffee," Knox says, casually slinging an arm over the back of his bench seat. "And what kind of pie do you have?"

Roach-filled is my guess.

"Cream," she offers, nodding as if she admires his bravery.

"What kind of cream?"

She and her baby blue, food-stained outfit shrug, uncertain. "Vanilla?"

"Just what I was in the mood for," he replies with way too much enthusiasm.

"Sounds about right," I scoff.

He narrows his eyes and reads her tag. "Just coffee and pie, Helene."

"It's Helena," she corrects, and I reexamine her name. Ah, I see the issue. There's a small crust of something—possibly a booger—that makes it look like an 'e.'

She moseys off, diligently scribbling because coffee and pie are apparently kicking her ass to remember.

Okay, fine, Booger Girl didn't do anything to me. I'm in a bad mood because Knox offered to rescue my wife. And she accepted. As if I wasn't right there—half-naked and dripping wet, protecting her with my life.

God, why am I not just shooting him in the balls already?

Knox cracks his knuckles. It's a nervous tic he picked up after his partner was shot. At least, that's what his psych file says. Along with some disturbing shit about enjoying chick flicks and crocheting.

"Look," Knox says, sounding more irritated than concerned. "Let's skip the pleasantries. Spare me the threats. I'm sure you've got your gun on me, so just get to the point and go away. Why are you here?"

"Because you're going to tell me where my wife is."

"Or what?" he asks, underwhelmed. "You shoot me?"

I hold up my phone, turn around, and snap several selfies with him. "Or I post these on every social media outlet for the world to see with the hashtag #1FED."

Aggravated, he lowers his voice and leans in. "I'm undercover," he seethes.

"Are you?" I feign surprise.

"It's a little ironic that you were able to track me down in the middle of bumfuck Illinois, but have no idea where your wife is." He makes an exaggerated motion, his fingers splaying outwards as if his head is exploding. "Mind-blowing."

Which means she's probably been right under my nose the entire time, and I've been too blind to notice. Like a stupid little lovestruck puppy that someone should put out of its fucking misery.

Whatever.

I sit back, letting the cracked vinyl dig into my spine. "Tell me where my wife is before Helena returns, and you'll live to eat your salmonella pie."

"How about this?" He clasps his hands together, a smug look on his face. "You tell me why your name is all over dozens of your uncle's enterprises, and I'll give you whatever the hell you want."

What? I try to mask my shock, but my mind is racing. I've been trying to piece together all the businesses my uncle has conveniently inserted my name in place of his, but it's like matching scattered pieces of broken glass. "Which enterprises?" I ask.

"The two casinos out of town, the underground human

trafficking ring running out of the basements of a dozen bars, the money laundering operation in six different kids' dance schools—low, even for you. Do I need to go on?"

Hmm. My uncle's empire, and my name is all over it. The implications settle into every manipulative pocket of my mind.

If I play my cards right, I can cripple my uncle, and all I'd have to do is quietly take control of these holdings, since the dumb son of a bitch put them in my name.

I study Knox. Hell, would it be weird if I asked for a pen and paper?

"You drive a hard bargain, Knox. I want the entire list of locations and the safe house where you're keeping my wife. Then, I'll tell you what you want to know."

Helena returns with the coffee and pie. Okay, not going to lie. The pie actually looks good.

I hand her a twenty. "Don't come back," I instruct.

She snatches the twenty and tucks it into her sagging cleavage. "I wasn't planning to."

Knox whips out his phone. "It's in your inbox."

I check, irritation flaring. "Where's my wife?"

Chuckling, he sips the steaming-hot mop water they call coffee. "Nope. Tell me the grand scheme first. Then you get the address."

I blow out a breath and do something I never thought I'd do in a million years. I tell the truth. "Fine. I suspect my uncle is trying to set me up for an epic fall," I admit, more candidly than I should.

But when it comes to Kennedy, my heart insists on running with scissors all day long—carefree and blind.

Knox grins like a moron. "Try not to blow up all of Chicago while taking Andre down."

"No promises." I smirk. Are we . . . bonding? I shake off the thought in disgust and lean in, my composure regained. "Now, the address."

"820 North Halstead. Apartment 5b."

My vision narrows, and it takes every ounce of restraint not to pull the trigger. Whatever bromance was blooming between us gets killed real fucking fast. My voice drops to a lethal whisper. "That's your place."

"Relax, Enzo. I'm not fucking your wife. I handed her the key, dropped her off, and left."

"And I'm supposed to believe that?" The gun is at his head before he can say a word, and I don't give a damn who's watching. Not that anyone is. The place is empty, and Helena is probably snoring behind the counter.

He shakes his head and moves the gun aside. "It's the truth."

The fuck it is. God, my finger itches so badly, ready to shoot him, but I can't do it. The rage I feel in the moment is swept away under a tsunami of regret. Because what does it matter?

I'm at war with my uncle, and I'll probably be dead in a few days anyway. If my wife is choosing Knox over me, I won't stomp out her happiness like a petulant, sleep-deprived toddler.

Kennedy deserves love.

And, with any luck, I'll die swiftly taking down my uncle rather than dying slowly and pathetically of heartbreak.

"Now," Knox clears his throat anxiously, "my mark will be here any minute. Are you leaving, or what?"

With a resigned sigh, I pocket my gun and pray that the pie gives him the worst diarrhea of his life. "I am."

I head out and send a quick text to Striker.

ME
Where's my uncle now?

STRIKER
Monaco.

ME
Have the jet ready in 20.

STRIKER
Yes, sir.

Chapter Thirty-Seven
KENNEDY

I PUSH open the heavy door to Dante's club. Dim lights cast fleeting shadows over the opulent leather booths and the glistening marble bar. It's nearly empty, a stark contrast to the last time I was here when the place buzzed, body to body, pulsing with music.

"Kennedy?" Dante emerges from a hallway, his surprise evident as he kisses me on the cheek. "I didn't expect to see you. Enzo isn't here. He's"—he considers his words carefully—"a little fucked up."

"He is?"

"Just, after your little couple's therapy session went south, he decided to go after our uncle. Something about photographs. He's trying not to involve us, but I'm pretty sure he's about to get himself killed." His eyes meet mine. He winces. "Too soon?"

I smirk. "A little." A flutter of nerves kicks up in my chest. Stop stalling, Kennedy. Just ask. "I, um, have this flash drive, but I don't own a computer, and I can't risk anyone else seeing what's on it. At least, not until I do. Do you think you can help me?"

He rubs the back of his neck, suspicion etched around a twisted grin. "You don't own a computer? Then why do you have a flash drive?"

"It's not mine," I reply, sheepishly.

His eyes light up with intrigue. "Is it porn?"

Awkwardly, I shrug. "Honestly, I'm not sure. It belongs to Knox." *God help me, what if it is?*

"Ooh," He rubs his scruff, mischief burning behind his bright eyes. "Hacking into FBI property feels like a felony," he says, chuckling as if it's the best idea ever.

I sigh, pulling the drive from my pocket. The second he catches sight of what's written on it, his smile vanishes, replaced by a deep, intense frown.

Enzo.

Chapter Thirty-Eight
ENZO

"Ready kid?"

The air is thick with the acrid stench of sweat and the metallic bite of blood. My heart slams against my ribcage, each beat a ticking countdown to my first fight.

In my mind, I'm already there—dancing through the jabs, delivering surprise kicks, executing every move Mullvain drilled into me.

Left hook, right jab, keep my guard up.

Breathe.

Focus.

This isn't just about proving myself to my father or placating my uncle. This is about making Mullvain proud. And, if I'm being honest, earning some serious bragging rights when I finally meet his pretty daughter one day.

The referee pats me down for weapons, his one good eye sharp and assessing, the other a lifeless void beneath a brutal scar.

His hands are rough, patting me down with a thoroughness

that borders on invasive. "You sure you're ready for this, kid?" he growls, his breath a mix of stale beer and legendary regrets.

I nod, swallowing the lump of fear in my throat. "I'm ready."

"Once you're in the cage, that's it. No one comes out until one of you wins and the other one is dead. Whatever's thrown in the ring, try to grab it with your hands." He raises his hands, clenching them into tight fists. "Then it's yours for the fight. Otherwise, you'll be defending yourself against it."

Not exactly comforting, considering he's missing two fingers.

The crowd is a frenzied beast, their roars and cheers electric and terrifying. The air crackles as I'm led through the sea of people, the cage a shadowy outline ahead.

Each step fires pure adrenaline through my body. My pulse thuds loud in my ears in time to the deafening roar of the filthy rich and deeply depraved.

The cage door slams shut with a resounding clang, and then I see him.

My feet stop cold.

The rush of blood freezes in my veins.

He's the biggest, most ruthless man I've ever laid eyes on. Monstrous, towering, and twice my height. Shit, my entire body weight would probably fit in one of his legs.

It's the moment I realize just how hard my uncle fucked me over, and how life as I know it is about to nosedive into the worst part of hell.

"Mullvain."

The man who's shaped every punch, every move, locks eyes with me, his steely green gaze wide with panic.

"Stop the match!" Mullvain's voice cracks with desperation as he pleads through the cage to Andre.

Uncle Andre chuckles, his eyes glinting with that trademark cruelty. "You know the rules. Not until one of you is dead." He glances at me, then back to Mullvain. "Well, did you show him the ropes? Or does that happen now?"

"No! I won't fight him. He's just a kid!" Mullvain's voice is swallowed by the crowd's roar, and the bitter desperation in his eyes is haunting.

A buzzer blares, and Mullvain turns to me, his form seeming to grow three times in size, eyes wild, teeth gnarled. "Defend yourself!"

"What?"

He grabs me by the neck, hoisting me up until my feet dangle. It's a move we've practiced a dozen times. His voice drops to a whisper, concealed by the roar of the crowd. "Look terrified."

"I am terrified."

"The entire routine. We need to play it all out now." Regret is etched in every line, every glance. "You're gonna get hurt."

"And then what? The man said one of us has to die."

Defeat washes over his face. "We keep going until I figure out what to do." Without another word, he hurls me against the cage.

And, as usual, he was right. It hurts like hell, knocking all the wind from my lungs.

He kicks me in the side. To him, it's a gentle tap. To me, it's agony. I recoil in pain.

"Move!" he barks. On command, I do. Like a petrified jackrabbit fleeing a hungry wolf.

The cage is small, and our pre-orchestrated moves quickly lose steam. "Well?" I ask, breathless, as he throws me into a headlock.

"I'm thinking. I'm thinking," he mutters, tossing me over his back. I land in a tuck and roll, coming up on my feet.

As a desperate last resort, I kick him in the nuts. I mouth sorry as he doubles over, slowly sinking to the ground until we're eye to eye. "How long does it go on?"

His face drops. "Until one of us is dead."

We start to stall, and the crowd jeers every second we do.

"What if we just stop? Call a truce?" I suggest, my voice barely audible over the growing boos.

His eyes darken with resignation. "Then we're both dead. Two guards are just itching to shoot us down." He grabs me by the back of the neck. "Brace yourself."

I do, but when my entire body slams into the floor, bones crack, and the taste of metal floods my mouth. All I can think is, he's going to do it.

Mullvain has to kill me.

I'm about to die.

When a gun lands next to my hand, with the initials AD *etched into the handle, I don't think. I grab it.*

The roar of the crowd swells like a wild animal, bloodthirsty and demanding more.

Heaving and gasping for air, I struggle to my feet, the gun pointed at Mullvain. Tears blur my vision, making it hard to see what I'm aiming at. "I won't do it!" I scream to Uncle Andre.

"Then you're both dead." My uncle casually points to two guards high in the stands. "I thought you were ready."

I shift my aim to his fucking face. But the second I do, Mullvain grabs the barrel and shoves it against his chest. "What are you doing?"

"They'll kill you, kid."

"Let them! I don't care. I'm dead anyway, and I'd rather

take him down, too." But when I glance back, my uncle is gone, vanished behind the thick wall of people.

He smacks my face. Tears fly. "What are you waiting for? Do it!"

"I can't," I beg, crying.

Mullvain's grip tightens on my face, not in pain, but to lock my attention onto his eyes. "She's my heart, lad. They both are. One day, remind them of that." I don't need to ask who he means. His daughter. Two daughters. Our pact. Our secret. Fight Club.

The gun slips from my grasp into his. I don't hear it go off. I only see his eyes, filled with a plea.

Then, the weight of his body crashes into me, and the world blurs.

The crowd's roar crescendos, the buzzer sounds, and the ref drags me to my feet and raises my hand in the air.

My eyes drop to Mullvain's.

He's gone.

Chapter Thirty-Nine
KENNEDY

FOR MOST OF OUR FLIGHT, I'm a total basket case.

And not because of my fear of flying—Enzo cured me of that—but because of the sick, gnawing feeling that no matter what I do, I'm about to lose him.

Every time I take a breath the video replays in my mind, squeezing my heart so hard, there are no tears left.

Da is gone, ripped from my life all over again by that damned video.

And Riley is who knows where. Knox assures me she's safe, so I slide my baby sister to the back burner and deal with the issue at hand.

Enzo.

My wounded beast of a husband. And the love of my life.

"We'll be in Monaco soon," Dante reassures me. I force a weak smile, my gaze flickering to Smoke, Dillon, and Mateo.

"Are we sure he's there?" I ask, trying to keep the desperation out of my voice.

Smoke nods. "He's there, all right. Checked in yesterday and took an entire floor—three penthouse suites."

"Why?"

Smoke scoffs, amused. "Oh, in case you didn't know, Enzo hates people."

Mateo glances at his phone, his expression grim. "Our guys have intel on him. He's due in the high roller's room at the casino soon, betting big and crazy. Probably trying to lure out Uncle Andre."

"Thanks," I say, smiling meekly. I understand the dangers of having all the D'Angelo brothers in one place. Enzo once mentioned that Smoke's wedding was the first time they'd been together in years, all of them. And I know putting them at risk isn't what Enzo would want.

But they nearly came to blows trying to decide which ones were going and who'd stay behind. So, instead of wasting time letting them kill each other, we figured it was better to preserve their strength and save all that D'Angelo brute force for Enzo.

And, from what I understand, we're going to need it.

"I still don't understand," I say, drained and exhausted. "Enzo is going to gamble his life to get more of these"—I hold up the photos—"away from Uncle Andre?"

The weight of the photos feels like a ticking bomb. Each one shows me in twisted, pretty dresses, none of which I can recall.

"Not just of you," Dante replies, his voice low and grave. "Our sister, too. Uncle Andre's weaknesses are gambling and cocaine. Enzo's weaknesses are the women in his life—you and Trinity. He'll do anything to destroy every last photo, if we even know how many our uncle has."

"And he can't get to Andre directly. The fucker's too heavily guarded. The only way is for our uncle to come to him," Dillon adds. "The problem is Enzo's sort of an all-or-nothing guy."

I study the images again until they blur into a confusing mess. Something's off. I just can't figure out what. *Ugh*. All I know is Enzo is about to put his life on the line for them, and I can't let that happen.

Get killed, don't get killed—hey, buddy, you're married now. Wifey has a say.

THE FLIGHT FEELS ENDLESS, SEEMING TO STRETCH ON for days. I've called the girls twice, but I have to call once more before gearing up for the battlefield.

Instantly, Lili shows me her best twirl while Sofia proudly holds up a tray of Italian cookies she "baked all by herself." Pleased as punch, Dory stands behind her, giving Sofia all the credit with a knowing wink.

"They look delicious, Sofia," I say, genuinely impressed with how far the two of them have come in such a short time. "I can't wait to try one."

"Will Enzo read to us tonight?" Lili asks, worried, and she and Sofie wait on bated breath.

I want to say yes, but what if he doesn't? The double-edged sword of disappointment looms over my answer as Dory cuts in. "Who wants to go to the zoo?"

Both girls squeal and bounce around excitedly as I say thank you. They hang up in a rush of blowing kisses, and once again, and my shoulders relax. Crisis averted.

For now.

We land, and the drive to the casino isn't long. The grand façade of the hotel comes into view, adorned with intricate carvings and lush greenery framing the entrance.

Inside, crystal chandeliers dangle from soaring ceilings, and every detail, from the gilded moldings to the exquisite floral arrangements, screams opulence. In my jeans and T-shirt, I half-expect them to show me to the DoorDash pickup entrance.

The valet helps me out, and the men lead me to a private sitting area. "We'll split up and find Enzo," Dante says.

Smoke nods. "I'll check with Dorian."

"Dorian?" I ask.

"He's the concierge and Enzo's right-hand man around here. If anyone knows where Enzo is, it's Dorian. Be right back, Kennedy."

I sink into a chair, anxiety twisting in my gut. Just as I start to feel utterly helpless, I spot him. My heart pounds, and I'm staring so hard I almost topple out of my seat.

Andre fucking D'Angelo.

The man whose fingerprints are all over my father's death.

Two beautiful women are draped over him at a private table across the way. I should tell the guys, but my feet are already moving, driven by a force I can't control.

Then, without warning, he's on his feet, heading down a hall. I pick up speed, rounding the corner just in time to find myself outside in a garden, grabbed by two guards.

"Well, well, well," Andre purrs. "If it isn't the new Mrs. D'Angelo. Here to beg for mercy?" He chuckles.

His hand grips my chin, and the second it does, a voice booms from behind. "I suggest you remove your hand before it's shot off."

Gun drawn and eyes blazing, it's Dante. Not the carefree Dante I've come to know. This man is a thousand times more lethal.

"You and what army?" Andre sneers.

Suddenly, Andre and his men are surrounded as Smoke, Mateo, and Dillon materialize from out of nowhere.

Andre pulls his weapon, too, and now everyone has a gun except me.

A calm-looking man in a fancy suit and thin mustache strolls over, and I'm debating whether to warn him to get away from this ticking time bomb of a standoff when he says, "Mr. D'Angelo?"

Everyone turns, confident as they all respond, "Yes?"

"Mr. Andre D'Angelo," the man clarifies, his voice steady.

Andre steps back and nods. "What?"

"Good news, sir. The high roller table you requested just had an opening. You are free to join." He holds up what looks like an engraved invitation. "Unless, of course, there's an incident." His gaze sweeps over the drawn guns, disapproval clear as if a headmaster is scolding unruly students. "Then we'll have to ask you to leave the hotel."

"What's the buy-in?" Andre asks, his grip on the weapon unwavering.

"Normally, a hundred thousand, but the person who can't make it forfeited his deposit," the man replies smoothly.

The look on Andre's face confirms what the guys suspected: gambling is one of his greatest weaknesses. He takes the invitation, and with a final glare, storms off.

The brothers lower their weapons, and shift their focus to me.

I brace for the inevitable lecture of *what the hell were you thinking*, but it never comes. All they ask is, "Are you okay?"

My heart swells. It's been so long since I've royally fucked up, only to have all be forgiven. Like a band of big, burly brothers stepping in for *Da*.

I nod, still a bit shaky. "Come on," Dante says. "We'll take you to the room."

AFTER A SHOWER AND SOME FOOD, I COLLAPSE ONTO the bed, staring at my phone. Enzo still hasn't called or texted, but each of my new brothers has. Dante's last message reads:

> DANTE
> Still no sign of Enzo.
> High-roller game our uncle is invited to starts in an hour. We'll be heading down then to see if Enzo's there.

Exhausted, I flip through the photos once more and do a double-take.

This is me.

And it's not.

All of a sudden, everything clicks. The puzzle piece I couldn't see, staring me in the face.

I clutch the photos and look at them again, one by one. Carefully scrutinizing them, making sure I'm not wrong. Then I grab my suitcase and my best battle dress.

> ME
> Count me in.

Chapter Forty
ENZO

"Last game of the night, gentlemen," the dealer announces, the final cards gliding across the green baize in front of each of us.

This is why I love Monaco. It's where I saw my first stripper and had my first fuck. It's discretion and power all wrapped up in one, and high stakes have jack shit to do with cards or money.

Betting big means betting it all. A car. A house. A man's wife for a week of depraved, no-holds-barred submission.

A man's life.

Power doesn't just exchange hands; it dances, whirls, and intoxicates with the potency of sex and the addiction of a drug.

"Your poker face hides a lot, Enzo. But not everything," Uncle Andre says as he studies his cards. His eyes lift to his dwindled pile of chips, and his sly, calculated grin remains intact.

My poker face hides a lot. He should know. Right now, I'm thinking about twelve inches of serrated steel slicing through his throat.

But I keep a clear head and offer nothing more than a nod of acknowledgment.

To my left is a prince of some wealthy but irrelevant country. To my right, a Belgian financier. And next to him, a recently engaged nouveau-riche tech mogul.

Uncle Andre's flowery words aren't worthy of my attention at the moment. My gaze has drifted to the woman who just entered the room. My eyes roam every part of her, but not her face. Never again her face.

That angelic face has tortured my dreams and toyed with my sanity, and tonight, she chose red.

Red.

A red dress.

That damned red dress and the way it teases her thighs and caresses every alluring curve of her body . . . I swear, she'll be the death of me.

I steady my pulse as she takes two steps in my direction. The gold band on my finger suddenly weighs a fucking ton. But it's her wedding ring that breaks the spell. As soon as it catches the light, my jaw clenches, and I blink back to the game.

Of course, it catches the light. How could it not? The damned thing is as big as the moon and cost me more than my yacht.

She's worth a million times more.

Shut up.

In my periphery, her lean legs and come-fuck-me stilettos step closer, and my dick throbs with approval and need.

Not you again. You're the dumbass that got us into this mess.

The problem is, she's not alone. My brothers are here. Dante sidles up beside her, and Dillon has the audacity to lead her in by the hand. Does he think I don't notice his other hand is on the small of her back?

I see you, fucker.

I suspect Mateo is lurking about somewhere. And Smoke, no doubt, is with him.

At least Trinity is smart enough not to enter this war zone. And make no mistake. This is a war.

It's her scent that hits me first. Those tender notes of floral and citrus and . . . *her*.

"Can we talk?" Her voice is barely above a whisper, and her perfume wafts around me so tightly it strangles my senses.

God, I want to say yes.

Every fiber of my soulless being demands I say yes.

But my mind locks on the thought of her again—of her begging Uncle Andre for mercy. Dorian overheard every word, and if he hadn't delivered the invitation when he did, who knows what would have happened.

She's a Mullvain. Ready and willing to do anything for me and I know I have to let her go.

All thoughts of us—a future—snap apart like a leg in a trap. Except it isn't a leg. It's my heart.

I do what I do best. What I'm known for. I crush all her precious hopes away. "Unless you're here in a reverse harem situation with my brothers, you're wasting your time."

"As long as we have your permission." Dante smirks, patting me once on the back.

I take a needed breath and refrain from snapping his fingers in half.

Concentrating, my jaw clamps down tight enough to break a tooth. I toss back the rest of my scotch and motion for more. I study the cards in my hand and remind myself that the banker has a jet I've been eying.

The tech geek tugs at his collar. "Do you take bitcoin?"

I roll my eyes. For fuck's sake. Annoyed, I turn to the Belgian host of our room. I translate the request. "*Acceptez-vous les crypto-monnaies?*"

He shakes his head. "*Non.*"

I repeat. "No." *Moron.*

The tech geek's wife-to-be stands behind him in a white slip of a dress that accentuates her massive breasts and a diamond choker around her slim neck.

Hmm. If he offers her up, I don't care what the Belgian says. I'm saying yes. She'd look absolutely ravishing on all fours, wearing nothing but that necklace with my dick down her throat.

While the rest of them watch, of course.

Especially *her*.

My wife.

Her red dress is now flanked by my brothers, and it feels like sharpened fingernails against the inside of my chest.

Yes. Another woman is what I need. Preferably, a few of them at once. That would teach the one and only Mrs. Enzo D'Angelo not to fuck with me. Dangling a skimpy red dress in front of an outraged bull . . . She gets what she gets.

God, stop thinking of her.

The dealer deals me another card, and it looks like I've just been dealt my winning hand. A smile tugs at my lips. I toss out another pile of chips. "Raise."

"I'm out," says His Royal Highness, angrily tossing his cards onto the table.

Pussy.

"Me, too," the tech guy says.

I pass a glance at the virginal, wide-eyed beauty standing behind him.

Pity.

The Belgian twirls the edge of his mustache, deep in thought. Slowly, he nods to the attendant, who presents a solid gold chip with the imprint of a jet on it.

Considering I'm pretty sure his hand consists of at least one numbered card—probably a three—I nearly come on the spot at the thought of his jet being mine.

Or maybe it's my *Bella's* hand sliding across my shoulder. She's asking for a punishment.

She's about to have that red fucking dress ripped off her and have her soft skin and toned body slammed up against the nearest wall until she's begging for mercy and finally realizes once and for all who's boss.

I am.

And all I need is to hear her say so while I'm driving into that sweet, tight body of hers.

One last good fuck is exactly what I need. To fuck her out of my system.

For good.

Ever the cock blocker, Uncle Andre clears his throat, snapping me from my millionth fantasy of her today.

I cast a wary glance at him as he pretends to thoroughly inspect his cards . . . as if the past three minutes have magically changed his hand. I raise a brow. "Well?"

With feigned nonchalance, he taps his cards on the table before shoving his stack of chips into the center.

A smirk graces my lips. "You seem to be a bit short." Like the rest of all five-foot-three of him.

"Not exactly." Andre's meaty hand slaps an envelope onto the table.

The chips lose all their luster against the crisp parchment pouch.

It's about goddamned time. I kick around his request. "How many?"

"Just one," he says, eagerly adding, "You'll like her in this pose. It's one of my favorites."

I study my hand carefully, my face a mask of composure. Any allegiance I had to my father's brother died so long ago that I don't remember it at all.

Briefly, I consider lighting the envelope on fire and shoving it up his ass. I know nobody here would waste a drop of sweat, spit, or piss to put it out.

As if reading my mind, he adds, "*Your* new favorite."

I love dirty secrets. They make the best leverage. Too bad this time the secrets are *Bella's,* and the leverage is my life.

Before I can stop myself, I hold the envelope up to the light, the shadow of its contents a subtle threat to my composure.

With a calculated move, I secure the envelope in my breast pocket. "Consider this one a gift. But if I win, I get them all. Every last one."

Uncle Andre takes a sip of his aged whiskey, his grin souring as he speaks. "Fine. And if I win, you owe me."

I owe *him?* The words grate against my skin like sandpaper on an open wound. I know why he wants this. I'm the biggest thorn in his side, and he wants a blank check. Me, with an electric leash around my neck.

So be it. Anything for my wife. But I won't make it easy.

My Belgian friend silently folds and pats me on the shoulder. He's bowing out because he's smart enough to know better than to tiptoe across a D'Angelo family squabble—and the line of fire of an all-out war.

Losing patience by the breath, I snap. "I'm not sliding my neck into the guillotine to try it on for size. Name your price now for every last photo, or fold."

His fat fingers snap for an attendant, who places a pad of paper and pen in his hand. My uncle scrawls his demand on the sheet of paper, folds it up, and sets it on the pile.

As soon as I reach for it, his hand slams hard against mine. "I wrote it down. My price. We play out the hand before you look." He leans in, taunting me with his tone. "It's called gambling for a reason."

The thing is, people think I'm reckless. But I'm calculated. Every step. Every angle. Strategic moves executed with patience and precision.

But with my wife here, I'm distracted. I can never concentrate when every curve of her is blocking my view of the chessboard Uncle Andre has laid at my feet.

I tap an annoyed finger on the table and scan the room.

My brothers want peace.

My uncle wants me under his thumb.

And my wife? Well, she wants me dead.

But first things first. I want something, too. And I want it so badly that I'm willing to trade anything for it. My sanity. My soul. My life.

"Enzo," she cajoles softly. But I can't hear her.

All I hear is the sound of blood raging in my ears.

I focus all my attention on Uncle Andre. *You want me, motherfucker? Then let's do this.* In a rush of adrenaline, I go with my gut. I flip over all my cards and slam them down. "Call."

He does the same, and my face falls as soon as I see his hand. *Fuck.*

Chapter Forty-One
ENZO

Four.

Fuuuckkk.

Granted, in the grand scheme of things, he could've written anything down. Ten. Twenty. A hundred.

Note to self: when blinded by rage, don't gamble on the number of men you'll be fighting in a goddamn MMA match.

With a deep exhale, I pour another glass of Macallan 72, letting it slosh over the sides before tossing it back. It's roughly the price of a Mercedes, but damn, it does wonders for taking the edge off.

A series of light knocks taps the door. "Go away!" I bark. When that's followed by a thunderous round of loud ones, I get more direct. "Fuck. Off."

Don't they know I'm about to go balls-to-the-wall with four freakishly big men, and I don't need to see them? What I need is to pass out and get my beauty rest.

And I definitely don't want to see her.

It was bad enough that *Bella* left me, but for him? She's

been shacking up at Knox's place all this time, and to add insult to injury, she didn't even take Titan.

It's a big, fat, fist-sized dildo slap in the face. So, back to my original statement.

I. Don't. Want. To. See. Her.

I also don't want her to see me die, so there's that.

"Open the door," Smoke calls out.

"Please, Enzo," Kennedy says, her voice all sweet and innocent. I've seen her take my cock. That girl is definitely not innocent. No, sir.

"Do not make us break it down," Dante warns.

"I'd like to see you try, fuckers!"

And because wishes really do come true, they break down the door to my suite and saunter in, smiling and unapologetic.

Dillon takes my drink like the jerk he is. "I think you've had enough."

"Well, I haven't. You want to know when it'll be enough? When those four fuckers are pounding on me tomorrow like I'm a chicken cutlet, and I feel absolutely nothing." I snatch the glass back, downing it in one go, then slump against the wall.

Andre has won. And the thought of that eats me from the inside out like flesh-eating beetles.

"Can I have a word with my husband?" the angelic voice says. Her words are soft and sweet—a siren's song—and her perfect mouth is all I want right now.

But having her here, witnessing what's about to go down—my inevitable death—is too much, even for me.

I grab Dante by the collar with both hands. "Get her out of here."

"Make me," he dares, stubborn as all shit.

I pull back my arm, ready to throw a punch, but his knee grazes my balls just enough to make me see stars. The next thing I know, I'm on the ground, wincing in agony. "You're dead," I growl.

"Tough talk coming from a guy eating carpet."

The next thing I know, I'm being hoisted into the air and dropped onto the bed, the dizzying effect nearly making me hurl.

"We'll be outside," Dillon says.

When her soft body curls up next to mine, I resist. Correction, I *try* to resist. My dick is all in. "Go run to Knox."

She slides down one spaghetti strap, achingly slow, exposing one luscious tit, and then another. "I don't want to run to Knox."

She hikes up her dress and straddles me as I prop myself up on my elbows, defiant. "You need to go." Because if we do this tonight, there's no way I'm leaving her in the morning.

So, I crack open my heart. The gloves come off. "I'll be dead tomorrow, Kennedy. You need to leave."

Her full lips pout as she undoes my pants. "How would you rather die, Mr. D'Angelo? By four men in a cage, or me, slowly fucking you to death?"

Is this a trick question?

She knows exactly what she's doing with that raspy voice of hers, calling me Mr. D'Angelo and all.

But enough is enough. Playtime's over. No more Mr. Nice Guy.

I throw her onto her back, flipping her so fast she gasps. "*Bella*, I won't tell you again. I. Don't. Want. You. Here."

"Why not?" she purrs, playing with my tie.

This woman. She frustrates me. She antagonizes me.

She shatters me.

Her father's death is on my hands, his blood. I've hurt her enough. If she has any feelings left for me, I need to destroy them all.

Otherwise, Kennedy will stay. Like her father before her, she'll try to save me. Then my wife will watch me die.

Her father's death changed me forever. It killed all the parts of me that mattered.

And I can't let that happen to my *Bella*. Not now. Not ever.

"I killed your father," I wrench out.

There's a long pause before her hands cradle my cheeks, her kisses so soft there might actually be poison in her lipstick.

Which, of all the ways I can think to die, would be perfect. Other than Option A, of her slowly fucking me to death, of course.

"You didn't kill *Da*," she whispers against my mouth. "He sacrificed himself. To save you."

At this point, she's teary, and I am, too. A drunken flood of emotions slams into me with such force, I know what I have to do.

Finally, I say the one thing that I know will drive her away from me. For good.

"I don't want you here, Kennedy. Because I don't want you."

Chapter Forty-Two
KENNEDY

HE SAID it with his own two lips. "*I don't want you.*"

It was so, God, I don't know... cute. Heroic.

But the thing is, I know exactly what Enzo is doing. His carefully constructed plans are all so crystal clear.

So, I let him say it.

Just before I undo his pants and tear off the rest of his clothes.

His golden eyes stare up at me, beautiful and blank. "I said I don't want you."

"I heard you," I whisper against his chest, my lips trace down the line of his abs, savoring every ripple until I reach that tantalizing patch of happy trail.

With deliberate slowness, I take a long lick of his gorgeous dick.

He hisses, words strangled in his throat. "Goddamn it, *Bella*, I don't want to hurt you."

But that's when his actions betray him. He grips both sides

of my head, and with raw need, thrusts his cock deep into my throat.

Enzo is right. I know him better than anyone. Even better than himself. And this—all of this—is him.

Unhinged and out of control, he's like this only with me. Every moan, our melody. Every touch, a match strike on kerosene, white-hot and potent.

He needs me, and I need him just like this. The villain, fucking my mouth, forcing himself deeper, telling me what a filthy, dirty girl I am.

He tears my clothes to shreds, rips off my panties, climbs on top of me and shoves himself deep—*thrusting, thrusting, thrusting*—until my legs are forced wide and I'm taking him to the hilt. I know I'll never get enough.

I crave every part of Enzo. The chaos. The fire. The rage. And every inch of him that threatens to tear me apart.

Because Enzo Ares D'Angelo is my husband, and while he may have claimed me, make no mistake—from his beautiful heart to his goddamned gorgeous dick—I've claimed every piece of him right back.

The god of war is mine. And no one and nothing will take him from me. Not his manipulative uncle, not four thugs in a cage. Not even himself.

Because I'm a Mullvain.

A Mullvain saved him once—my *Da*. And a Mullvain is about to save him again.

Enzo finishes reading to the girls, his voice morphing into so many characters I'm convinced he's been secretly taking acting lessons. "When are you coming home?" Sofia asks, her pouty lips trembling.

Enzo's face goes ghostly pale, but before he can say a word, I jump in. "Soon. Very, very soon." We say our goodnights and the girls disconnect. Regret etches itself into every line of his features. I kiss him and say, "I know what you need."

Then, I grab a stack of photos and hand them to him. His expression hardens instantly. "Burn those," he orders.

"Look at them," I insist. "Figure out what's wrong with them."

"Other than they're seriously fucked up?"

"Just do it."

After twenty minutes, he tosses his hands back and gives up. "I need a clue."

I show him another picture. Upside down this time to see if that helps. "Better?"

"Perhaps if I were Picasso."

Reluctantly, he examines another one as we feed each other ice cream. I force him through it, picture after picture. None of these are overly suggestive, but they all have the same glaring error.

When I hand him the next one, he refuses. "Enzo, I promised you that none of these photos can ever hurt me."

He puffs out a breath. "One hint," he insists.

I smile and move my lips to his ear, feeling his arms wrap

tightly around me. I whisper the hint, the clue that's been right in front of his face all along. "*Da*'s last words."

It takes a minute, but when his mouth curves into a slow, knowing smile, I know he gets it. He doesn't say it. He doesn't have to.

Da's words are with us both.

She's my heart.

Chapter Forty-Three
ENZO

AFTER A STROLL through a metal detector and satisfying pat down, we march into the fray. The crowd is amped up, their roar like a war cry. Each of my brothers moves into position while I size up my opponents.

Yup. Four fucking tanks. From Uncle Andre, I'd expect no less.

Uncle Andre steps over to me as I'm about to enter the cage. "Don't fall too fast. I've got eight figures on this game. Nine if you can last at least twenty minutes." He chuckles. "And your bet?"

I smirk. "Ooh, I'm betting that when this is all over, the look on your face will be like you've been fucked up the ass with a battering ram." The words wipe the smug grin right off his face. "Will you be up in VIP?"

The VIP box at the top has everything he needs. Booze. Coke. Bullet-proof glass.

But it's not him I'm taking down today. It's this entire fucking game.

I step into the cage. The door clangs shut behind me.

Just before the buzzer goes off, Diaz pipes my mic into the system, and my earpiece transmits everything I say. "Ladies and gentlemen, can I have your attention?"

The feral crowd quiets, a ripple of confusion spreading through them.

My uncle's frown deepens.

"The game is permanently ended."

Curious murmurs ripple through the crowd, quickly followed by boos and jeers. Someone even throws a piece of meat at me. What is that? Wagyu?

Seriously?

One of the human tanks cracks his neck, a grin spreading across his face. "And here I thought this would be a challenge."

I blow out a breath, rolling my eyes. "Trust me, we're all disappointed."

I motion to my brothers who are all in position.

Since I first stepped into this ring at the age of fifteen, things have changed. Enormous monitors now line the walls, and my uncle's sniper team has expanded from two to four.

Their rifles are trained on me, while my brothers' weapons are locked on them.

"Now," I say.

Four shots ring out, and for a moment, the crowd roars, thinking the bloodbath has begun. But then they see me, still standing and very much alive.

Then, panic sets in. Like privileged rats fleeing a sinking ship, they scatter, a flash of diamonds and the clicks of designer shoes as they scramble over each other and run for their worthless lives.

I step forward and, with surgical precision, blow a kneecap off each of the men caged with me. I want them alive, to set an example.

"You brought...a...gun..." Tank A groans, writhing on the ground in agony.

"Yup, sure did," I say, smirking. "Not sure why I didn't think of it before."

"How—?" Tank B chokes out, his voice a strangled mix between a gasp and a squirrel lodged in his throat.

And he's right to ask.

Guns are strictly prohibited, except by my uncle, of course. They tend to end the match too quickly, like a turkey shoot in a barrel. Hence the reason for the thorough and somewhat intrusive body search.

My pat down was about halfway through when I shoved a knife into the guy's throat. I could've gone for the gut, but he was about to scream for help, and I was crunched for time.

Very, very satisfying.

"Metal detectors..." one of them mutters.

"Oh, you know what I did with the metal detectors? I unplugged them! So, yeah, I have a gun," I say patronizingly as I wave my gun in the air.

I look at the crowd, who for the most part have vacated. Though a few idiots are still taking bets.

My eyes land on Andre, perched high in his VIP tower as I wave. "You're next, asshole."

Angrily, he holds up more photos, as if he has an endless supply. Now, I know exactly what that bastard did. He showed our father pictures of Trinity, which is what pushed him to start talking to the Feds.

When Tank C or D—honestly, who's keeping track—summons what's left of his strength to grab at my leg, I shoot him in the head.

It's like they never learn. Rock beats scissors. Scissors beat paper. Bullet beats dumbass. How tough is this to grasp?

Uncle Andre starts banging on the glass from his ivory, bulletproof-tower, brandishing his handful of incriminating photos. I look back up. "Oh, you mean like these?" I grab my own handful from my back pocket and flash them right back.

The thing is, family will never scrutinize lewd photographs of someone they love. Anyone with a conscience and a heart wouldn't. That's why I didn't see it. Nobody did.

Kennedy's heart.

The delicate heart-shaped freckle along the soft curve of her neck. The one she's had since birth.

A digital photo would've been too easy to detect it—closer looks at pixels and shit. But fake photographs, printed in a dingy basement and manipulated with ancient fucking film, that's a different story. The more yellow and blurry, the more authentic they seem. But it was an illusion.

It wasn't Kennedy. It never was. And it wasn't Trinity. Just their faces slapped onto the bodies of real victims. Girls and women I vow to spend the rest of my life avenging.

My voice lowers, deadly calm. "Let me be clear. If I see another fake photo of Kennedy or Trinity or any other member of my family, the rest of your operations will go up in flames, just like this one."

He flips me off, and I smile. "I suggest you and anyone else who wants to live get the fuck out of here. I've got enough C-4 strapped to this place to send it to space, and it detonates in"—I check my watch—"twenty minutes."

My *Bella* reminded me who I really am. Not some sap who enjoys long walks in the woods and candlelit dinners.

Into vanilla? Move it along.

I'm Enzo fucking D'Angelo, and for the woman of my dreams, I'll blow up the world.

Epilogue One
ENZO

"Don't be nervous," she says, looking me dead in the eye like the total boss that she is.

Sofia. My *diavoletta*.

I straighten my tie. "I'm not nervous," I insist. But who am I kidding? I couldn't be more nervous if I was the one actually giving birth.

The door creaks open, and I swallow the lump in my throat. "Well?"

Kennedy, my beautiful wife, grins widely. "Soon."

In three months, my old life has faded into a blur, replaced by this whirlwind of sticky chaos that drives me to the brink of sanity and well beyond. Half the time I'm a ruthless tyrant hell-bent on torture, and the other half, I'm a walking, breathing teddy bear, doling out hugs.

Oh, don't get me wrong. I still relish the thrill of showing a scumbag what pain really means, whether it's with car battery clamps or something more creative.

There's a certain satisfaction in sensory deprivation and

ripping off fingernails that ignites something deep within me—every single day. The silent terror in their eyes, the way their minds unravel under the weight of darkness and isolation—it feeds my soul in ways nothing else can.

With my psychological framework, it's a miracle that Sin was able to make the adoption go through.

But when Sofie and Lili took Truffles for a walk and came back with a second dog—a little cinnamon-chocolate mix-a-poo they immediately fell in love with and already named—I knew I was done for.

Cocoa.

They named the floppy-eared girl pup Cocoa. Cocoa and Truffles. How could I say no? Seriously, I'm asking. It was like my heart banished the word from my vocabulary.

And even when I mustered the physical strength to utter that dreaded two-letter word, my little *angioletta* Lili hit me with those big, sad eyes and prayer hands. She actually said, "Please, Papa."

Papa. It was the first time either of them had said it, and let's be real, I'd have a better chance standing my ground against a fucking cattle prod.

I choked back the tears, trying to keep it together, and sniffled out a squeaky, "Yes." I swear, my heart does all kinds of shit it never did before.

They cry, and it squeezes. They fall, and it feels like it's going to explode in my chest. And don't even get me started on when they smile at me. It's like getting skewers to the heart, one after the other.

So, in just a few months, the family I never anticipated in a million years has grown. Truffles and Cocoa became instantly inseparable, and now we're expecting another addition because Cocoa is pregnant.

"Have you picked out names?" Smoke asks the girls while his wife, Katarina, and Dory prepare a feast in the kitchen.

Sofie thoughtfully says, "Mascarpone."

Lili cries out, "Cannoli!"

"Only two?" Sin asks.

I jump in with a little context. "Unlike big dogs, a half-pounder like Cocoa might only have one or two buns in the oven."

"You look blue, bro," Dante says, slapping me on the shoulder. "Maybe you should try some Lamaze breathing. *Hee-hee-hee-hoooo.*"

I glare at him. "Do not make me kill you in front of the girls."

Dillon hands me a glass of champagne and glances around at the blue and pink balloons and streamers. "Are we seriously having a baby shower for a dog?"

Mateo shakes his head. "It's the Trinity years all over again." He looks around. "Where is she?"

Sin smiles. "Father Marc drove her to the airport. They're picking up Leo, Ivy, and their brood."

I chime in, "It's the first time their tribe meets ours. Z's kids will meet Sofie and Lili, and everyone is excited. We've got tents set up out back, and I'll be arm wrestling Leo to see who gets to read to them all."

Smoke chuckles. "Just so we're clear, I have no intentions of patting either of you down. So, no weapons."

Suddenly, Sofia wraps both hands around my leg and growls up at "Uncle" Smoke. I'm not sure what that's all about, but I kiss her head, knowing this will make for an interesting first day of school.

Then my wife reemerges, radiant and glowing. "We have puppies!" she announces, all smiles and a little weepy.

We all file in, the girls first, then the rest of us. I'm last because I need a few minutes alone with my *Bella* to make sure she's all right.

Before I even ask, she's already nodding, reading the concern etched on my face. "I'm fine. Just emotional."

My hand automatically finds her belly, and she looks at me lovingly. I kiss her lips, losing myself in this woman the way I always have. Since the first moment I laid eyes on her, a spark of want and possession ignited so deep, it could only be love.

Machiavelli once said it is safer to be feared than loved, but only if you cannot have both. For all my life before Kennedy, I ruled by fear. But now, with a growing family and this woman who brings me to my knees by my side, I choose both.

"What's with you two?" Dante asks, taking a breather from snapping photos and makes his way over, smiling as he notices my hand around Kennedy's belly.

"Nothing," we both say in unison. Innocently, though, I don't move my hand. That wish is too fragile and precious to voice out loud, so for now, it remains a quiet secret between us.

But I suspect my *Bella* will be right behind Katarina in the baby parade. The cat's already out of the bag on that one, and she's just starting to show.

"I took a ton of pics for Riley," Kennedy says hopefully. It's been a difficult time. Riley's not ready to talk to anyone about her sister marrying me—the man responsible for her father's death—and from her point of view, we understand. Still, it's been months.

I kiss her lips. "Give it time. She'll come around," I assure *Bella*.

She better. Kennedy has no idea the surprise I have in store for her: a baby moon in Elafonisi Beach with the kids, the dogs, and her sister. A trip which is currently on hold until Riley returns.

My *Bella* nods and shifts her attention to the girls, joining them as the laughter of two little girls fills the room.

The moment she's out of earshot, my demeanor hardens. "You're taking care of it?" I ask in a low voice. Riley missed the adoption. If she misses the birth of our child, it would devastate my *Bella*, and that's not happening.

Dante nods. "It's handled." The situation is delicate, and I know it. It took Trinity four years to speak after her attack. Patience is my strong suit. As a family man and a torturer, it's a trait that serves me well.

My brother, though, not so much. People mistake his smile for being easygoing. If only they knew.

Get on Dante's bad side, and he makes my temper and thirst for blood look like a domesticated pussycat.

I pat Dante's shoulder. Weeks ago, I told him to handle it, and I know he will. "Your assurance is all I need. I trust you implicitly."

Bella waves me over, and I join them, staring down at the infant pups, which look like strange little wriggling potatoes.

"Aren't they perfect, Papa?" Lili asks.

I brush the curls from her face. "Not as perfect as you and your sister, but they're a close second."

Kennedy looks up at me, and I see the glint in her eyes—the fire. In a few short hours, I know that one of us will be in total control while the other will be tied up and slowly tortured for hours.

A slow grin spreads across my face. Who'll be begging for mercy? I haven't got a goddamned clue.

Hate sex with Kennedy is heaven. But her like this—supercharged on hormones and eager to please—it's like having my entire body doused in kerosene and set on fire. It's so next-level, so beyond anything I've ever felt or experienced...

My addiction for life.

"She's my heart." Mullvain's words echo from the back of my mind.

And with a shaky breath, I respond to thin air, the way I always do. "Yes. And she's my heart, too."

Epilogue Two
DANTE

I TRUST YOU IMPLICITLY.

Is Enzo fucking kidding me?

I run a club with a taste for the dark and depraved. Who would trust me?

I'm pretty sure my brother will have my balls in a vise if he even begins to suspect all the ways I want to punish this little petulant child for every last one of her sins.

From the rich leather seat in the private room at my bar, I shake my head. Who hands a bunny to a wolf and says, "Take care of it?"

When she strides into my lair, auditioning to be a dancer, I warn her off. But when she protests, burning with defiance, I open the door and show her in.

Silly Feds . . . thinking they could keep her safe. I'm more dangerous than any man she's known. And now, she's in my domain.

My club. My rules.

Still, the situation is delicate. The girl has Handle With Care tattooed all over her incredible body—so much so that it's taking every last ounce of my strength to stay in control.

But if the girl wants a high-paying job with ironclad guarantees no one will find her, done. Because I want something too. And it all begins with locking her into a binding contract with a few small rules.

Rule One: Tell no one.
Rule Two: I select her outfit, complete with a blindfold.
Rule Three: No other men in her life.

Why the blindfold? Call it a little trust exercise. For us both. That and clients enjoy a certain amount of anonymity.

Why Rule Three? Because I'm a possessive prick, and that Fed Knox is already on my last nerve.

And if she breaks the rules? I sip my single malt, a smirk playing on my lips. Let's just say little girls shouldn't break rules. Yet every inch of me thrums with the certainty that she will.

God, even from here, Riley smells like heaven and moves like hell. Sin wrapped in the body of an angel, innocent and broken and definitely more trouble than I need. Unconditionally off-limits. Irresistibly forbidden.

She's young. So fucking young that my mind spins with a million different ways to *"take care of it."*

The devil on my shoulder smirks. *You're goddamned right, I'll take care of it.*

I rub my chin and study her, the way her body sways in perfect rhythm to the slow, sad ballad. My newest obsession is marked off with bright yellow Do Not Enter tape. But as long as I just look with my eyes, no harm, right?

I let the whiskey burn a line down my throat, exhaling as I tally up all the ways I'm damned. Because if she stays, deep down, I know it's not a question of *if* Riley will be ruined. It's *when*.

The music dies down. Her shiver is a mix of nerves and discomfort in what's probably the tightest outfit she owns. "Well?" she asks, biting her full lower lip as she crosses her arms.

"Well, what?"

She yanks off the blindfold, eyes blazing with bravado. "I have the job, right?" Her wide, innocent eyes lock onto mine, her voice quivering just enough to betray an intoxicating mix of hope and fear.

And she's right to be afraid.

What sweet, little Riley fails to realize is the job has been hers from the second she stepped inside.

And she has only one client.

Me.

Thank you for reading *SINS & Temptation*, the last book in the trilogy! I hope you loved Enzo and Kennedy.

Grab more books in the series today!

The *SINS* Series in order:

SINS of the Syndicate

SINS & Ivy
SINS: The Debt

SINS: The Deal
SINS & Lies
>> **SINS & Temptation**

Coming in 2025
SINS: The Contract
Preorder at All Retailers NOW>>

NEED ANOTHER ANGSTY ROMANCE? TRY OUT THE Boys of Bishop Mountain!
1-CLICK>> MARKED

Eight years ago I nearly died.
And it wasn't that I didn't remember her.
I didn't recognize her. There's a difference.

She was a kid.
And I was a soldier . . .
Two seconds from deploying with her brother for our third, and final, tour.
One I wasn't sure I'd be coming back from.

She thinks I don't remember.

That kiss was beautiful. Innocent.
It kept me alive when I thought it might be my last.
How could I ever forget?

So, shove me off all you want, country girl.
Because you've just landed in my sights,
And you're about to be mine.

1-CLICK>> MARKED
KEEP GOING FOR A SNEAK PEEK >>

READY FOR ALEX DRAKE AND HIS OBSESSION, Madison?

1 billionaire.
1 month.
1 bed.

Get The Alex Drake Collection Now>

★★★★★ *"What a fabulously sexy hot read!!!"* Top 40 Goodreads Reviewer

★★★★★ *"Talk about heat!! 5 Burning Stars!!!"* Amazon Reviewer

Join Lexxi's VIP reader list to be the first to know of new releases, free books, special prices, and other giveaways!

Free hot romances & happily ever afters delivered to your inbox.
https://www.lexxijames.com/freebies

Marked

BOYS OF BISHOP MOUNTAIN

Chapter One
JESS

HAVE you ever believed that if you wished for something hard enough, you could make it happen?

I did. It all started when my mom used to say, "Never underestimate the power of a wish." Then she'd hold the fluffy-white dandelion in front of me as my cheeks puffed with air. "Blow, baby girl!"

And I would. Wasting a universe of wishes with reckless abandon on books, candy, and toys. It's like slots for toddlers: The more you wish, the more chances you have of one of those wishes coming true.

It took a few years before I got serious. Doubled-down on just one wish. What was it Hannibal Lecter said? We covet what we see every day? Who knew the words of a fictional psychopath could ring so true?

And see Mark Donovan, I did.

My brother's best friend. Yeah, try not seeing him. Dark, carefree waves that melted down to eyes that changed with his mood. Golden caramel at his happiest. Moody winter green when he was brooding.

He was it. My first big wish. My first epic fail.

Every night for a month, I wished I would grow up to marry him. And then I did the unthinkable. With my little-girl outside voice, I said it. "I am going to marry you." Said it straight to his beautiful boy face.

Considering I was six and he was twelve, it went over like a loud fart in a packed church. What started with a wince morphed into uncontrollable laughter, culminating in Mark doubling over on the floor.

Oh, that last part wasn't from laughter. It was from my angry little-girl fist jabbing a full-force punch square at his balls.

This cautionary tale taught me two things. First, boys apparently can't breathe without their balls. And second, wishes aren't meant to be trite or trivial. If only a few wishes are meant to come true, make each one precious. Make them count.

When my dear, sweet parents made their way to heaven—a pain so raw, it hurt just to breathe—I had faith. For every dandelion I plucked, I wished messages could make their way up through the clouds, delivered by the wind.

I wished Nana Winnie was as happy as a lark, cutting out crazy patterns for her latest quilt. I wished our old Labrador retriever, Saint, was with them, running fast and free to catch a Frisbee from my dad. I wished every time I sang to the clouds, my mom could feel the love I poured into every note. Knew how much I missed her. Missed them all.

When my brothers moved away, lured by the military, I

wished them back. Brian showed up the next day, the Rock of Gibraltar by my side ever since.

How? I have no idea. Considering he's a sniper at the beck and call of the Army, I can't imagine how he worked that out. But we both knew it couldn't last forever, and the lifeline he cast me was beginning to strain.

In five short days, he returns to the other side of the world, and the last thing he needs to worry about is me.

So, today's dandelion is for a job. Not just any job. Just a small promotion that keeps the lights on and cements me in place, home on Bishop Mountain.

On my day off, and armed with the fluffiest dandelion I could find, I close my eyes and imagine my mom holding it out. My small smile makes way to a gust of breath. I blow all my fears and doubts away, letting the feather-soft wisps fly free on a breeze.

One wish. One shot. And one man who can make it all happen.

Chapter Two

JESS

"Have you seen Tyler?" I ask, standing a respectable distance from the customer side of the bar.

Anita frowns as she side-eyes me while flipping a shaker with finesse. "I thought you were off."

I shrug. "I am." Though I have no idea why. I pause for a beat. "But I wanted to pick up my check." I can't help my envious stare at her nametag. ANITA MAE, BARTENDER.

She nods, her smile knowing. "And call dibs on my job?"

I scrunch up my face. "Too obvious?"

"Uh, it's called initiative. You're a Bishop. I'd expect nothing less." She notices the space I've created between me and the bar. Bartending in the great state of New York at eighteen? Totally legit. Taste-testing even one drop of alcohol? Not so much.

And as I am the last of the Bishop children to work in this establishment, let's just say I don't want to be the one to eff it all up with the liquor authority.

"You're not a kid anymore, Jess. Step on up!"

Proudly, I do. With a lighter, she demonstrates a technique called *flaming an orange peel*. With the strike of a match and the flick of her fingers, a fireball showers the drink, then vanishes behind a small trail of smoke.

"Doesn't that burn?" I ask.

She shakes her head. "You're not really lighting the peel as much as spraying the orange oil against the flame into the glass." She walks me slowly through the motions. "See?"

I nod. Rumor is, her promotion is in the bag, which leaves her job up for grabs. It's a long shot, but I've been practicing. Thank God for YouTube.

She peers over thick-framed glasses. "Master this trick. People eat it up, and the tips flow like water." She gestures grandly to the wall of liquor and art-deco accents. "This will all be yours someday."

Fascinated, I glance around. "There's so much to learn."

She tosses a small notebook on the glossy wood. "Here. You want the job? Memorize this."

Flipping through, I realize it has to be fifty pages of customized cocktails from the *Adirondack Sunset* to *Donovan's Deadly Twist*. But when my gaze hits *Bishop's Breeze*, I pause, and my eyes well up. I expected it to be a drink created by Brian, Rex, or Cade—any one of my brothers—but it's not. It was written by Henry.

Henry James Bishop, my father. My fingers skim across the page as I inhale pride and exhale sadness. Vodka. Lemon. Honey. Club soda with a splash of Moscato. I choke up. I can almost see him making it for mom.

Anita's warm hand covers mine. "Anything I can do?"

Rewind time. Stop them from getting in that car.

"No," I say softly. *Not unless you can bring my parents back.* It takes a breath before the pain subsides and a few blinks to dislodge an annoyingly stubborn tear.

"Lunch?" she says kindly.

I decline with a hopeful grin. "Rain check?" Considering I'm blowing all my money on my gift for Brian, I will absolutely take a free lunch IOU.

Sharp, jabbing pains erupt in the lowest point of my gut. *Not now.* I suck in a breath to stave it off. A hard pinch comes again, a tight twist. I hug both arms against my belly, wrestling the pain away, grateful that Anita's too busy to notice.

"Hmm . . ." She fills a thick glass mug with whatever's on tap. "Tyler?"

She thinks for a moment while I try not to double over in pain. Or cry out "*Mercy*" to the gods of pain.

Month after month, my periods are ten times worse, and over-the-counter medications are barely making a dent. With any luck, the extra-extra-strength medication I got at the drugstore will kick in any second now.

While I bite my lip like a bullet, Anita ponders on. "Tyler . . ."

Maybe it's the repeated knife jabs to the gut talking, but if one more person says they haven't seen Tyler Donovan, I'll throw down like a toddler. I'm two seconds from unceremoniously face-planting onto the questionably clean floor, arms and legs flailing about in full-on meltdown mode.

Anita sets a pink-and-purple drink at the pickup station and a mug of beer next to it before sliding her glasses to the tip of her nose.

"So, you have to see Tyler?" she sings suggestively. Or hopefully. I swear, the woman is vying for the official title of Cupid.

The knife jab below the belly subsides to a dull ache enough for me to play along. "Obviously, because Tyler knows how to make a girl truly happy."

She gives me the hairy eyeball. "You're lucky you're legal," she says, smirking as she waggles her brows.

"All I need is a few minutes alone with him. Just me and Tyler so he can"—I deadpan— "pay me." I lower my voice and clasp my hands in prayer. "And pitch him a dozen reasons for why I'd be perfect for your job."

By her outrageous yawn, she's underwhelmed. "Boring." She leans in confidentially. "Moment of truth . . . which one?"

"Which one what?"

"Which one of the Donovans melts your butter?"

Which? How can she ask me that? I mean, they're all friends with my brothers. *Which* makes it weird.

Wide-eyed, Anita smiles expectantly as I think it through. Anything to take my mind off the pain, though it's eased up enough that I'm no longer tasting blood from my lower lip.

Ignoring my childhood faux pas of a wish, I run through the list.

There's Tyler, who's inherently sexy because he has my paycheck. He's the older, wiser, kinder of the Donovan brothers. His sandy-blond waves are always as carefree as his soul, and his twenty-seven-year-old smile warms you from the inside out. One day in the not-too-distant future, this business will be his kingdom, an attractive quality that the vagina of every eligible bachelorette in the tri-county region has zeroed in on.

Hunk-worthiness? A ten and a half. On the date-worthy

scale, I can't even go there. He's almost paternal. Or a really hot uncle you hope will find his forever match. Whenever I come in, he's always checking to see how I'm doing and if I've eaten. Thanks to this place, I have.

Then there's Zac, the youngest and three years older than me. A young McDreamy in his own right; his looks are totally wasted. The man has been my BFF since forever ago, but he never dates. Between studying at New York University and launching his own mogul career, you'd think the man was thirty-one, not twenty-one.

Over summers and holiday breaks, he returns to Saratoga Springs to shake things up. Moving the inventory system from the caveman era into the next millennium. Shifting the ordering to the cloud and ensuring it takes everything from Venmo to Bitcoin. And launching a spruced-up website with candid shots that always manage to blow up Instagram, which he often credits me for.

Every chance I get, I snap outrageous photos and videos, and at Zac's insistence, they've posted every single one. Food photos. Tyler clowning around, serving a bachelorette party in nothing but a black apron. Well, he had shorts on, but you couldn't tell from the front. Even simple things like Anita plopping dry ice into drinks at Halloween.

Zac says I have raw talent. I call it an obsession with Mrs. D.'s food.

Zac will forever be my biggest cheerleader and best friend, but something more? Let's just say our one and only test-the-waters kiss was all we needed to be eternally friend-zoned. Plus, I'm not sure he'll ever settle down. Core-of-the-Earth-level hotness? A thousand percent. A compulsive workaholic? Ten-thousand percent.

And last, but not least, there's Mark. The very same Marcus Evan Donavon my child mind thought I could marry. Silly girl. I couldn't possibly marry an ass, and make no mistake, that man is an ass.

As if reading my thoughts, Anita asks, "Ooh, is it Mark?"

Heat flares up my neck to my cheeks as I scoff. "Mark? Mark hates me."

"He does not."

"He even gave me that stupid nickname."

Anita coos at me. "It's adorable."

My palm is affronted before I am, and it flies in her face. "Don't even."

Her hands raise in surrender as she smartly backs up a step. "Okay, okay. Just saying, he's not terrible on the eyes."

When Anita gets googly-eyed for Mark, I gag. She grabs a ticket and pulls a highball from the shelf to work on her next drink.

All I can think is...Mark? Really?

I mean, to look at, yes. Agreed. If Mark had a mute button, he'd be the perfect man. The problem with him—or rather, the biggest problem with him—is that his looks far overshadow his tiny, little pea-brain. That and his two-sizes too-small heart.

Have you ever seen a man too beautiful to exist? Sure, in and of itself, it's not a reason to hate him. What I hate is that Mark wields it like a weapon. Whenever he walks into a room, I feel the need to dispense chastity belts with reckless abandon.

Again, I'm not talking about your garden-variety good looks, as in he looks great in a pair of jeans with an insta-swoon dimple that could launch a thousand ships. I'm talking about a legs-locked, knees-weak, heart-stopping level of sex appeal that would stand out in a sea of Hemsworths. The irony is that with all that heat, Mark is too cold.

Anita pops the cork on a bottle of Moscato and works on a Bellini. "Well, if your heart's set on Tyler or Zac, you're SOL. I just remembered that Tyler isn't here. He and Zac went fishing with their dad before Zac returns to school."

I nibble my lower lip again, worry twisting my gut.

"Nope. Don't do that," Anita says, frowning.

"Huh? Do what?"

She waves an accusatory strawberry-margarita painted fingernail in my face. "That thing where your brows pinch so hard, they nearly touch. Trust me, you're too young to start with the permanent angry line." She wipes down the bar. "You worried about Brian leaving?"

"No," I lie, lifting a defiant chin. "Brian has been here long enough. Having him take care of me since my parents—"

My mouth dries, sand filling my throat before I can say the words. I breathe through it until words come out.

"Anyway, the military gave him all the leave they could. I'm an adult. I've graduated. I'm a big girl, and my brother's a big boy. We can take care of ourselves." I say this out loud at least a dozen times a day, because any day now, I'll believe it.

Anita places a bowl of mixed nuts between us and pops a few into her mouth. "Then what is it?"

Deflated, I sigh. "I have five days to get Brian his going-away gift before his deployment."

"That should be plenty of time."

"I need to be able to afford it first. It costs my entire paycheck."

She lifts a brow. "All of your paycheck?"

I nod. "Along with the engraving, yes. I caught him drooling at the jewelers over some stupid-expensive tactical watch. After an insane amount of searching, I found a pre-owned one, but I have to pick it up today. The owner already has other buyers." I'm about to show her on my phone, but my battery's already low, and I still need to use it to find this guy. Wiggling my fingers at her, I say, "Give me your phone."

Anita hands it to me, and I pull up the Laney Jewelers website, then scroll to the right photo. With a two-toned whistle, she approves.

I smile. "And then hopefully, I'll have time to get it engraved before Brian leaves."

"You mean Brian and Mark. What, no gift for his bestie?" she teases.

My lips quirk as my narrowed eyes respond for me.

"Hey, if push comes to shove, girl, I've got you." She holds up a paring knife. "Seriously, how hard can it be to scratch two Bs on the metal band?"

"What I had in mind is a little more than his initials, and this watch is worth weeks of my life," I say indignantly as I lower her knife-wielding hand. "As skilled as you are with slicing and dicing, how about we leave the pretty letter carving to the experts." I tap the counter, not sure what to do. "Who can I get my check from?"

"You can get it from Mark."

"What? Mark's here?" My brows pop up as the name of my

arch-nemesis rings through the air. Or is it just nemesis? "Mark never comes here. And why isn't he fishing with everyone else?"

Smiling, she shrugs. "Mrs. D.'s working out the details for the Whitney wedding. I guess he's filling in."

"Perfect." I let out a frustrated sigh. "Any idea where he is?" Anita shakes her head as I slide off the leather stool. "I guess I'll stop looking for Tyler and hunt down Mark."

"Hang on." She fishes cash from the tip jar and hands it to me.

Blinking, I stare at her. "What's this?"

Her hands grab mine, shoving the bills into it. "A bunch of tourists went all out at brunch. Take it. I don't want you not to have a paycheck. You'll be working this side of the bar soon enough."

Emotions overwhelm me as I stare down at the twenties, tens, and fives. This isn't just how Anita is. It's how everyone is here. Always looking out for me when I suspect it least and need it most. Everyone here cares for me. In return, I have to care for them back.

Counting it quickly, I split it right down the middle and toss half back in the jar. "Thanks," I say, rushing out of there before I'm a blubbering puddle in the middle of the floor.

Sternly, I wipe my cheeks and make my way down the hall. I can cry when I'm at home. That's what showers are for.

Scowling, I mutter under my breath. "Yoo-hoo . . . Satan. Come out, come out, wherever you are."

Where Tyler and Zac are wholesome goodness wrapped up in sunshine and smiles, Mark is the polar opposite, ready to fight, run, or fornicate at a moment's notice. His brothers are easygoing sails on tranquil waters, while Mark is a storm.

And those eyes. Shamefully, I've stared at them more than once.

Some men were meant to build castles while others were born to slay dragons. That's Mark. A hot-blooded fighting machine who can't turn it off. It's what makes him the best. And the broodiest.

When Brian entered the Army, Mark rushed in after him, besties since their stupid blood oath in the fifth grade. Seriously, how deep did they need to cut? They both required five stitches each. But that was them. Two beautiful idiots pridefully counting every last scar.

It's the reason why no matter how hard I try, I can't avoid Mark. Like my brother's shadow, he's always around. A personal tormentor, ready and eager to strike at will.

I pop my head into the break room. A few waitresses are eating a late lunch and gossiping about customers.

Gasping, Kara looks up at me. "I thought you were off," she says, offended at my very presence. "Tyler said you needed a personal day." Her eyes roll to a resentful stop. "Must be nice."

Why would Tyler tell them that? I ignore her, and not just because Kara's an ass, but because convincing Kara that Tyler is wrong would be as fruitful as convincing Mark I should be a bartender. There's no point. It'll never happen. But I still need to pick up my check. "Have either of you seen Mark?"

"Oh my God," Starr says as she whips back her pink hair. "Is Mark *Danger Zone* Donovan here?"

Kara claps and squeals like a seal, while I rub my temple, praying that the migraine she just spurred up goes away. High-pitched and hopeless, she carries on. "He's so lickable. I heard he now holds the record for the most confirmed kills."

Confused, I stare. "How does that make him hot?"

She smirks. "You wouldn't understand." She scans me up and down before dismissing me with her eyes. "You're too young."

"I'm only a year younger than you, Kara."

She scoops her breasts into her crossed arms, forcing cleavage that even her overstuffed push-up couldn't tackle. "There's a world of difference in a year."

Perhaps to a dog.

"Trust me," Starr says. "His brothers are princes, but Mark Donovan is a full-fledged demi-god." She licks her spoon suggestively. "I've got something that sharpshooter can aim at."

She sucks her finger, amplifying the point. I dry heave and leave the room. Only God knows where that finger's been.

Kara calls after me. "Tell him we're looking for him, too, okay?"

Their giggles echo wildly as I shake my head. *Sure. Why not? Because maybe if I offer two semi-virginal sacrifices to your demi-God, he'll give me that promotion I desperately need.*

"Jess?" I hear Mark say. His deep, gravelly voice flows effortlessly down the hall, though I don't see him.

As I approach his office, the door is ajar. I slide a hand on the handle, pausing as soon as I hear, "What about her?" Because Mark isn't talking to me, he's talking *about* me.

The door is cracked ever so slightly, an obvious invitation to listen in. His heavy footsteps move farther away, and I nudge the door a hair, wide enough to peer inside.

Framed by the large picture window at the other end of the office, Beelzebub stands in all his glory: dark blue jeans, crisp white shirt, and chestnut-brown hair mussed to perfection. The million-mile stare he sports is fixed somewhere off in the distance as he presses the cell phone to his ear.

It's wrong of me to stare. But I can't not stare. I mean, it's hardly the first time I've seen Mark Donovan. It's just the first time I've dared to unapologetically stare at his ass.

He shifts in place, and the move is hypnotic. Did he bulk up ... his butt?

I knew he did some heavy lifting, but this is ridiculous. I mean, once, when traffic was blocked, he and Brian lifted a fallen maple to the side of the road. By themselves. So, yeah, I get it. Muscle mayhem. But now, his arm bulge alone has his shirtsleeves within an inch of their lives. It's as if he graduated from bar-belling trees to tanks.

"What?" he snaps indignantly.

I shouldn't hang on his every word, but I do. Who's he talking to? Is someone complaining about me? Because I've been crushing it. Taking double shifts. All smiles. Amped up like an Energizer bunny. Nobody works as hard as I do, and not just for the tips. I have the Bishop legacy to maintain.

And yes, I may have mixed up an order here and there, or spilled one tiny little kid's milk. But I fixed every last mistake. And the *milk spill Boomerang clip* the kids posted got a ton of love on TikTok. Granted, the putrid dairy after-smell was wafting about for weeks, but thankfully, it's gone. Almost.

"No. No way," I hear Mark say, chuckling. I frown hard. I know that laugh. That's his evil laugh.

It's the laugh he had when he and Brian set a rope snare and trapped me in it, which, in my defense, I was eight. It was also the laugh that accompanied that nasty bowl of foul-tasting jellybeans and his insistence that girls couldn't eat them. He knew what he was doing. Throwing down a double-dog dare in the face of the female race. Well, I ate every last one. And whoever decided that vomit and boogers were palatable should be shot.

He also had that very same annoying laugh when he came up with that stupid nickname—

"Choir Girl?" he says with a scoff.

Fire fills my face as my grip on the door handle tightens.

This is the same man who tosses nicknames like *babe* or *princess* at every walking vagina in town, but for me, I'm simply Choir Girl. I mean, sure, I was in the church choir. And not just because everyone there was nice or that they handed out cocoa and cookies after every performance, which I lived for, but because Mom was there, too. It was our space as much as anyone else's.

"Me with Choir Girl?" He says it as if disgusted. By this point, I'm already inappropriately one foot in the office and charging straight at him. But Mark doesn't notice and just keeps going.

"Not with a ten-foot pole," he says with another scoff, and half of my heart shatters as he goes from being cold to cruel. "Make that a hundred-and-ten-foot pole. She's too"—he pauses for a moment for just the right word, the wheel in his mind landing on—"Jess."

Seriously? It's bad enough that he's banished me like a dwarf planet in my own brother's solar system. Why talk about me at all? Oh, that's right. Because he's Mark.

I bite my cheek, my face burning with more emotions than I can count. Frozen with indecision—to leave or to knee him in the groin—I blink away my stubborn tears just as he turns around. "Not even if the fate of mankind was dependent on my dick connecting with her vag—"

His mouth snaps shut, and I narrow my eyes.

He hangs up. For the longest second in history, I stare down the first man to make my *Vow to Hate for All Eternity* list. And that's not just my period talking.

"Jess," he says with a huff, annoyed. "Ever hear of knocking?" He walks over to his desk.

He did not just say that. *Ever hear of not talking shit behind someone's back, butt-munch?*

My mouth falls open, and I can feel every last one of my freckles catch fire. "Oh, I'm sorry, Your Royal Highness. Is that the proper etiquette? Knocking so I don't disturb you being an asshat?"

"Asshat?" His steps stop cold. He spins, facing me. "Well, this asshat happens to be your boss for today, Jess. That is, if you were working, which you shouldn't be. How about you come back tomorrow?"

Is that why Tyler told me to stay home? Because of Mark? When I could've used those tips? I feel my anger rise to a dangerous high as I stand my ground. "How about you give me an apology?"

When he rolls his eyes, I poke him in his dumb, stone-hard chest. *What am I doing?*

His eyes dart to my finger, then to my eyes. "I—" I take a breath, my chin defiant. "I deserve an apology," I snap.

He edges closer into my space. "Haven't you heard? In life, you never get what you deserve, Jess. Only what you can negotiate. Move it along, Choir Girl."

Again with the name? "Make me," I say in total stupid-brazen disregard for my stand-in boss. But I can't back down. Instead, I step up to him, toe-to-toe. I'm keenly aware of the childishness of my action considering the man has, oh, I don't know, a yard of height on me.

My stare-down is feeble, pathetic, really. I blame his eyes. They're gold now—charged and deadly—like some wild exotic cat I'm stupid enough to be in a staring contest with.

Two knocks chop at the door.

"Come in," he barks.

"Hey, hey, hey." Brian's voice is too familiar to both of us, but neither of us budges. My brother wraps a casual arm around me as if the death-glare crossfire isn't happening at all. He pulls me back and leans over to Mark. "I thought we had a talk about this."

I whip my head to Brian. "A talk about what?"

"Nothing." Mark's reply is quick. Too quick. He retreats behind his desk. *Coward*.

I turn my attention to Brian, breaking down his resolve with my angriest angry eyes. "What talk?"

He shrugs, his guilty smile on full display. "Nothing," he says, rushing me out of the room with both hands on my shoulders. "Mark and I need to chat, sis. See you later."

Before I get too far with a protest, the door slams in my face.

"*Argh*." I stomp my foot. I still need my check. Maybe if I'd taken Anita up on that lunch, I wouldn't be consumed with hangry rage. Between my hunger and my period, there's only one solution: full-blown annihilation. Crazed, I plow down the door, guns blazing.

"Why'd you hang up on me?" Brian asks Mark.

"What?" I glare down my enemies, Tweedle Dumb and

Tweedle Asshat, trying to make sense of why Mark's dick and my vag would ever come up in their conversation.

What the hell?

When Anita asked me about Mark, did I say, *"Me? With the dildo of the century? Not even if my vagina was on fire and his dick was the only way to put it out."* Wait, that came out wrong. And of course, I didn't. At least, not with my outside voice.

Instead of being a half-decent person, Mark clasps his hands and cocks his head in that arrogant way he always does. "Remember our little talk about knocking, Jess?"

It's as if his balls are begging to be kicked so hard, they lodge in that vacant space where his brain should be.

Fire licks at my good senses. I'm so ready to hand him that perfect ass of his on a platter, but the second I open my mouth, he adds, "I'd hate to see you lose your job for something as trivial as manners."

Stunned, I stare. *He'd really fire me over this?*

And what about Brian? Instead of standing up for me, my idiot big brother is just standing there. Like a big, dumb oaf, he's doing nothing but warning me with his eyes and a slow shake of his head.

Brian's right. I know he's right. He's leaving in a few days and taking this worthless sack of shit with him.

I should stay calm because I don't want this job, I need it. And not even for the money. Without it, I'm more or less alone. Rex is stationed in New Jersey. Close, but never close enough. And Cade is away in some god-forsaken part of the world that feels as unreachable as the moon.

Tears threaten fast. Too fast. As soon as he says, "Well, what do you know? Even choir girls have manners," no-holds-barred atomic anger wins.

I see the stack of checks on the desk, miraculously in alphabetical order. Mine's right on top. I snatch it up and stuff it in my pocket.

"Go to hell, Mark Donovan." And once again, when faced with the most beautiful man I've ever seen, my brain snaps in two, and I do the unthinkable. "I. Quit."

Pulse racing, I rush out of the room, determined not to cry like a girl or beg for my job. How did today end up like this?

I should've spent today planning the sendoff of the century for the brother of the year. Instead, I'm stuck spending the better part of it finding a new job and hating the both of them.

Asshat, one.

Choir Girl, zero.

Chapter Three

MARK

A FIST of fucking titanium flies from out of nowhere and slams me square in the chest. "Ow." My tone is pure *what the hell?*

It's true, I know better than to pick a fight with Jess. And I am technically the grown-up. Well, with her being eighteen and all, I guess she's a grown-up too. But I swear to God, that woman gets under my skin like lava-coated chiggers. Or maybe it's the guilt.

Brian and I know the price of his extended leave. It was a deal with the devil. Saying our next mission will be dangerous is like saying the Pope sometimes prays. There's a good chance we'll never see our families again, and the last thing I needed was to face off with Jess and her big, blue, soul-searching eyes. Hell, I can't even bear to look my mother in the eye.

Guns blazing, Brian lays into me. "You fire my sister five days before our next deployment?"

I didn't fire her. She quit. But with Brian glaring me down, there's no use arguing that technicality. Flustered, I point a finger at him. "This is your fault."

"My fault?"

"For giving me the fucking third degree and accusing me of making a play for Jess. Which she overheard. Thanks a fucking heap."

"Ah." He flicks a speck of dust from the desk. "How was I supposed to know you'd have that conversation with the door opened?"

I wave both arms in the air. "Now you know. And Jess was eavesdropping. *Again.* Her own bad habit brought this on."

Brian gives me a *don't fuck with the Bishops* face. "I can't have your back if things aren't square with Jess."

I rub at the ice pick driving into the base of my neck. "Well, technically, she quit."

When Brian hits me this time, he doesn't hold back. The man packs a punch like a battering ram. "Fix it, fucker."

I look at him as if a dick sprouted from the top of his head. "How? You know your sister. She's earned every last flaming strand of that red hair of hers. Fuck, we haven't spoken in years, and this is our reunion." I huff and lift my chin to the sky. "She hates me."

He shrugs. "Well, considering your first conversation in years is to threaten her job, her hating you seems validated."

"Is it my fault you made me say I wouldn't make moves on your sister with my outside voice?"

"Is it my fault you'll hump everything from a hydrant to a lamppost, and it wasn't exactly a stretch?"

I gesture at the door. "Clearly, you had nothing to worry

about." I adjust my pants from behind the desk. *Yeah, that's a bald-faced lie.*

"Clearly." Brian shakes his head. "You can't talk to her like she's twelve. She isn't."

Duh. One look at her ass told me that.

I remain stone-faced as Brian continues to lambast me. "You don't understand. Jess is stressed, too. With all the shit she's going through—" He clams up.

My ears perk up. "What's she going through?" I ask, tiptoeing as I pry.

He shakes it off. "Nothing. Just, *er*, woman stuff."

Enough said. The last thing I need to hear about is the world of Jess's uterus, though it does explain her flying off the fucking handle. With Jess, Moody is her middle name. Plus, with how full her breasts are and—

Where the fuck did that come from? I scramble to wipe the image from my mind. *Can we change the subject already?*

Brian drones on. "She's not a child anymore. And you're only filling in for the day, dickwad. Don't make me call your mommy on you."

"I know she's not a child."

While the very full-grown woman was busting my balls, it took every sheer ounce of willpower to avoid staring at those full, pouty lips. *Fuck*, she can't come back here. At least, not while I'm here. This is my funeral in the making.

Hmm. I think it through. Because I also can't *not* bring her back. Brian would murder me—*Saw* movie style.

I offer a solution. "She can consider herself on paid vacation until we leave. This way, the two of you can spend some time together."

And she'll be far the hell away from me.

Brian socks me again. Playfully, this time, but considering he gave it all he had the last round, I wince. "I guess you'd better find her and tell her that."

My eyes shoot wide. "You're her brother. Why don't you find her and tell her?"

"Because it's not my mess. It's yours. And we have our entire next mission to clean up after each other." He winks, the smartass, and heads for the door. "You know my baby sis would love to tend bar," he sings at me on his way out.

I throw a stress ball at his head. And miss.

He chuckles. "And they call you a sharpshooter," he calls out as he closes the door behind him.

Fucker.

I scroll through my phone until I find Jess's number, filed under "CG." I shoot her a text and wait her out.

Can we talk?

An hour later, after a thorough review of Zac's new inventory system, I check my phone. Still no response from Jess, so I try again.

I really need to talk to you.

By the time I've finished reviewing next month's menus with the staff, getting the seating arrangements for the Whitney wedding changed to accommodate nearly two hundred people instead of one hundred people, and reconciling the accounting for the month, my brain is fried.

I blow out a breath. Not a word from Choir Girl.

So, I do the unthinkable. I apologize.

Sorry I was an asshat. Please call back.

A text pings back, but the small surge of relief is instantly snuffed out. It isn't Jess. It's Brian. Even his text looks unhinged.

Did you talk to Jess???

Brian sends me a screenshot. Her phone finder app has her pinned on possibly the worst street in Albany. Without even speaking to him, I know Brian's about to lose his shit. Hell, my heart's beating out of my rib cage, and I'm half a breath away from losing my own shit.

What the fuck is she doing there?

Keep calm, I tell myself. If I'm panicked, Brian will panic tenfold.

I lock my voice into casual mode and call. "I've texted her several times. She hasn't returned my texts, but that's nothing new, considering her nickname for me is sometimes Satan. Have you tried calling her?"

"Yes, dumbass. Tried that first. I'm heading that way, but I'm home." The Bishop home is buried in a southwest pocket of Adirondack Park—at least an hour and a half from Albany. His voice rises, unnerved. "I need you to—"

"I'll take care of it. I'm leaving now."

I grab the nearest keys and rush out the front, nearly plowing down Anita. "Sorry, I'm in a hurry."

"Wait." She blocks my path. "Did Jess find you?"

"Yes," I grumble, irritated. Now I just need to find her.

"Oh, good. I know she was worried about getting that watch for Brian."

Impatient, I mutter, "What watch?" as I move around her and make my way to the truck.

Anita keeps pace, shoving her phone in my face. "This watch."

I check out the price tag. All her paychecks for two months wouldn't cover that watch. "How is she paying for a four-thousand-dollar watch?"

"She isn't. Some guy is selling his old one."

Of course. Because that's what people do. Sell four-thousand-dollar watches for a fraction of the price. It happens every day.

I get in the truck, slam the gas, punch the dashboard, and shout, "*Fuuuck!*"

Ready for more of Mark Donovan & Jess Bishop?

1-CLICK NOW>> MARKED

About the Author

Lexxi James is a USA Today bestselling author of romantic suspense. Her feats in multi-tasking include binge watching Netflix and sucking down a cappuccino in between feverish typing and loads of laundry.

She lives in Ohio with her teen daughter and the man of her dreams.

www.LexxiJames.com